Out of a Southern African Furnace

Dr Thomas Bagot

DEDICATION

Andrew, Jo, Judy, Natalie and Wendy without
whose help this book would not have been
possible.

3rd Edition
Baclesit
Nov 2014

Copyright © 2013 Dr Thomas Bagot
All rights reserved.
ISBN-13: 978-0-646-55279-8
ISBN-10: 0646552791

Out of a Southern African Furnace Synopsis

A page turning corporate thriller. Life and death situations arise in an international but remote community, in Botswana, Southern Africa, where technical complexities, human weaknesses, and strengths, are used by self seeking corporate power brokers, to fraudulently gain from the endeavors of a farming family, the de Bruins and Charles Obenta a tribal leader, and his people from a Tswana village, Ngami.

What Ben de Bruin had found would have been of value to almost anyone with the resources to claim it........

Turning with great difficulty Ben grasped for the case that contained the key to their family's hoped for fortune. Gasping with pain he managed to drag the case up ....

The partners are at the end of their tether with only a friend of Ben's, an engineer, Peter Connor, to rely on. A ruthless, beautiful and sophisticated international management and engineering expert, Rebecca Rosslynn, is paid to be the respectable front for unbridled efforts to stop Peter and destroy the partner's hopes. An awkward young Tswana, Joseph comes to play a critical part in the events.

The interplay between the various interests provides a constantly moving story as the proponents are drawn from their lives by the key interests, into and out of the heat of a campaign to acquire the wealth.

ForeWord Clarion Review
Out of a Southern African Furnace

Four Stars (out of Five)

Out of a Southern African Furnace. ....Can a consulting technical expert who is up against time constraints, hostile colleagues, and scheming corporate interests succeed?

The story is set in a remote part of Southern Africa and opens with Ben de Bruin in his car, injured and nearly unconscious. The book begins with violence and danger before proceeding into the story of the events that lead to de Bruin's accident.

De Bruin is part of a South African family with mining interests. His relatives can't understand why the family business seems to have gone awry. What they don't know is that the corporate power brokers involved want the business to fail, so they can profit from its resurrection. The de Bruins suspect foul play, but they are not sure what is going on. They call on Peter Connor, an engineer, to conduct an independent investigation. Meanwhile, the corporate interests have brought in their own consultant, Rebecca Rosslynn. Rosslynn is an international management consultant and engineering expert charged with making sure her assessment shows why the mining operation should be shut down.

The book begins with de Bruin's accident and then goes into more procedural matters, but just when the reader is lulled into thinking that the danger is over and that the story is focusing on the the power plays between the consultants and plant management—an element of danger creeps in again. Connor finds that he is a target because the corporate interests do not want him to finish his investigation.

.... The story is not weighed down by the technical details, and it shows a great appreciation for both the landscape and the mingling of cultures that takes place in South Africa.

Kirkus Indie Review
Out of a Southern African Furnace
3rd Edition

In Bagot's novel, the reader is vividly drawn into a world of high-stakes politics and money in modern-day Botswana, specifically at an ore mine near Lake Ngami. Opening with a car accident that traps geologist Ben de Bruin in a car with his agent, Rob Jamieson, Bagot's novel explores the domino effect of destruction after de Bruin raises questions about the Ngami mining company, which he works for and in which his family has a vested interest. Specifically, de Bruin wants to know why it's so poorly mismanaged ....
Experts from around the world are called in to consult, such as Peter Connor, an engineer, and Rebecca Rosslynn, a business consultant and operator from Australia. Connor, Rosslynn and de Bruin realize all too soon that even a mismanaged company can be powerful —and dangerous. Bagot provides a fully realized world that speaks to his background in mining. The novel clips along at a nice pace, and Bagot deftly builds conflict, moving it ever onward. It's also interesting to see the central conflict from multiple viewpoints, particularly that of Rosslynn. The local tribal concerns regarding the company are likewise intriguing.
....

An intelligent, informative thriller that looks at deadly corruption in southern Africa.

1

Ben was barely conscious. He was trapped. Caught between the twisted steering wheel and the driver's seat. One leg was held by something he could not see. The seat belt buckle would not release. He was bleeding, from his head, right hand, and leg.

He turned his attention to Rob. Forcing himself to stay conscious by taking deep breaths. The family's agent was lying motionless against the crushed passenger door and did not seem to be breathing. Ben called him but there was no reply. He could not reach far enough to check the agent's pulse.

He looked around for the case, "Oh God," he prayed, "please don't let the sample case have gone through the window," then he saw it, caught between the passenger seat and the back seat. He reached out and succeeded in getting a grip on the handle of the smallish case. Gasping with pain he managed to drag it up and wedge it between the door and the Land Rover's steering wheel. It contained the key to a fortune.

He closed his eyes briefly and slipped into unconsciousness.

A few moments earlier, Ben had been driving the Land Rover along a remote track and Rob had been dozing in the seat next to him. They were returning from a three week trip without proper bathing facilities.

The vehicle was as dusty and tired looking as its occupants felt.

The smell of his own perspiration had irritated Ben as much as did Rob's. They were on their way to the village of Ngami in Eastern Botswana, Africa. In countryside largely filled with low bush made up of a variety of small trees.

He knew they were nearing their destination when he began to notice a change in the landscape, the flat plains, that make up much of Botswana, were beginning to fill with kopjes.

In the dawn's early light the piles of rock, making little hills, looked at times like vastly magnified ant heaps. No two were alike. They seemed to have been formed in isolation; some from contiguous barren rock protrusions, others from great slabs of rock and huge loose boulders, piled against each other. Soil amongst the rock provided footholds for grass, bush and trees.

As they approached the wide river, that sometimes flowed through the district, they began to notice that the size of the trees was increasing, some were quite majestic. Large sycamore figs, anabooms, rain trees, nyala berries, fever trees, marula, boerbeans, and other species grow along the river's course.

The track was becoming dangerously rough, because of protruding rock, washes, and potholes; formed by the district's occasional and sometimes heavy rains; and they had to negotiate up, and down the occasional steep gully.

The rockiness of the terrain near the kopjes made cultivation difficult. Domestic animals ranged among them; and the little hills provided a home for several species of wild animal; leopards, impala, baboons, and others. So Ben had to be on the lookout for these as he drove.

Ben, a lean tanned geologist of thirty-eight, with Rob Jamieson, their agent, was on his way to a meeting with Charles Obenta, a trusted associate of the de Bruin family, and an Ngami tribal leader. They carried details of a valuable platinum find.

To say that Ben was pleased with his discovery would have been an understatement.

As he had absorbed the immensity of what he had found, the hope, that he had started out with, had turned to concern; about, how to prevent the loss of the information. What he had found would have been worth a fortune to anyone with the resources and facilities to claim it.

Their vulnerability was not only due to the value of their find. Their efforts in Botswana were in conflict with the ambition and greed of a powerful magnate, Jack Anders, who wanted the orebody for himself.

As they rattled and jolted along the track, Ben was drowsily thinking that he should have taken the vehicle back to the rental agency at the airport when he had first realized that it was in poor condition. Suddenly his heart constricted and he was wide awake. Lights had appeared in his mirror and were coming up quickly behind them. He tried to accelerate but soon knew that he could not outrun the following vehicle. He wondered if he should pull over.

"What the hell is this idiot doing?" Rob asked, shaken awake by Ben's attempt to travel faster, fear harshening his voice.

"I think the bastard's trying to ram us," Ben answered. "He must have very big tyres to travel like he's doing."

Rob looked anxiously through the dawn light, at Ben's drawn face, crowned by a thatch of slightly curly hair, lit by the tailing headlights.

That there was any other vehicle was surprising. They were far from regularly maintained roads, and the chance of coming across any sort of traffic at any time of day was negligible.

Ben licked his lips. They were dry from the many days they had spent in the sun, from thirst, and now, from fear.

"He must be some sort of maniac," said Ben as the gap between them closed. His head jolted as they were hit from behind. The unexpected vehicle then repeatedly rammed the back of the tough Land Rover.

They could just see its heavy reinforcement in the early light. As they had thought, it did have huge nonstandard wheels and tyres.

Ben said, "Hang on to anything you can Rob, tightly, this is really looking bad."

To the left of where they were driving, the track dropped away sharply, over broken rocks, to the riverbed, now dry, because the rains had long gone.

Then a steady force drove them forward. Ben's hands were wet from perspiration. They slipped on the steering wheel.

He thought of swerving to get away from the powerful following vehicle, but there was no room to do so. His clenched teeth were hurting his jaw. He then tried braking, but the imposed force overrode his efforts; and their vehicle was pushed steadily toward a steep drop. A slight swing to avoid a meandering cow, together with the increasing pressure from behind, and their Land Rover tumbled over the edge.

As the noisy drama unfolded, the sky became a mass of wheeling and screeching birds, frightened into flight, in huge flocks, from the trees. Their protests, at the violent activity below, competed with the noise of the vehicles, and then complemented an absolute silence.

Joseph, a small herd-boy of what was thought to be mixed Bushman, and Tswana ancestry, was far from home because of the dryness of the season. He had been listlessly looking around after he had woken, thinking of his limited future. He could smell and feel rain was near and wished that the weather would break.

Rain would decrease the harshness of the land, by providing the moisture needed to soften the earth, and germinate the next season's grass. Most importantly for Joseph, the new pasture would ease his daily task of finding food for the family's cattle.

His thoughts had included a familiar dream; of moving to a big city where people dressed beautifully, and lived lives of luxury.

The youngest of five children, his existence had always been hard and neglected. His mother was old, not so much in years, as in health and bearing. His father had lost interest in them before dying at the age of fifty.

His older siblings were not successful, even by the standards of the poorer people in Botswana. So Joseph lived in a world of dreams.

His make belief world was based on the few television shows he had watched. These had provided images of false lives, further removed from reality than any fairy story or local folk tale. His worldly experience of reality was limited to Ngami. He, like so many other people, simply did not have enough knowledge to enable him to differentiate between reality and electronic fiction.

The lights and the noise of the two straining engines had broken into Joseph's dreams. Vehicles were a rare sight in the area at any time, and he had never seen any reach the speed that these were going. The second vehicle, with its large wheels, bull and roll bars, made him think of some kind of monster. He was as afraid of its appearance, as much as of the danger it presented. It seemed to be trying to get closer to the one in front, like one bird attacking another. The roaring engines reminded him of protesting, angry animals. He shook his head in amazement, and then looking around at the cattle, realized that they were in the way of the oncoming spectacle. He dropped the dusty blanket, that had been protecting him from the coolness of the early morning, and sprang forward to herd the animals to safety.

He took a breath of relief as he got the last of the cattle out of the way, only to see another of the precious herd turn back toward the track.

At the same time the larger, following vehicle, pushed firmly against the back of the smaller four-wheel drive.

Joseph knew there was nothing he could do to save the animal.

But it survived, after Ben and Rob had been pushed off the road, the reinforced vehicle straightened, missed the cow and stopped over the slight rise.

The cow trotted back to the herd, seemingly unhurt.

Joseph was scrambling down toward the stricken Land Rover before he realized that the other vehicle had come to a halt.

When he did, he stopped for a moment, at the thought that he would be an unwelcome witness and should run away, but decided he had to try to help the people in the Land Rover. So he worked his way down the rock face as quickly as he could.

He found the vehicle teetering on the edge of a cliff, above another steep drop. He climbed cautiously onto the precariously balanced Land Rover. It rocked and Joseph froze.

Ben's unconsciousness was not complete, he was dreaming, about his brother James and his sister Clare when they were young children. They were sitting on the veranda of their Cape Dutch home with their grandfather. The old man was recounting their family history. A story, made familiar by the old man's regular retelling; about how the family had come to live in the Cape in the seventeenth century. His grandfather had repeated a tale of their religious persecution in Europe, with a familiarity that made it seem as though the events had occurred in his own life.

In the telling of this dramatic story, the majesty of France had come alive for the children.

For most South Africans the Huguenot problems in Europe were a remote tale, about some of the people who had settled in the Cape.

To the de Bruins, the story was their own. The problems their ancestors had faced as a mixed Catholic and Huguenot couple under King Louis XIV of France had resulted in the relinquishment of entitlements to a farm in France and the acceptance of a pension, to settle in the Cape. The old man had told the children how, starting with the allowance, their forbearer had bought land, near Paarl in 1685, and had developed it as a family farm from uncultivated bush.

A bush that was then populated with wild animals and small numbers of San or Hottentots. A tribe who have now become integrated with the many other, different settlers in the Cape.

Ben's dreams shifted their focus, to their father's funeral, and their inheritance of the farm, which was, at that stage, rundown. It had been plagued, like the rest of the country, by the sanctions that had been applied to have apartheid removed.

The uncertainty of the people and the country, that carried over from the apartheid period, and its aftermath, had moulded the de Bruin's lives, as much as their heritage. Ben, his brother James, and sister Clare, had decided to make the best of the situation by using their separate skills to rebuild the farm; and they had managed to redevelop their inheritance, into a successful winery.

The dream evaporated into clouds of pain, and then returned, to include Ngami and their excitement at the prospect it had, at first, offered the family; of how they had mortgaged the farm to invest in the project, and how their dreams for the project had turned into a steadily worsening nightmare.

Ben regained consciousness and forced himself, through another cloud of pain, to get his cell phone out of his pocket. When at last it came free, he found he could not work it; because one of his hands was covered in blood and the other feelingless.

The driver, of the freakish looking and heavily modified vehicle, got out after stopping, and walked to the edge of the rocks to look down at the Land Rover. He could only see the front of the crashed vehicle. He needed to get the samples and information that Ben had in his possession, so he climbed awkwardly down the rocky face. This was difficult for him, because he was seriously overweight. His rifle was awkwardly slung around his fat shoulders. Eventually he found a ledge on which he could rest. Looking about he realized, to his annoyance, that he was below the crashed vehicle. It overhung the ledge he had found.

He started to creep around below the vehicle, his legs screaming in protest at the unaccustomed exercise. As he got below the Land Rover, it started to move. It groaned, creaked and tilted toward him.

He quickly squirreled back into the open.

Joseph had caused the movement. He was climbing onto the Land Rover. The creaks, groans and motion stopped him. He leaned back and the vehicle steadied. He then lay flat and crept slowly forward again, to get his head above the driver's window.

Ben, in the Land Rover, heard Joseph, felt the vehicle move, and was filled with hope, until Joseph's small, dust covered face, crowned by equally dusty hair, appeared in the blue space of the window. The hope faded, Joseph looked far too small to help.

"Hello sir, me Joseph, herd-boy. Are you okay?"

"I think Rob is dead and My leg is caught."

"You get out?" asked Joseph in his limited English.

Although Joseph could only say a few words in English he could understand what Ben was saying, he shook his head doubtfully and answered, "Man from other car coming. Very dangerous."

As he got away from the vehicle's shadow, the other driver, moving to climb back, up the rock face, the way he had come, heard the voices, without being able to pick up what was being said. He stopped, listened more carefully, and heard Ben say, "Can you take this case and look after it, it's very important." This was clearly the case he had been told to get back to his employers.

Ben painfully lifted the case up toward the small boy.

A dusty hand reached down into the cabin space and the vehicle creaked ominously. Joseph froze, he was frightened for himself and the man. Moving slowly he managed to get a grip on the bag's handle and pulled it free of the cabin. He inched backward, the vehicle tilted and steadied.

The would be assassin struggled to free his rifle, but could not see Joseph.

"Get help, run, Charles Obenta," he heard Ben say hoarsely.

Joseph understood what was required, but was not sure where the help was supposed to come from. He did not know how to ask. He knew Charles Obenta by reputation as a most important person.

He awkwardly tried to console Ben.

Ben thanked him warmly, despite his pain, but asked Joseph to go quickly.

Joseph complied, and scrambled off the unsteady Land Rover with the case.

When he was on solid ground, Joseph thought about what he should do. The cattle were his family's only possession. He knew he really ought to go to them, but, frightened of the driver of the other vehicle, he decided to head for the village along the riverbed.

He looked at the Land Rover again and saw there was a gap where he could wedge something, to help steady it. He found a suitably sized stone and carried it to the edge of the ravine, fitted it carefully between the rock and the crushed metal, tapped twice on the vehicle to say good-bye, and left to climb down the cliff.

After he reached the dry riverbed, he headed off at a loping pace toward the village.

The shred of hope Joseph had provided heartened Ben. If Joseph looked after the bag's contents, Ben's effort to save the family's investments would succeed, but only if his brother, James, knew where they were. He wished, yet again, that he had explained the details of what he was doing to his brother. He tried to use the phone again and failed.

The rattling, banging, and subsequent steadying of the vehicle, as Joseph rammed his wedging stone into position, then the good-bye tap, helped lift the injured man's spirits. He steeled himself to try to work the phone again.

The other driver saw Joseph as he headed off down the river bed. He tried to get a sight on the boy, but Joseph was moving too quickly; and then he was out of sight.

His size, made it too dangerous for him to climb down the way Joseph had gone, so he decided to drive ahead and ambush the boy. He stopped long enough to report, using his satellite phone, the departing boy's direction.

He was given instructions; to first get the samples and the information that Ben had been carrying, and then to make sure that no one survived the incident.

He returned to his vehicle and drove for a few minutes in the direction Joseph had gone, stopped at a point where he could get to the riverbed, scouted around for a few moments; to find a position that would give him a good view of Joseph as he rounded the bend. He then settled carefully, balanced his rifle on a rock and sighted toward where he thought the fugitive boy would soon appear.

2

The trip that ended in Rob Jamieson's death came about as a result of a series of coincidences.

Three weeks before the two men were forced off the cliff, GVN, the operating partner of the Ngami project, had called a board meeting, to discuss their presentation to an upcoming World Bank review of the project's funding.

Ben read the minutes on the flight to Ngami, and then stared out into the empty sky.

The project was a complex mining and ore recovery project in a remote location. Not on a major road system, it had not had rail access when it started, and there had been many mishaps and accidents.

The net result was that it had never achieved its design production; four thousand tons of a matte a month, containing significant percentages of platinum, nickel, gold, and cobalt. They had never reached the target at any single time, let alone for a continuous period.

The mine, that provided the ore to feed the process plant, consisted of an underground operation that used traditional drill and blast narrow tabular reef mining methods, called the standard breast mining approach.

In this method, scrapers are used to clean the stopes. The underground workings are accessed from a twin shaft system.

Mined ore is transported, by rail, to a conventional ore-pass system, with separate rock handling facilities for reef, and waste, and then from the shaft head frame to primary crushers, secondary crushers and then mills to reduce the particle size.

Gravity separation, floatation cells, and spray drying; concentrate the ore and remove water from the concentrate, before it is fed to the smelter.

The Ngami board had eight members and a secretary. The de Bruin brothers held two of these directorships.

Ben de Bruin worked for the company on remote exploration sites, as a geologist. His brother James ran the family farm which they had used as an asset to purchase their holding in Ngami.

The operation itself was run by people who belonged to the renown GVN corporation, who had been paid for their contribution, competence, and effort, in shares.

When Ben disembarked from the flight at Ngami airport, on his way to attend the director's meeting, he met Andrew Riley, one of the few Ngami people who he knew well.

After they had collected their luggage, Andrew asked Ben to dinner, and he accepted.

"Do you have a vehicle here?" Andrew asked as they walked away from the baggage trolley.

"No, I'm going to hire one."

"Would you like a lift?"

Ben declined, saying he needed to go to Francistown, and that he would hire a four wheel drive.

On the way to the parking lot Andrew belatedly phoned his wife and asked her if his bringing Ben to dinner was okay.

She jokingly chastised him for not asking her first, and then added that she would love to see Ben again. She concluded with, "I'll invite a few other people."

After the two men parted at Ben's hired Land Rover, he rolled down the window, to ask, "What time Andrew?"

"About six if that's okay with you."

"That'll be fine. See you later," Ben called.

As Ben wound the window back up, with difficulty, he noticed that other aspects of the four wheel drive seemed to have been subjected to more wear and tear than he would have expected in a hired vehicle. Not wanting to return to the hire desk, he sighed irritably and drove on.

Andrew Riley's wife, Ann, welcomed him when he arrived for dinner, one child on her hip, and several others tumbling around in the background. She was even more beautiful than he remembered, so much more so, that he had to catch his breath.

"We don't see much of you in Ngami, Ben," she said.

"No. I work in the north of the country."

"Related to Ngami?"

"Not entirely, there are some fascinating archaeological mysteries north of here that I'm working

24

on, but I am also prospecting for the company up there."

"The archeology sounds interesting, I'd like to try that."

"Perhaps one day?" he said with a slight smile.

"Go on Ben let's meet the others."

"How about you, how's the robotics going?"

"As you know I'm only working for two days a week. I'm also doing a Masters that's related to using remote controlled vehicles in mining."

"Sounds interesting."

"It is."

The Riley family, like many others, had come to Ngami, from various parts of the world, on lucrative contracts.

This step, in each of their lives, would allow them to establish themselves more easily in Europe, than if they had continued their careers in their home countries.

One of the many anomalies at the Ngami site was that large numbers of people were breaking these lucrative contracts, without the main benefit of the contract, a generous terminal bonus.

Without Ann Riley's continuous pressure, Andrew would certainly have been among the many who had left early.

Ann showed Ben to the lounge of the generously proportioned house and introduced him to Father Murphy, a priest. The man's slightly bloodshot face made Ben think that the priest might be inclined to enjoy one too many drops of malt. He stifled the thought. Trying, instead, to think about the loneliness that such lives as the man's have involved and about how much good he probably did in the remote community. He asked a few courteous questions and then subsided into the role of interested observer, while the priest and Andrew discussed their common hobby, model aircraft.

After ten minutes listening to the discussion of model airplanes, Ben decided to go and ask Ann if he could help her.

The highly efficient Ann had not needed any direct help. She chatted to him for a while before asking him if he would help her by picking her some tomatoes from their extensive vegetable garden, that was visible through the kitchen window.

"Where do I find them?"

"Off to the right behind the corn."

He walked out, through the kitchen door, across an open space, to the garden itself; through neat rows of peppers and eggplants. Past the potatoes, several rows of healthy looking corn, and some other plants he did not recognize.

Eventually finding the tomatoes in a corner of the garden, behind the corn, he selected several bright red examples and put them in the basket that Ann had given him. He sampled a few of the smaller ones with relish, while he worked. He found that picking the tomatoes was surprisingly more exciting than finding tomatoes in a shop. There was a pleasure, in the almost forgotten smell of the plants, their appearance, rough stalks and in choosing, and sampling some of the smaller ripe red tomatoes as he picked them.

Ann called from the window as he made his way back through the rows of peppers, "Ben could you get us two paw paws as well please, they're against the back fence."

"Two Paw Paws?" he asked trying to restrain himself from making some not-so-funny remark, to the beautiful Ann, about the possible size he should consider, and failing, put up both hands facing toward her indicate the rough size of a paw paw, he asked, "How big?"

"Go on man, just get two," she replied. "Three if you like, if the idea of two paw paws is too much for your overactive brain."

Suitably chastened, Ben walked to the fence where the paw paws grew, in two neat rows, like scruffy little palms, some as tall as him, and some smaller. Most of the little trees had a number of fruits in various sizes. They were colored from a dark shade of green, through to bright yellow, and deep orange. There were at least a dozen that seemed ready to eat. As Ben picked the second paw paw, about half the size of a football, and, about as orange as he could find, a neighbor noticed him.

The man was big and balding with a great beard and bushy eyebrows. He had a handkerchief tied across his bald-head and had been digging in his garden. He looked, to Ben, like a character off a Toby Jug. Like someone's idea of a nineteenth century sea captain. His face was flushed from the sun, digging and probably, Ben thought, good quantities of some form of liquid refreshment. He was sweating profusely but smiled most benevolently.

Ben intuitively liked him.

"Hello mate, I haven't met you before, you here on holiday or something?" the man said in a pleasant Yorkshire sounding accent. "Stealing the Riley's paw paws?" he added.

"No," Ben said smiling as the large fellow ambled across to him, having found something more interesting than digging.

"Don't worry about it mate, we all do, they've planted enough of the damn things to feed the whole village and they do. Are you a relative?"

"No. I'm here to attend a meeting about the difficulties in getting the plant up to full production," Ben started to explain, but got no further.

"Well I never. I'm sure at least a part of what's going on is underhand," the large man said.

"Oh?" Ben replied.

The Toby Jug character was silent for a moment, seeming wary of talking. He mumbled to himself, then appeared to decide to share his knowledge and went on to explain his theories about the company and why it did not work, including information about himself as he spoke. He explained that he was a civil engineer who had worked on many major projects around the world.

The Toby Jug character explained that the management were not trying to fix the problems, and were deliberately neglecting the plant, and mine, so that it would be forced into bankruptcy.

"Why would they do that?"

"They could then reopen the operation using a better source of ore."

"Who is they?"

"That I can't say but they must be high up the tree."

Ben shook his head in doubt, but the man certainly seemed convinced about what he was talking about. As he listened, he was almost, but not quite, thinking that what the man was describing could not be done. He could not believe such an apparently obvious fraud would be likely or even possible.

"You seem to know a lot about it?"

"They're looking for the ore now."

"Is that unusual?"

"Not the company geologists, someone else. They've got exploration work going on, to the northeast of the existing operations."

Ann called Ben to dinner from the window.

He excused himself, feeling like a drowning person and returned to the house.

Two other couples had arrived while Ben was in the garden and he was introduced to them when he reentered the lounge room.

He distractedly acknowledged the others.

One of the new arrivals, a slim man, who seemed to be in his thirties, with a flushed baby face and prematurely silver gray hair, sat opposite Ben at dinner. The man smiled incessantly, showing large, perfect, white teeth. He told Ben that he and his wife had only been in the country for a few weeks and that he was responsible for the construction of a major road in the district. As his story unfolded Ben had even greater difficulty concentrating, than he had when he first arrived.

The second family were more less forward.

Ben eventually heard that they owned a farm, on the lake near the town, and had apparently settled there in the nineties. The attractive Tswana woman explained that she had once worked for a mission in Francistown and had been given a scholarship to study in England where she had met her husband. They had returned to Botswana when her husband had been offered a contract to work on the furnace and had later established the farm.

The farmer went on to say that they had done very well out of their venture and invited Ben to visit the farm, explaining in detail where it was located.

Ben asked if they relied entirely on the farm for their income.

The man replied that he worked with Andrew Riley on the furnace, in the smelter department, from time to time, to earn cash when the farm was quiet.

Ben asked about the furnace problems and was surprised at the extent of the man's knowledge. He made a mental note to ask Andrew about some of the theories that the man expressed.

The priest was also interesting, he surprised Ben with his worldliness over the evening.

The slight and clearly intelligent man had told some amazing stories about his immensely large parish.

Thinking about the information on geology, that the neighbor had provided, Ben had asked if he knew anything about prospectors working to the northeast of the property.

The priest said he knew about them, that they were American, but not much about what they were doing. "I've been told they are visited regularly by Willers the GVN security person," the priest added. "My parishioners have asked if they work for the company, as Willers does. They're puzzled by the fact that the work the men are doing is clearly geological, yet none of the Ngami geologists seem to go near them."

Ben stood to leave at eleven, before the others.

At the door he thanked Ann and Andrew for the dinner and made his way back to the hotel, trying to work out how he would to deal with: Firstly the reported clandestine prospecting, due to his background as a geologist, he could check this on the ground by visiting the area himself. And secondly the comment that there was a campaign of deliberate neglect in the management program being run by GVN, the corporation who ran Ngami for the partners.

The latter investigation would have to be carried out by someone with enough knowledge of all the facets of the complex operation, there were not many people who could do this, that he knew of.

3

During the restless night, following Ben's dinner with his friends, he decided that he would take a closer look at the area where the Americans geologists, that he had heard about, were supposed to be working. Such an exercise would not be too much of a deviation from what he had planned for the weeks ahead.

When he woke, he thought about phoning his brother, James, to discuss this exploration, and the need for it, but decided he needed to be more certain about the problem before he worried the badly stretched farmer, possibly unnecessarily.

He had also decided on someone he could ask to carry out the checks needed on the plant, but had not had time to contact them by the time the board meeting began.

The meeting was opened by Jack Anders, the managing director, a tall elegantly dressed man, who was based in Johannesburg and only visited the site occasionally. He started in the formal way such events usually, do and at first very little of real importance was discussed.

The issue of the upcoming World Bank meeting, that was due to be held in four weeks, was then raised by Jack Anders who finished with, "We need to be frank about the disastrous situation with the smelter."

Ben asked, "What do you mean by frank?"

"The smelter's hopeless and we need to say that at the World Bank meeting."

"So you're suggesting that we should go in there and trust that after you tell them the smelter's useless, they'll say, 'carry on boys here's some more money?'"

Anders, startled by Ben's curt tone, looked at him with surprise. Ben had never confronted him before, he usually said little and was thought of, quite correctly, by Anders and the others, as being little other than a straight forward, polite farmer turned geologist, who, not having enough knowledge of operations, completely trusted GVN.

"What's wrong with the truth Ben?"

"The truth? I'm not at all convinced of that. We've got problems, but that they're suddenly intractable? You people are employed to manage Ngami, perhaps we should tell them instead that we're going to change managers," said Ben.

"That's a bit sudden."

"Not as sudden as blithely taking the chance of their shutting Ngami down completely."

Anders hesitated.

Ben went on to say that he was formally refusing to agree that the project could not produce what it should.

This was supported by his friend and associate, Charles Obenta, the senior tribal representative on the board.

They asked that their requirement, for an independent opinion of the project's potential, be minuted.

"We've had several capability studies, so that'd be a waste of time at this late stage," replied Anders.

"The only people you've had here are from Binnett, your agents, they've reported to you; and you've assured us, after each exercise, that you were dealing with the cause of the problems. I want someone I know to look at the project's capability. Someone who knows the operation, and has previously assured me that it is capable of producing what it should."

"Who could you find to do that at such short notice?"

Ben, normally in awe of the tall, slim, and very elegant managing director forced himself to continue, slowly, clearly, and deliberately, said that he intended to employ Peter Connor, who had worked on the commissioning of the Ngami plant; and, who had successfully improved several other problematic facilities.

Anders paused, looked at Heldebron, the site general manager, and then the other members of the board.

Seeing their concern, he decided that he decided to agree, and said, "When can he be here, there's very little time before the meeting."

"I'm waiting to hear from him."

After the meeting, Ben thanked Charles for his support.

Charles nodded and asked, "Why were you so set against Anders in there? You've always relied completely on his judgement."

"It's not just the smelter production that needs addressing. There's an investigation into reserves being run by someone else," Ben said and told him what he had heard at the Riley's about the geological work.

"And our security people visit them?"

"That's right."

"Hell Ben, that's a really bad situation. I didn't know anything about that."

"Neither did I, and in both cases it's a worry. Why don't either of us fully understand what is happening?"

"If you're right we're in a much worse position than we thought. We've perhaps been too trusting in leaving the whole exercise in the hands of GVN."

"You would not find anyone in South Africa who did not trust them," said Ben.

"Something very odd is certainly going on. I'm hoping that it doesn't involve Anders himself, but I'm beginning to think that it's the only answer that fits."

"If it does, what are we going to do? He's very influential," said Ben.

"I don't know, but we have to do something. When will Peter Connors be here?"

"I'm still arranging it."

"As Anders said in there, we don't have much time."

Ben had phoned his brother James, after the meeting and told him what had happened.

"There's so little time," said James, "have you contacted Peter Connor or his firm and ask him to do the work?"

"You'll need to do that James, I've got to check something else here."

"How do I find him?"

Ben had spent some time before the meeting tracing Peter and had found that he still worked for McNeil Associates, as he had done during the Ngami commissioning, so he was able to give James the contact details for the engineer, concluding with, "It's not likely that he'll be free, so you'll need to do some serious convincing."

"I'll do what I can Ben but I don't know how to apply much pressure to either Peter or his firm's managing director."

"I think what you'll need to do is convince both of them that we're going to be bankrupted if Peter doesn't get here."

"I'll try."

"I'm sure that Peter will help, if he knows how desperate we are, and McNeil is a very reasonable sort of person."

4

Gerry Heldebron, the general manager of Ngami, had been successful in getting as far as he had with no support system and few formal qualifications. Anyone who had ever worked for or against him would attest to his ability to keep to his own agenda.

Ben's success at what was supposed to have been a rubber stamp meeting had conflicted with every aspect of his nature.

He and Jack Anders walked in silence to Heldebron's office from the Ngami board meeting, both furious at Ben's effort to block their plans.

"Another review and by someone they choose will be like putting an unguided missile in here," said Heldebron, as they walked into his expansive office

"We've got to stop them," Anders replied.

Heldebron ordered coffee.

They continued the discussion after they were seated in the two comfortable chairs that faced the office's long window overlooking the bush.

Taking a sip of the excellent brew, Anders asked, "Do you know this Connor they're talking about?"

"No, but I've heard people talk about his efforts being good. He works for McNeil Associates."

"I can't possibly keep up appearances in head office with anyone saying that Ngami is viable and we've mismanaged it."

"No, it would be disaster. How is your young cousin Michael doing? More specifically, how long before he takes over managing the GVN corporation from you?"

Jack Anders held another position, acting managing director of the GVN corporation.

"He's a quick learner, he'll be wanting more control soon, so I don't have much time. I just can't afford to have any sort of blow up."

"You had to accept Connor's motion."

"I know."

"Can you tell McNeil to keep Connor out?"

"I could try, and it would certainly make it very difficult for the de Bruins, but I don't want to make waves at the corporate level in GVN."

"There's something else we could do, to make sure that this mess is seen as a just that," Heldebron said and stood up.

"What's that?"

"I've seen something about a nickel plant closure by someone who works for Binnett Consulting," Heldebron said.

He stood and strode across the office to his bookcase, searched for a moment and then selected a Binnett Consulting journal from the many that were stored there. He brought it back and opened it on the heavy wooden coffee table.

"So what does it say?" asked Heldebron.

After pointing out the main aspects of the article to Anders, Heldebron said, "This Rebecca Rosslynn gets the type of result we want. If we could get her here, she'd finish off anything Connor might say."

Jack skimmed through the article and said, "Sounds interesting, perhaps dangerous though, what if the Binnett consultant doesn't reach the conclusion that we want?"

"This place is beyond hope and anyway they'll do as we say. We've worked with Binnett all the way along and they stick to our rules."

"But not with Australian members of the firm."

"She's just done the same thing in Australia," Heldebron said.

"I suppose it might be a good idea, let's just save it until we know they can get Connor. If they can't we might do ourselves more harm than good by bringing her into the equation."

"Binnett will do as we tell them. I've never had any problem with any of their people."

"I know but let's just see what happens about Connor. Everything will work out more easily if no review takes place."

"This morning's minutes will be published."

"That's true I suppose. Okay, find out about the woman in Australia. If she's definitely the type of person we can deal with we'll go ahead and get her here."

The two men parted and Anders drove to the airport. He needed more information on Peter Connor, so he contacted van Zyl who was another, close associate of his.

Van Zyl was located in an office at the back of an old shop in Francistown. It faced onto a neat back garden, its interior was spotless and it was expensively decorated. It was operating as the temporary heart of a very successful organization, which he and Jack Anders owned through untraceable subsidiary companies.

Jack explained why they had to stop Connor getting to Ngami. During the conversation van Zyl told him that Ben de Bruin had set out to check the geology North of the Ngami site after the morning's board meeting.

Will he be able to find anything in the timeframe?"

"Almost certainly, he knows the country very well."

"That would really wreck our plans. Why hasn't he looked before?"

"Presumably because he thought GVN had everything under control. What's set him off?"

"I'm not sure, the way he arrived at this morning's meeting fired up is a side to him that I haven't seen before, but, whatever's driving him, we can't allow him to find anything."

"I'll make sure he won't."

"Good."

Shortly after his aircraft arrived in Johannesburg Jack heard back from van Zyl.

"Peter Connor, the engineer they're talking about, is working on a site we have an interest in at the moment," said van Zyl.

"What's he doing there?"

"Checking on losses."

"This exercise in Ngami will make me independent of the corporation and set our joint efforts on an even better trajectory, so Connor must not get to Ngami. Stop him, perhaps try doing it gently at first but don't waste time. He must not be allowed to start work on the Ngami site."

"I'll make sure he doesn't get there."

5

Ben had checked out of his Ngami hotel; after his successful attempt to get the Ngami project review approved and, had spoken to both Charles and his brother.

He then drove to Francistown, to see Rob Jamieson, their agent intending to supplement his knowledge of the geology of the area in which the unexplained prospectors were working.

Although satisfied with his performance at the meeting, Ben was feeling overwhelmed by the extent of the effort needed to bring their future back from disaster.

In Francistown, Ben parked his hired Land Rover next to the agent's office on a quiet section of the main street and strolled toward the office thinking about the area's history. Currently an administrative center for the Botswana government, Francistown had arrived in the new millennium with the same justified confidence as the rest of Botswana. It had been the center of a historic mission and was a significant outpost during the last phases of the British Empire. The town had also played a central role in a 19th century gold rush and looked colonial and yet strong and modern. It was a growing tourist hub; an interesting and well managed African town, that encapsulated the atmosphere of the continent with its colonial past. A past that was almost entirely good.

Jamieson's receptionist welcomed Ben with a large smile. She had worked with him for quite some time and appreciated his quiet ways. She told Ben that Rob would not be in the office for another half hour.

He left her saying he was going to get supplies.

As he walked down the street toward a general store Ben passed several women sitting along the pathway selling souvenirs, vegetables and other odds and ends.

The old fashioned store reminded him of his childhood, of shopping days on holidays, in a time when similar stores were the norm in many small towns in Africa.

As he wandered around the big, old and spotless shop, he was fascinated by its wares, set out in neat orderly sections. Quantities of cloth of every possible color were stacked opposite women's clothing of every type. The shelves that ran almost up to the high corrugated iron roof.

Bata and other footwear filled another area.

Heavier items such as cooking utensils, iron pots of the three-legged variety and gardening hardware were at the back of the extensive building.

The grocery section smelled of spice.

Dry goods; such as flour, salt, many different types of beans, and an amazing variety of dried herbs were displayed.

A huge selection of canned foods filled both sides of several aisles.

Ben made a list of what he would need for three weeks in the bush, and left it, to be filled, with one of the shopkeepers, thinking that it was an efficient way to shop.

He then strolled back to the Jamieson office to find that their agent had arrived.

"Sorry I'm a bit late, I've had trouble with one of the crew that we have working for the government, on a new warehouse," said Rob Jamieson, after welcoming him.

"No problems Rob, I've bought some of the things I'll need for the trip that I'm planning."

"I was surprised to hear about this exploration trip. Has something else gone wrong with Ngami?"

"Yes. I've discovered that there are prospectors looking for ore reserves that we've not been told about by GVN. Something that could be more serious than the poor plant performance, which is likely to sink the project on its own."

"When will you hear about the World Bank finance?"

"We've got a meeting to discuss the refinancing of the project in a few weeks time."

"So what are you planning?"

"I've always thought that the ore body continues to the North East of the mine. The mining company, GVN's reports say there is no easily exploitable ore in that area."

"You mean they're giving you and the rest of the shareholders false information?"

"It seems unlikely, I know, but I've been told that it's happening."

"How could you know that?"

"There's an exploration program in the area being coordinated by the Ngami security people that we haven't been told about."

"That's not necessarily GVN though?"

"Whoever it is I need to make sure that any new ore is not claimed by someone else or Ngami and our company will lose out badly, without the production problems entering into the equation."

Jamieson and his wife held a large block of the shares in the company and were as desperate to see the project succeed, as was Ben.

He offered to help in any way he could. "It's very rough country, perhaps I should come with you?"

"Can you spare the time?"

When Rob replied that he could, Ben agreed.

Ben then phoned his brother James to ask if he had managed to get Peter Connor to review the smelter operations.

"You only just asked this morning," James replied slightly irritated.

"Sorry James but I'm really worried."

"So you've said and I agree. I've spoken to McNeil. He's not keen on the exercise."

"James there's no other option, I've told the board that he is coming, and I don't know where else we could find someone who knows what they are doing and knows this plant. Then of course they would have to have enough credibility."

"So he's the only possibility?"

"That's right."

45

"I'll do what I can. McNeil did say that he would talk to Peter."

"Could you approach Peter directly?"

"I'll see what I can do."

"Where are you going yourself?"

"I've been working on an interesting prospect for a while and I also want to check something that I heard about while I was at dinner the other night, about Ngami's reserves," said Ben, still not mentioning the details of the conversations he had had at the Rileys about the prospectors.

"Oh I see," answered James, noncommittally, as he thought about how to get in touch with Peter without offending McNeil. What Ben was doing was assumed, by James, to be a part of Ben's routine geological investigations.

Ben's conversation with Rob Jamieson and his call to James had been listened to by van Zyl.

Van Zyl possessed a unique and deadly set of skills, not readily obtainable, even in Africa. Nondescript, grey looking, with thin hair and a sharp face, he had been trained by the South African Bureau of State Security, to carry out exercises in espionage, blend with a crowd and carry out ruthless assassinations. He did not have to employ people to do his dirty work, although he did so when possible, but he always made sure that his own proficiency was not lost, due to lack of practice. Ready to disappear at any moment, he was wealthy. His fortune scattered around the globe. His nimble life-style matched his career, and sheltered his interests. He intended to become richer still, and Ngami was a part of that plan. He employed several very dangerous people and could, at a moments notice, arrange some rather unpleasant experiences for anyone he did not like.

The moment Ben finished his conversation with his brother, van Zyl contacted someone he used who was based in nearby Bulawayo, across the Zimbabwe border.

He arranged for the person to put an end to Ben's geological expedition and remove him from the position of contention he now held.

6

Rebecca Rosslynn, the skilled operative that Heldebron wanted to engage to carry out a review of Ngami, was an engineer with a Master's Degree in Business Administration. Her influence greatly exceeded the average for the consulting industry. She was considered to be a very distant at best, or perhaps more accurately, a ruthless operator.

She saw herself as cool and analytic, deliberately kept clear of the extraneous aspects of people and problems, and carried out the requirements of the terms of reference of her assignments to the letter.

After Anders had left for the airport on the day of the Ngami board meeting, Heldebron called Wilson, the person in charge of Binnett Consulting' South African office about getting Rebecca to Ngami.

"Wes we need a another review of Ngami." he said.

"Another investigation? I'm not one to avoid work but surely you don't need to know any more about Ngami?"

Heldebron explained what had happened at the Ngami board meeting and what he and Anders had discussed about their needing someone to confirm, yet again, the project's problems.

Heldebron then went on to say that they had read about the work Rebecca had done in Australia and that they particularly liked the story about her recommendation, that a project similar to Ngami be closed.

Wilson agreed with their opinion. "Rebecca Rosslynn is well known within Binnett as someone who achieves required results. I'll get back to you with an answer."

Although operating from Sydney, Australia, Rebecca's life had been shaped by wealth accumulated, and lost, in South Africa. Some of her outlook could be traced to her history. A business failure had led to the loss of her grandfather's company and the associated wealth. This had forced the family into poverty. The set of circumstances that had led to that failure had never been fully explained. The event had made a huge difference to her existence and she usually tried to keep its memories at bay. Her family had all suffered, partially because of the extent of their loss and partially because of their loss of status in the community. They had been forced to turn to charity.

The request for Rebecca to carry out a program, to confirm that Ngami should be shut down, was relayed to her by Binnett's Australian principal.

It had come on the Tuesday after the decisive Ngami board meeting, as she was waiting to be met by Ed Chalmers, a friend and associate, with whom she was going to lunch at a restaurant on a wharf near the Spit Bridge on Sydney Harbour's northern shore.

Ed had seen that she was busy on the phone when he arrived and had walked slowly toward the waterway end of the wooden structure, to kill time without interrupting her. Turning back at the end of the wharf, he thought, not for the first time, how extraordinarily beautiful she was, and how she always seemed to attract attention. Even conservatively dressed, as she was, her clothing barely concealed an attractive figure, that was crowned by her lovely pale, almost translucent, face. In its own right it was noteworthy, character filled and beautiful. Framed by shining soft black hair it was exceptional. Eventually she straightened, turned and strode along the wharf toward him, still talking animatedly.

He pictured her deep brown eyes, protected by unbelievably long eyelashes and of her soft warm lips that he would very much like to have kissed, a prospect that had so far eluded him. He could not understand why anyone so attractive was so completely remote. Rebecca had always rejected his slightest attempts at developing their casual friendship and business relationship into something more personal.

She finished her conversation at that moment and completed the remaining distance between them with as much style as someone on a catwalk, making her conventional dark business suite look like something special. She greeted him warmly, kissing him lightly on the cheek saying, "Hello Ed, how are you?"

"Good and how's your day been Rebecca?" he answered, trying to ignore the fresh smell of her perfume and the tickle of her hair as her lips brushed his cheek.

"Unusual."

"What happened?"

"They want me to go to Africa this week."

"Who does?"

"That was Chris Bain he wants me to go back to the office to discuss the assignment after lunch."

"Africa's a long way for anyone to go on an assignment, isn't it? Which part?"

"Southern Africa, Botswana. It's on the northern border of South Africa, a few hours flight from Johannesburg."

"Why the hurry? You'd think they would have enough experts there, wouldn't you? South Africa's quite industrialized, isn't it?"

"They've only just phoned and I've not spent much time thinking about those aspects. I'm not sure if I can afford to take the time away from what I'm doing here. I'm trying to decide whether I want to go at all."

"Such a rush and so many questions, perhaps you should find out a bit more, before you get involved?"

"I'm going to speak to the South Africans later today. There's another reason I want to go, there's something that I've always wanted to do in South Africa."

"I suppose you've got family there?"

"Yes, distant though. It's not that. I'd like to know what caused the failure of my grandfather's company."

"Was it something more than the usual problems that companies run into?"

"I'm not sure, I was very close to him and I feel as though I owe him something. When he died last year he said some things after the failure that in retrospect were a cry for help. I want to know what really happened, if only for his sake."

"I suppose that's a good reason to go, but if I were you, I would make very sure that the assignment you're going to be working on is okay."

"I'm usually very careful."

"I know but it's just that I've burnt my fingers badly by leaping into situations that seemed, at the time, to need me and me alone. You've done so well. You don't need to prove anything. You certainly should avoid unnecessary risks."

They arrived at the restaurant as he was speaking.

The harbor was full of yachts taking advantage of the perfect day. Eighteen footers skimmed across the sparkling blue water, using advanced materials technology and clever design to reach incredible speeds.

One toppled near them and they watched with amazement at the speed with which it was righted.

The lunch was pleasant but not relaxing for Rebecca. She thought disconsolately about Ed as he tried to cheer her. She really liked him and was aware of his more than business interest in her, but could not bring herself to lower her barriers. A feeling of emptiness had become an irritating and recurring aspect of her life. When it took hold of her, she became withdrawn and seemed to lose focus, her goal driven life became confused and she, on occasion, could not remember the reasons behind her ambitions.

She went back to the office feeling more lonely and unhappy than she had at the start of her day.

As arranged, she went straight to see Chris Bain, the head of the Australian branch of Binnett, a tall, slim and distant man of about forty with a bland disciplined personality.

Rebecca had never found him to be approachable. She had, however, always treated him with the respect that she felt his position deserved.

They exchanged greetings and he went ahead with the reasons for the meeting, wasting no time on pleasantries.

After he had explained the request, and they had discussed what he knew about the work, he phoned Wilson.

"What's the time there, now?" she asked as he was looking for the contact number.

"Morning, he should be in his office."

Wilson answered almost immediately.

Chris switched the phone to conference mode and said that Rebecca was with him.

After greeting Wes Wilson she thanked him for the request for her help and said she was flattered at such a personal enquiry, made from so great a distance.

"The clients have read that article about your work in the nickel industry, in the Binnett journal. They have a similar project in Botswana, that also cannot be made to produce. It's been lingering at thirty percent of full production for four years and they want it written off.

"The Australian plant was very complicated."

"So is this one. That's why they need somebody who has experienced the same difficulties, so that the report they produce will provide an opinion that will be watertight."

They then went on to discuss general aspects of the project and the assignment's scope and location.

Rebecca asked if he could send her a copy of the proposed terms of reference.

"I'll email them," he replied.

"I'll call you back when I've read them."

The information arrived within minutes.

"So you want to prove they've done everything they can to save a project that has no chance of succeeding?" she said after reading the email and calling Wilson back.

"That's right."

"But if it has failed, what would you expect from me?"

"It has never produced more than a third of what it should."

"So what's the need for someone like me?"

"The project is managed by GVN, as part of a partnership, of three entities. The one, a family company, will be bankrupted and the other, the local tribe, would be saddled with some of the debt and lose their hoped for profits from the project. They are employing someone they know to review it's prospects."

"And organization and management are okay?"

"Nothing they've done has helped."

"Is there a design problem causing the lack of capability of the plant?" Rebecca asked.

"There must be, but I'm not an engineer."

"Most such problems can be engineered out."

"That's true and we've had literally dozens of consulting managers, engineers and technicians look at it."

"Are their own staff okay?"

"They've employed the best engineers and metallurgists from South Africa and internationally."

"And nothing has resulted in any improvement?"

"Nothing has worked. The main shareholders, other than GVN are, as I say, going to lose a great deal and are simply refusing to recognize the reality of the situation. Technically it's a failure and there's a complete lack of interest among the people working there"

"Why can't you use someone local?"

"The farming family and the Tswana, are about to employ a well recognized South African engineer, to investigate the potential. As I have said, GVN are responsible for running the project and are convinced that the problems cannot be solved. They want you there because you're internationally credible and your opinion will provide them with a counter balance to his evaluation."

"I've heard of GVN, they've got operations in Australia and we do work for them. So the other shareholders are being too optimistic?"

"That's right."

"No problem with that then, that's what I do."

"Good, so you'll take the assignment?"

"What about our plans here?" Interjected Chris Bain.

She had been thinking about this and her current projects were of a fairly routine nature and were being run by good managers. "I should be able to set things up so that I'm not missed too badly."

"You're not worried about the human side of the exercise?" asked Chris.

"Not in the least, if they can't get it working it's their problem."

"So you want to go?"

Conscious of the need to cover herself and the truth of Ed's comment that when someone tells you that you are the only candidate for a role, you need to be very sure that they are not setting you up for something unexpected, she hesitated.

"One problem is that we don't have much time," said Wilson.

She was silent for a few moments more, and then agreed to take the assignment.

Wes Wilson thanked her and then added, "Rebecca there is one point that does need to be understood about the exercise, and that is that it is not intended, by the clients, represented in the main by Gerry Heldebron and Jack Anders, to be a study."

"You've said that it's hopeless."

"Yes I have, but you need to know that Anders is a seriously important customer and moves in all the right circles in South Africa. Heldebron the general manager is no lightweight either and has a very tough reputation. They want the project closed, nothing more and nothing less."

"You've told me that it it's hopeless, what else is likely to result than a poor conclusion?"

"I just wanted to make sure you understand that we are not trying to solve some problem."

"I understand. I'll carefully delineate a systems approach that will confirm the facts of the failure."

"Right Rebecca. I'm looking forward to meeting you and working with you. Can you let me have your travel details when you're ready."

7

"Are we getting anywhere?" Rob asked on the morning of the third day of their prospecting expedition.

The search for additional ore, in the area North East of Ngami, had been a slow and torturous effort for him. They had traveled long distances during the first two days and he was beginning to regret his decision to accompany Ben.

Ben explained that his slow and methodical approach was necessary and was providing him with enough information to steadily improve his knowledge of the geology.

"It sure doesn't feel like it," answered Bob. "Why did we start off by heading north?"

"Not quite the same area?"

"No."

"Not the same exercise, Rob it's just something else I've had on my agenda and it was very successful. Sorry, I should have explained it better."

They had stopped near a water hole while they were speaking. Their Land Rover was parked on a flat rocky section next to a kopje. The water hole was in a dip, well below the surrounding country, surrounded by steep rock banks, making it inaccessible to hoofed animals. A kopje shaded the pool for most of the day, which, Ben supposed, was why it still had water in it.

"This is the spot my receptionist said was well worth a visit," said Rob.

"It is unusual," Ben said, and, getting out of the vehicle, he continued, "The formations around here are clearly exposed and what I'm looking for, a major fold, definitely has occurred here."

"Oh," replied Rob, none the wiser.

"We're on the right track."

They walked together around the kopje, Ben looking at the rock formations and Rob fiddling with his phone. Noticing that there was a slight indication of a signal, he called "Ben, my phone's got a bit of a signal, you said you wanted to phone your brother."

Ben phoned James and asked what was happening about Peter Connor.

"I haven't been able to speak to McNeil again."

"James you must get him there and soon. Call him now and ask if you can employ Connor directly. I'll wait here until you phone back."

James phoned back a few minutes later and said that he had persuaded McNeil to consider releasing Peter for the work, provided the engineer agreed with the idea.

"So are you going to contact him?"

"No. McNeil will talk to him first. He's going to do that now."

"I'll wait in this area to hear what happens."

At the time, Peter Connor was on his way to Springvale, in the Gauteng province of South Africa.

His journey from Johannesburg near the centre of the province took him through vast fields of maize, planted straight, green rows.

The maize, taller than a man, had long leaves. Each leaf seeming to form the same shaped curve; each stalk crowned with tufts of string like flowers.

He knew that similar land made up from the rich soils in barely undulating fields produced an abundant supply of food, for vast distances around the city. In country so familiar to Peter that he normally never took much notice of its quiet beauty.

A tall, broad shouldered man, Peter's normally smiling lips were turned down at the corners.

Springvale represented an unwelcome turn in his career. The assignment had started on the site a week before. At the personal request of McNeil.

Peter had found signs of major fraud and had returned to Johannesburg the previous day to discuss this with McNeil's accounting specialists.

Peter's thoughts returned to the present when he saw the Springvale smoke stack, through the thinning morning mist. He traversed a slight rise in the plain and saw the industrial complex itself. He thought that the structures looked as though they were floating on the fields of maize. Like flag ships of the new age, ready to move off, perhaps to capture another part of the once unspoiled land and bend it to their will. The industrial might had overcome the maize, which in itself had been an accompaniment of successive incursions. Hundreds of years before, small plantings of crops, by migrating tribes, had provided the first breaks in the endless savannas to displace herds of game, zebra, wildebeest, buffalo, and antelope.

The first human settlers of these spaces were thought to have been related to the Bushmen or Hottentots. Fossils had shown that these were the earliest known humanoid inhabitants of the planet.

Matabele, Nguni from the North had replaced these earlier settlers.

Having grown up in the province himself among the descendants of the African rulers who preceded the arrival of the Afrikaners, the Matabele, Peter knew their story well.

The Matebele, in the area, had been attacked by Shaka in his ruthless conquest of Southern Africa. This attack by the king of the Zulu, another branch of the Nguni, had resulted in a move North by the Matabele, who had then settled the land near and in the states now known as Botswana and Zimbabwe. Their arrival there had been greeted by clashes and massacres in the already populated lands. The tensions from that period remained until the present times and are reflected in some of the stresses that can be found in present day Zimbabwe.

Peter sighed restlessly. He wanted to escape himself. His own feeling of discomfort, with the world he knew so well, had come about fairly suddenly, as he imagined the movements of these earlier people would have done.

His progression from his childhood on his grandfather's farm near Rustenburg, to the present, had never been smooth and he had learned to be cautious of emotion-based opinions. He had, however, always, firmly believed in the future, however difficult the path toward it had seemed. 'Don't take risks, work hard, get promoted, look after your family, and help build the country, would have described how he thought.

In terms of where he belonged, in the South African rainbow, the determinedly independent people, with whose culture Peter could most closely relate, were those who had moved into the land left largely vacant by Shaka.

They had come in a partially religious journey or trek from the South, in the nineteenth century. The Afrikaners, or Boers as they called themselves, had moved north when Britain claimed the Cape from the Dutch and imposed a rule which had not suited them at all. They had then begun their migration in what was called the Great Trek and had firmly established themselves on the Highveld by the late nineteenth century. Among them were some descendants of the first British settlers including Peter's antecedents

The Afrikaner's more aggressive farming methods had resulted in larger plantings of crops.

The farming basis of the economy of Southern Africa had begun to take a lower profile with the discovery of gold and diamonds in the nineteenth century, after which the Transvaal Republic was claimed as part of the expanding British Empire.

The pretext for that invasion, on the part of the British Government, had been to prevent apparent discrimination, against the mostly British miners, by the Dutch South Africans or Afrikaners who had ruled the Transvaal Republic. That war had been won and those republics were no more.

British influence and fabulous quantities of gold and other minerals had originally, and still did, support the growth of what became an international success.

The years of colonial rule by Britain were then, for a time, replaced by another attempt at a farmer's or Boer republic at the end of the first half of the twentieth century. That state had barely survived forty years before handing over its reins to the country's latest rulers, at the end of the twentieth century.

The mixture of people who now ruled the country, nearly four hundred years after the first Europeans arrived in the Cape, with the Dutch governor van Riebeck, was complex and did not directly relate to the farmer mentality of the Afrikaner. The new rulers were having some success with aspects of the complex society but the going was not easy.

Industry's stark power now overshadowed the land, and its master's were those Peter followed, sometimes with difficulty. He sometimes wondered if his problems could possibly come from trying to apply his simple philosophy to the complexities of commerce. South African industry had thrived on cheap labour that had always been available but which now flowed in a seemingly unstoppable stream from the North, and the country had an abundant supply of resources. The farms had also developed with the industrial growth, to their present level of disciplined high productivity. These now compared favorably with those in the rest of the world and certainly set standards for the rest of Africa.

There was no doubt in Peter's mind that despite South Africa's disadvantages and its composition from a vast array of different peoples, or perhaps because of it, the country was easily the most prosperous on the continent and could go further, but his convictions were being stripped away in his career, and by his strong family centered philosophy being in an equal muddle.

His wife had left him two months earlier to go to Australia, with their children; Laura a ten-year-old girl,

Desmond, eight, and Nicholas the two year old. He tried on a regular basis to decide whether he should follow his family to Australia, or stay.

He thought, as he drove, of the day he and his wife had met in the sunshine on a church picnic, in the hills near Rustenburg. He pictured Christine's beautiful, finely chiseled face, glowing in the warm sunshine, her eyes; cornflower blue, her radiant smile, and her soft white skin, faintly freckled. They had married the year after their first meeting. Christine had worked as a teacher supporting him through parts of his career. His study had been largely part time.

Then he pictured their last parting, of Christine crying, but still determined to go. She had been hugging their daughter Laura; ten years old and so much like her mother that it was almost uncanny. Desmond who was a strong blonde boy had been hugging him. Nicholas, the two year old could speak almost perfectly and was gentler, had stood apart, baffled by what was happening.

The division between the couple had grown slowly. Christine had decided Australia was a better place to bring up children. The ever-present danger, the slow ecological destruction of South Africa and the encroaching overpopulation, unchecked, it seemed, even by the tragedy of the Aids epidemic, were all factors driving her determination. She was also convinced that Australia offered a uniquely good future, in a globally confused era.

She had gone there, without Peter, to investigate its potential, and had wanted Peter to go with her. His immigration papers had been completed and his visa approved, but work had held him back.

She had returned after establishing herself as a permanent resident of Australia and had begun a campaign to get Peter to return to the huge country with her.

While the aspects of South Africa that worried her were as much of a concern to Peter as to her, he held on to his belief that South Africa's technical and economic future were uniquely good, and would lead to better times. His understanding of technology and his work at improving efficiency and productivity would and did, he was sure, contribute to the country's future. He believed that increasing industrial strength could achieve more than erudite efforts, however well meant. So Peter had delayed, and this, together with the long hours he was working, meant that he never got any closer to leaving the country for the apparent promise that Australia offered and Christine had eventually said that she was going, whether he accompanied her or not.

Peter had never fully explained his greatest fear to her, that he had not wanted to start from scratch in Australia, which he thought was not all that different, but where he knew he would be completely unknown. Not having the right connections had made things difficult enough for him in South Africa.

His thoughts were interrupted by a call from McNeil.

He brought the car to a standstill on the side of the long straight road beside the fields of maize and climbed out, using the call as an opportunity to stretch his legs.

The call was a request that he return to Johannesburg to discuss undertaking a review of the Ngami project.

Worried, as he was, about the work, he was doing for McNeil, at Springvale, he was not happy about another direct request from the principal.

He had not spoken to the managing director since he had started at Springvale, and was not sure how much McNeil knew about the difficulties he was having there. He decided that he had no choice about what he did, and agreed to return to Johannesburg that evening to discuss the assignment in more detail.

McNeil thanked him and said he was looking forward to their meeting.

After opening the car door to get back into the vehicle for the return drive Peter stopped for a moment and folded his arms across the roof. He rested his chin on his arms and looked, for a few lost minutes, at the scene. He felt and smelled the warmth of the veldt. The fields of maize displayed a rigidity that was not unlike the way he lived. He sighed and got back into the car.

He was so structured and careful that it was almost foolish. He thought, not for the first time, about the many people he had worked with who managed to take a percentage of the revenue they were responsible for and wondered why on earth he was so bad at things that would make much more commercial sense.

McNeil phoned James de Bruin and told him he had managed to get Peter Connor to consider the possibility of helping but that more work on the idea was needed so he was meeting with the engineer that evening.

James thanked him.

"Okay James, I'll call you after the meeting with him."

James phoned Ben and told his brother what had happened.

Ben was delighted and asked if he should phone Peter himself.

"I've told McNeil it's your request and that we're desperate. Perhaps leave it until we find out what happens."

"Okay we'll camp in this spot this evening, its hard to find anywhere with enough of a signal out here. I'll phone you at about ten tomorrow morning."

"You should get one of those satellite phones, they work better don't they?"

"I keep meaning to."

8

The importance of the meeting between Peter Connor and McNeil, to the Ngami clan, and the de Bruins, could have been said to be reflected in the quality of the restaurant in which they met. It was very good, even by the high standards that South Africa can offer.

When Peter arrived, the maitre d'hotel showed him to the cocktail bar where McNeil was sitting, near a window overlooking the lights of Santon.

McNeil stood to greet the younger man.

The setting, the managing director's warm welcome, and his extraordinary personality made Peter feel as though he had been removed from his normal plane of existence.

McNeil was well known and well connected. His work was often in the forefront of industrial knowledge, and had been the subject of articles in international journals. Yet he could talk to someone like Peter, who was relatively obscure, as easily as he could to the leader of a country.

After he had welcomed Peter, he went on to explain the problems the de Bruins faced with the Ngami project. He also explained his concerns about getting involved while finding out how much Peter knew of the project and its potential.

Food and drink waiters interrupted their conversation to take their orders. McNeil ordered a prawn entrée with a grilled Cape Salmon to follow.

Peter asked for a smoked salmon entree, with prawns peri-peri as a main course.

"So Ben de Bruin asked for me himself?" Peter eventually asked.

The wine waiter brought a bottle of Pinot Gris before McNeil could reply and he waited until the wine was served before answering. "Yes, he was impressed with your work during the initial commissioning and now they need you to provide a credible opinion of the project's capability after a short review. They want someone who knows the plant, has a good reputation, and has proven practical competence."

"I did work there, but it's a big project. I was in charge of the commissioning for a while, but when you're in a senior position like that you know what's happening but can't necessarily deal with all the detailed problems. The type of work I do now, though, is well suited to dealing with complex situations."

"Ben has vouched for your competence to the Ngami board. He's told them you are someone who can realistically assess the capability of the plant."

"Yes I knew him well and we worked well together."

"James also asked me to tell you that Ben sends his best wishes and has asked you, as a personal favor, to accept the work."

"That's very flattering, but what if I can't see an answer, or it's something they don't want to hear?"

"I understand your position Peter, but you did say, earlier, that you are sure the plant can achieve what it's designed to do."

"Yes, it should be able to produce at full capacity. The design is complex but not that unconventional. There must be some problem, or detail, or set of problems at the root of the failures that's not being pinpointed or resolved. So management of maintenance or operations or both are faulty, but that type of thing can generally be fixed."

"That's exactly what they need to have established, by someone who will be able to ask the right questions and check the answers without too much research."

"Do you want me to leave this Springvale exercise though?"

"They're desperate, and, although I'm wary about getting involved, I have known James de Bruin most of my life, not as a close friend, but as someone I can trust and rely on. I believe that it's essential that they get a clearer picture of what's happening and I really would like to help him; but we as a firm can't get directly involved."

"What's wrong with fixing problems for GVN, we do it all the time?"

"Yes, but they ask us to. This is the other way around, we are being asked to pull someone else's solution out of a GVN problem."

"The other people are entitled to get our opinion though, aren't they?"

"Of course they are but GVN is established and well thought of, they are a major client of ours."

"You mean GVN is too big to be wrong."

"Too big to be told by a customer that needs them that they're making a mess of Ngami."

"So how do I do something that will help but that won't annoy the people at GVN?"

"Perhaps we could allow you to see what can be done to salvage the situation, on your own."

"On my own I'd have even more difficulty dealing with GVN."

"People and big name companies are not necessarily different in their ability to solve some problems. Big names are as liable to failure as are individuals, sometimes more so. I've said that you might be able give them an assessment of the problems on some kind of release from us."

"Sounds reasonable but I definitely don't want to leave your firm."

"No, I realize that. A separation of some sort is the only answer. You mean a lot to me, and to our company, but all of us need to move forward. If you could manage to do what no one else has done you would achieve a unique credibility. I'd make sure they pay you at the highest possible rate and we could also arrange to let you do the review on some kind of special leave. But I'll have to check that with our lawyers.

"Do you know anything else about what's wrong?"

"Only what I've already told you."

"The odd thing is that the entire operation seems to have been mishandled by GVN."

"You're right, they make mistakes of course but I've never heard of them losing the plot like this. You hear of problems all the time, but GVN of all companies seem to correct them."

"It seems as though there's something strange about the project, and yet no one knows anything about who or what is creating a negative agenda."

"That's about it."

"How big a disaster would the plant's failure be?"

"The loss of the venture would affect Botswana and the Tswana clan seriously. De Bruin Enterprises would be bankrupted and of course many smaller investors would lose money."

"What about GVN? If they were facing a loss they would use their expertise to rectify the situation. They're big enough to move people there from another of their sites."

"I don't know Peter."

"What does de Bruin think?"

"He's not at all reticent about that, he's convinced that there's something fraudulent going on at least."

"By GVN?"

"I hardly think so."

"Who does he suspect then?"

"He doesn't know, but since there are literally billions of dollars involved, it could be anyone or unlikely though it seems, the company itself. He says it would have to be people at a high level and probably more than one person if it's not the company."

"If it's fraud, and GVN are directly involved, I could be annihilated as much as you would be. If it's anything else I'd have to get the cooperation of GVN, and if you are not sure about trying to do that, then I surely should be very careful of what I'm getting myself involved in."

"I think where the review is concerned there is only one question you need to think about, and to answer, and that is whether you are interested in providing a professional opinion of the project's capability. It's not a long enough exercise to affect an individual carrying out a technical assessment. There is very little danger for you in doing that. With our firm's involvement it would become more of a threat to whoever is involved and that would make the danger more immediate."

While this sounded reasonable to Peter, he knew, from personal experience of politics on assignments, that were not nearly so critical, things could quickly become unmanageable if the people involved were sufficiently desperate about something as small as a personal error. With billions of dollars involved he had little doubt that dangers could evolve on a scale beyond anything with which he was familiar. However the benefits were real and the needs of the disaffected shareholders were something he thought he should consider. He knew and liked Ben de Bruin and had been genuinely happy among the people of Ngami. "I'd like to help them, but I'm worried about the risk," he said.

"Perhaps you should meet and talk to James de Bruin."

The entrée and main course had arrived in turn and had been enjoyed as the two men had continued their discussion. They were eventually shown the sweet menu, and agreed to order crepe suzettes.

When the elegant maitre de hotel arrived with the stainless steel trolley to prepare their crepes, they stopped talking to watch the culinary effort. The man lit the gas burner, added sugar, orange juice and grated orange peel to the stainless steel saucepan.

As the performance progressed, McNeil explained that he had selected the restaurant because they made crepe suzettes like no other place he had ever visited.

The aroma of sugar caramelizing and citrus cooking distracted them from the problems of Ngami. Prepared quantities of liqueurs were added to the pan, followed by thin crepes folded into small triangles. The pan was tilted toward the gas flame and the vapor from the liqueurs ignited into a blue-mauve flame with a muffled puff. The flickering blue flame floated above the creation for a few moments, forming a focal point between the maitre de hotel and a huge flower arrangement of Cape heather, protea's and strelitzia's.

"When would they want me to start?" Peter asked after they had enjoyed the crepes.

"Tomorrow wouldn't be too soon for them, let's check."

McNeil contacted James de Bruin as they left the restaurant and told him about Peter's interest and how he had been worried about some aspects of the proposal.

"Could he come down here and talk to us tomorrow?" de Bruin asked.

McNeil said that Peter was with him and conveyed the message to the engineer.

Peter agreed to travel to the Cape the next morning.

The necessary arrangements were made and McNeil had his office arrange a hotel room for Peter. He spent a comfortable night in Johannesburg and left for the Cape early the next morning.

9

The flight to Cape Town, early on the day after the meeting with McNeil, about Ngami, was routine. Peter hired a car at the airport and headed for the de Bruin's farm.

The journey from Cape Town Airport to Franschhoek, near where the de Bruin's farm was located, is beautiful. Not even the most widely experienced traveler would normally ignore it, but Peter hardly noticed the scenery. He was excited by the challenge of the investigation and the high fees. The possible independence that had presented itself both frightened and enticed him. An overall change of direction to that of a self-promoting engineer and entrepreneur was a step he had thought about but had never planned to take. As he well knew, the main players in design and construction in the country had changed completely in the time that he had first been qualified. He had no wish to become another bit player that would have to leave the stage when their part was up, however common the use of contractors was becoming.

Peter thought about the Ngami countryside as he drove. He and his wife had spent a few weeks there, while the plant was being commissioned.

A particularly memorable event during the stay was a camping trip they'd gone on. Their first evening of the outing was unforgettable. Having driven away from the village along the broad intermittent river, they passed through gaps in the wooded bank onto what they thought was dry sand. As they drove, a soft patch had snapped the Land Rover's side shaft.

Luckily they'd been warned to take a spare and set out to replace the part.

The misfortune turned into a magical interlude. As Peter and Christine had battled with their awkward mechanical task they watched the setting sun's shades of gold on the bush and kopjes, causing them to glow and cast long shadows, enhancing their size.

A length of the river, that was much deeper than average, ended near there, at the junction of two 'ranges' of the koppies, to form a natural 'dam'. This large, seldom dry, 'water hole' was known as Lake Ngami and had given it's name to the village and the project.

A variety of game wandered out to the water as they had worked.

They did not complete the repair on the Land Rover before dark and spent the night there, to be treated to a similar parade at dawn.

They explored the ruins of some ancient fortifications that crowned the tops of some of the kopjes, in the days following the repair. These rocky outposts were constructed like small versions of the famed Zimbabwe ruins, by long forgotten inhabitants of the area, to guard against marauders who had also faded into history. But they failed to find any trace of the ancient metal processing kilns they had been told about and which were supposed to exist around the kopjes and supposed that settlers, prospectors, and miners, who had pioneered the area had destroyed the more obvious of these.

Peter and Christine had talked as they explored, about the interesting and perhaps unique history of the landlocked country, now one of the most successful in Africa. The efforts of the ancestor of Botswana's first president and democratic leader, Sir Seretse Khama with two other tribal chiefs of the Tswana, and pioneering missionaries, had prevented Botswana's annexation, and development, by Cecil Rhodes, one of the final colonizers in the British Empire. The leaders of Botswana had, from then on, skillfully led the country to independence, and into the modern world, without the loss of the country's unique culture. Its people multiracial and multicultural, were now better off than most others in Africa, very much because of this leadership.

Peter's memories of camping in Botswana, faded when the de Bruin farm came into view. He slowed at the start of the long driveway to the house. Tall pine trees separated it from hundreds of acres of vines. He could smell the pine as he drove slowly toward the house. The rows of vines led away from the trees and vanished into the distance, seeming to melt into the mountains on either side of the valley. The setting struck Peter as South Africa at its best. A Cape Dutch home eventually appeared with white gables, thatched roof and small paned windows, to fit perfectly into the blue tinted backdrop.

Peter parked the car at the bottom of a wide set of stairs that led to the front door of the house.

James de Bruin emerged from the large, heavy, front door shortly after he had stopped and strode down the stairs.

He introduced himself and explained that he had been looking out for Peter.

The simple welcoming gesture by someone so obviously established made Peter want to help the farmer without hearing further details of what was involved in the work. He noticed as he shook de Bruin's hand that the farmer's black hair showed tinges of gray. His face was tanned and craggy, but he moved effortlessly, seeming very fit.

James led him into the Cape Dutch home after the warm welcome.

Peter remarked on the beauty of the house and asked how old it was.

De Bruin said that it had been built in the seventeenth century.

"That's older than many famous international buildings?"

"Yes, it is. It has some unusual aspects, like floors that are made from stinkwood that would not be affordable for anything but the best furniture now."

Peter said that he thought that the furniture looked as old as the house, and asked if it too was Stinkwood.

"Yes it is," De Bruin replied.

"Why is something so valuable called Stinkwood?"

De Bruin explained that, as Stinkwood's name bluntly implied, the wood did have an unpleasant smell when first felled, but that the bad smell quickly vanished after the wood dries to become attractive and hardwearing. "Now days there is very little around here, it comes from forests near Knysna, and special permits have to be applied for before it can be felled. One funny aspect of owning Stinkwood furniture is to tell someone what it's made of, and leave the room in a way that you can still watch them."

"And?"

"They invariably sniff it."

Peter laughed.

De Bruin's office was in a separate part of the house, at the end of a longish passageway.

Seeing the receptionist at her desk Peter was even more surprised that de Bruin had bothered to come out to welcome him.

De Bruin's office was as relaxed and homely as the farmer was himself.

Charles Obenta was waiting in the office and was introduced to Peter.

Charles explained that his first knowledge of the Ngami project had been an approach made to him, as a member of the tribal council, by the de Bruins, after Ben had located the ore deposit. The project had then been brought to fruition through hard work on all of their parts. The third partner, the GVN mining corporation, had been found to develop the resource and run the operations. Finance had been obtained from the World Bank with the de Bruin's mortgaging their farm, and guarantees having been made by Charles on behalf of the Ngami clan.

Peter thought that Charles looked to be about forty years old. He was about the same height as the other two men but thinner.

"As you know Peter, the initial stages of the mining and metallurgical extraction process went well," de Bruin said.

"Yes it did, the situation that it now appears to be in, really surprises me."

De Bruin spent a few minutes asking about Peter's background and ambitions.

"Where is Ben?" Peter asked.

"Doing some geological studies." De Bruin answered.

As the conversation progressed, Peter could not believe that a corporation like GVN would need to take advantage of people like the partners appeared to be and said so at the conclusion of their exposition.

"All we know about for certain is that the plant has not produced anything like it should."

"I'm sure there must be an answer to that."

"Nothing they've done seems to help and the morale is terrible."

"Well, it really sounds wrong. I could certainly look at it, and I've improved situations, working with unhappy people before," said Peter.

"So we've been told," answered de Bruin, who then asked Peter if he would spend two weeks on site to formulate a technical opinion of what was wrong and a further week writing up his findings.

Peter hesitated, then said, "I'd like to help but I'm worried about getting on the wrong side of a corporation like GVN. The review might not present too much of a problem, but making the changes will be a lot more dangerous."

"We are desperate and need you there almost immediately, and we don't have any other options. There's a meeting with the World Bank in three weeks time that we believe will be used to sink the project," de Bruin said.

"How can so much damage be done in one meeting."

"The original finance was provided for four years and that time is up."

"How will anyone benefit from shutting the project down?"

"I honestly don't know, but it's happening."

"And you and the others might lose everything?"

"Might is not the word, we will lose everything."

"Why don't you speak to GVN, explain your situation."

"Of course we can, and have done so, but only with those directors responsible for Ngami which is a small part of their interests. I really cannot believe it's GVN as a corporation. This is more complex and we cannot simply trot in there making vague statements. Major corporations don't explain their motives. They are there to make money."

"But not crush investors."

"GVN only have their own interests to consider. In finance there are always winners and losers. They would never stop explaining if they took note of every unhappy shareholder."

"Wouldn't it be most unusual to let a project, as big as Ngami is, slide into oblivion?"

"It's not really oblivion. Only the end for us."

"I need to get my thoughts fully settled. It's a big jump for me. I have to leave the security of the McNeil umbrella, and although as a temporary measure, it's still possible that the exercise will put me in too much of an exposed position, so I'd like to think about it for another day if I could."

"That seems reasonable Peter. So thank you for coming down here. So we'll hear from you tomorrow?"

Peter said he would let McNeil know what his decision was and thanked them both.

De Bruin walked with him to his car.

Charles left shortly after Peter.

His subsequent report, to the tribal council, on the meeting with Peter in the Cape, was relayed to van Zyl.

10

Peter parked and made his way to the Springvale plant's offices when he got back from the trip to the Cape. He was advised that McFarlane, the Springvale plant manager, was not available. He then asked the person at reception if he could see the operations manager. Another call confirmed that he could see the second in charge of the facility and was given a visitor's pass.

He thanked the security official who smiled pleasantly and wished him a good day.

The security section advised their principals when Peter Connor got to site and a specially chosen operative arrived to take over the department shortly after Peter got there.

Peter turned and strode out of the reception area, to head on up the stairs, irritable and on edge, then walked along the passage's dark uncarpeted floor, to the operations manager's office, where he found, to his surprise, that McFarlane, the site manager, sitting with his back to the door, talking to the operations manager across a large, unloved looking desk.

The office looked as worn out and untidy as the desk.

McFarlane turned around as Peter walked in and said. "So you're back Peter, I was rather hoping we'd seen the last of you."

"Pleased to hear it." Peter answered, feeling petulant. Trying but failing to cut his reply short. "I wasn't too keen to come back myself. How are you Mr. McFarlane?"

"I'm fine, no thanks to your bloody work." McFarlane's mean eyes flickered away. He started to turn his back on Peter and said, "As you've no doubt been told I don't have time to talk to you now, so I'll catch up with you in the conference room later."

Peter nodded. "Fine, I'll carry on where I left off," he said, and made his way back to the conference room that he had been using as an office. Barely having achieved enough acknowledgment to allow him to restart his work made him hesitate about what to do.

He slumped at the conference room table for a few seconds, opened his portable, and sat looking at the blank screen, thinking about what his best approach should be.

He decided that getting any contribution from the unhappy McFarlane would be unlikely so he would try to work from the invoicing information that he had been given access to when he was last there.

He returned to McFarlane's office and asked his assistant if she could let him have the invoices that he had already looked at, for the previous month's construction.

She understood his predicament and decided to help him where this did not conflict directly with McFarlane's instructions.

Peter had all the information he needed within a half hour.

Working his way through some of the statistics, he quickly found several anomalies in the construction costs that proved his suspicions and he was well on his way to tracing a pattern in these by the end of the day.

McFarlane did not call on him, as he had said he would, and when Peter inquired as to his whereabouts he was told that the site manager had left for the day.

That evening when he was finished, at about eight, he went to the company guesthouse, where he was staying, found some eggs and potatoes in the refrigerator and prepared a light dinner. Then sat reading a novel he had brought with him.

There was a heavy banging on the front door within an hour of his arrival.

He could not see anything through the spy-hole in the door so he went to the dining room window that faced onto the covered area. The banging became weaker and slower as he went. From the window, he could see a man slumped against the door, seemingly alone. Returning to the front door he unlocked and carefully opened it. The door was pushed toward him by the man's weight, he stumbled through and fell onto the spotless carpet, bleeding from a wound in his head.

Peter walked out the door to the fence. He was relieved to find that there was no one else in sight, in the well-lit garden, or in the street. As he got back and closed the door the man staggered to his knees saying. "I'm so sorry. I didn't know where to go."

He thought he recognized him as someone he had spoken to during his site inspections. A severe wound above the man's left ear was bleeding profusely.

Helped by Peter, he stood and managed to get to the kitchen before collapsing again. Peter knelt beside him as he lay between the door and the kitchen table and pressed a clean linen cloth to the wound.

"What happened?" Peter asked, as the badly injured man groaned and opened his eyes.

"The new Andselc supervisor," he mumbled and slipped back into unconsciousness.

Peter made him as comfortable as he could and called the doctor and security. The doctor and the company ambulance arrived within minutes of the call. No one from security turned up or phoned.

After the injured man was taken to hospital. The doctor turned to Peter and asked what had happened.

"I don't really know. He said something about the new security supervisor."

The doctor didn't comment. Violence and robbery were not unusual in the company village, but usually took the form of arguments that sometimes ended in fights. He had decided he did not want to know what had happened or to be further involved when Peter mentioned security.

He wished Peter a good night and left.

Peter returned to the house after the doctor drove off, showered and went to bed.

He slept fitfully and got up at first light.

11

In the morning, after the wounded man arrived on his doorstep, Peter went to McFarlane's office to find out what had happened about the injured man.

He was told that the manager had not arrived.

Returning to the conference room he double checked the anomalies he had found the previous day, in the plant's accounts, and having confirmed his suspicions, sent an email to McNeil advising the principal that he had found conclusive evidence of fraud at Springvale.

Having nothing else to check on in the accounts, he then went for a walk in the plant.

At the northern end of the building the construction of a new electric furnace caught his attention. He stood and watched as teams of workers, shirts off because of the heat, shining with perspiration, skillfully swung huge electric furnace parts into position, clearly happy and enjoying their work.

They called out instructions to each other and sang in unison when coordination was needed, making the complex project look like a game. Enjoying the rhythm of chanting rigger's songs and seeing their efficient work, Peter imagined how the skills he was watching could be multiplied to build a better future for the country.

He turned eventually to make his way back to McFarlane's office. When he got there, he asked the assistant if the manager had arrived.

"I don't know where he's gone Peter," she said and then added, "I wouldn't wait around for him if I were you."

Peter, frowning, shook his head.

"How are you getting on Peter?" she asked, understanding his frustration.

He told her about the assault.

At first she looked down at the papers in front of her, then looked directly at him and said, "Violence is so much a part of our lives now Peter that we sometimes hardly notice it." Peter was so intense; she liked him and wished she could help him.

"I certainly noticed this."

"No, I mean others, like me, in this case."

"What do you think I should do?" he asked, puzzled by the odd reply.

"Well, Peter," she said after a short pause, "I would forget it happened." Peter frowned and was about to continue.

Looking uncomfortable, she raised her hand slightly to stop him and said, "I can't talk about it Peter, I think you should leave security to handle their own problems. I shouldn't say so, but I overheard something they said about you yesterday and I think you should steer well clear of them, they can be bad news," then, not waiting for his answer, she picked up some work and moved it to a folder.

Peter thanked her pensively and walked slowly back to the conference room.

He phoned the hospital to find out about the injured man and was told that he was in a coma.

Unable to concentrate on anything properly, he decided not to wait for McFarlane and called the person in charge of security.

The man politely asked Peter to come and see him.

When Peter got to the security building, which was set apart from the operations offices, he was directed to the office by the person at the front desk.

The supervisor stood to greet Peter when he walked in.

Tall and well built with fair hair and brown eyes, he introduced himself as Dirk Coetzee, and asked Peter to sit down.

Peter accepted and after a brief conversation about Peter's assignment Dirk enquired into what Peter wanted to see him about,

"You know that one of your people was assaulted yesterday and turned up at the house where I'm staying?"

Coetzee answered, "I had meant to call you and say I'm sorry about your involvement in what happened last night, but I have not had time. The man was injured because he left me no choice about how I dealt with him. There's a great deal at stake here and I had clear instructions to bring him into line. He refused to obey my instructions and deliberately provoked me. He has himself to blame."

Peter was surprised by the Coetzee's attitude. "You know what you're saying Dirk?"

"Of course I do, sir."

"But surely Dirk, that man had been hit very hard with something very solid."

"We all have problems and there is no room for softness in our operations. No one is above discipline Mister Connor."

"Unless he attacked you?"

"He raised his hand, I've warned him before, several times. The man's a troublemaker and troublemakers have no place in our organization," he said pointedly enough for Peter to be taken aback.

"Are you threatening me?"

Dirk nearly said yes.

Peter could see what the open-faced man was thinking and felt coldly furious. He could not decide how to answer, or how to deal with the clearly implied authority over his own actions. He was beginning to understand the personal assistant's reluctance to talk. He said, "Well Dirk I have to report the matter and I'll give you a copy of the report."

The supervisor agreed, looking satisfied rather than chastened.

Surely the whole thing can't have been set up? But, if so, why? Peter thought as he walked away, feeling more fear than concern.

Dirk reported the encounter to his superiors, after Peter left.

McNeil rang at about eleven and asked Peter what he intended to do about the assignment to Ngami.

Peter explained his hesitation briefly and McNeil asked if he could come back to Johannesburg to discuss what he was doing and what he planned.

Peter agreed to meet him for lunch at the restaurant they'd been to before Peter's trip to the Cape.

McNeil was already seated at the restaurant when Peter arrived, and the maitre d'hotel showed the engineer to his table.

After Peter was settled they spoke for a while about generalities and then Peter told McNeil about the assault and the attitude of the security supervisor.

McNeil listened sympathetically and then asked for more detail about the commercial problems at Springvale.

"It looks to me as though they're charging twice for some materials."

"Who is?"

"The management."

"McFarlane was completely uncooperative?"

"McFarlane seems almost deranged."

"The main difficulty with McFarlane was thought to have been related to his ineffectiveness. Can you show me the documentation for the deliveries?"

Peter showed McNeil copies of invoices and bills of material for the construction on his laptop, explaining what had apparently happened.

"It looks conclusive," said McNeil.

"Could you get auditors to cross check what I've showed you?"

"I think I might get Eileen from corporate control to look at it. What you've indicated is right up her alley and she understands the technical aspects better than almost anyone in that area."

"Now about Ngami. Are you going to take the position?"

"I'm worried about being sunk by the corporate or whatever powers that the de Bruins are facing."

"We'll give you special leave Peter, so if the exercise comes off the rails you won't be stranded."

Peter thanked him.

"So can I tell de Bruin you'll take the position?"

"Okay, if I've a way back, I'll review the plant's prospects, but any salvage effort that I might find to be needed are likely to be much more dangerous."

"I understand, let's deal with the first part first, I'lll talk to de Bruin," McNeil said and phoned James de Bruin to confirm his arrangement with Peter.

Shortly afterwards Peter received an email from de Bruin with the contract details and terms of reference for the assignment.

McNeil, with Peter's approval, arranged for his temporary release and for a shelf corporation to be purchased in his Peter's name and he then accepted the assignment in an email providing the new company's details.

De Bruin sent an order for the investigation, that stated that the outcome of the work in thee weeks time, would be a report to be presented initially to the de Bruin enterprises board and Charles Obenta, and then to the meeting with the World Bank. The sum to be paid for the work was considerable.

Peter phoned James de Bruin and told him that he would also provide the site management with a summary of what he found, before writing the report, and that this would take place about two weeks after he started, as he would normally have done with such a review.

James agreed and said he would arrange for Peter's access to the site and would call back within a few minutes.

He then contacted the site on what should have been a formality. This was met with a delay, the respondent saying he would call back.

James received the promised call in a matter of minutes and was advised that Peter did not satisfy the Ngami security standards.

"But he's worked there before."

"He's been reported as having had problems with security on another of our sites."

James checked with Jack Anders and was told, after another delay, about Peter's problem at Springvale.

"What problem at Springvale?" Asked James.

"He's had some sort of security problem there."

"I'll call you back," said James rudely.

He phoned Peter and asked about the security problem he had had at Springvale.

Peter explained.

James thanked him and said he would get back to him.

He sat back and sighed. He decided to speak to Michael Anders the cousin of Jack and the major shareholder of GVN. He knew that Michael had only just returned from a long familiarisation period overseas, undertaken as part of his preparation to eventually run the GVN corporation. He had known Michael for a long time, and had a closer association with him than was generally known. This had come about because James had helped Michael through a traumatic stage of his life, when the magnate was still a schoolboy.

James received a sympathetic, if impatient, hearing.

Peter and McNeil, growing weary of waiting, had stopped in a coffee shop to wait for the return call.

After hearing from James, Michael, impatiently, went to see Jack.

After a short delay, while Jack phoned someone, Michael was told a version of the security story.

"This is bloody ridiculous man. I know the de Bruins personally. Do you want me to get this bloody Connor in there myself?" he said straight over Jack's attempted justification. He was very busy himself and badly needed every minute to handle his own work.

"I'll get him there don't worry," Jack answered, awkwardly for him.

Michael phoned James and told him that Peter would be allowed on site while Jack looked on.

After he finished the call he said. "Jack that is the least relevant thing I have ever had to do in my career, I do not want to have to repeat this exercise in any way. What can they possibly think of you to come to me like that? What the hell is going on there?"

"Security picked it up."

Michael shook his head and walked out of the office.

Having received no news, Peter and McNeil had returned to the principal's office and had just sat down when James phoned them at last.

McNeil listened to what James said, thanked him, asked him to hold on, and then told Peter that he had been cleared to go.

"So when do I leave for Botswana?" Peter asked.

"You talk to him," he said and handed the phone to Peter.

Peter repeated the question.

"Right away, if it suits you, they never close the operation," answered de Bruin.

"Monday be okay?"

"That'll be fine."

Peter thanked him.

"So you're on your way?" asked McNeil after the call.

"Looks like it. Thank you for your trouble."

"You're more than welcome Peter, and, although it's been a bit of an odd exercise, you've handled Springvale well. I think, based on your work, we should be able to eliminate the problems there."

"Thanks, I'll help if you need me there again."

After getting Peter accepted onto the Ngami site, James de Bruin sank back in his chair, pleased at having recruited Peter but more worried than ever about the situation that they were facing. He felt rather than knew that the security barrier was only the first hurdle. He was concerned, considering what had happened to the security guard at Springvale, that they might start encountering physical danger in Botswana.

He tried ringing Ben but his phone was out of range.

12

Peter drove slowly away from the car park at McNeil's office, thinking about the failing Ngami project, his agreed part in the exercise, and the many aspects that worried him.

He was drawn out of his reverie at the first set of lights.

In the one-way street after the corporate car park, a man walked through a red light, onto the crossing, in front of the car.

Since he was travelling slowly Peter had plenty of time to stop; there was no one behind him, so the delay, at a green light, was only a slight irritation.

The person seemed crippled or a drunk. He shuffled forward, staggered and then repeated the exercise in the opposite direction, effectively blocking Peter's way.

The light, for Peter, changed to red, so he had to remain stationary. The man's condition was far too common a sight, amongst the wealth Johannesburg represented, he pretended to ignore the antics of the odd pedestrian, and looked around at the people standing at the intersection.

One face caught his attention. It was ugly, with eyes that seemed to be struggling to focus, affected by a deep scar across the left side of the man's face.

He was standing at the edge of the pavement holding some form of frame and his whole attention was concentrated on Peter.

Peter froze, he was looking at a hunter about to make a kill, and he was the quarry.

The man raised the frame and rushed at Peter's car.

Peter forced himself to stamp on the accelerator; bumping the staggering jaywalker with the car's left fender. He flinched at the thud but kept accelerating, through the red light, turning left in the direction of the traffic. He could not afford any sensitivity. He'd heard of too many people being killed in Johannesburg, after being forced to stop, in similar situations.

The man with the scarred face had the agility of a cat, as did the supposed cripple.

The steel frame crashed into the door frame, missing the driver's door window, its target, swung around, and broke the back door window.

A third man fired a pistol at Peter.

The bullet shattered the window that the frame had been supposed to break, and, deflected by the glass, just missed Peter.

The scar-faced assassin, who had lost his balance, swung back toward the pavement, bumping the gunman and causing a second shot to go wide.

Peter's car scraped the side of a crowded minibus in the crossroad.

The wide frightened eyes of the passengers looked out, helplessly, thinking they were about to join the country's horrific accident statistics.

As the car leapt away, swinging to the left, in the direction of the minibus, the gunman took careful aim for his third shot at Peter.

The long barrel of the exquisite instrument of death did not waver as he squeezed the trigger.

Luckily Peter swerved away from the minibus, as the man fired, and the third bullet missed him.

He swung in front of the minibus and the assassins could no longer see him.

The gunman turned and cursed the scar-faced man, saying he had missed because the window glass deflected the bullet. It was supposed to have been broken. He put his weapon into its holster, still muttering, and the three would be killers disappeared into the agitated crowd.

Peter, barely able to drive, pulled over a few minutes later, in a quiet area.

After a few moments spent gathering his thoughts, he reported the attempted car-jacking to the police using his cell phone.

He was told that such events were hard to trace, and that they doubted they would be able to find the perpetrators, but that they would contact him if anything came from their investigation.

Peter shook his head trying to clear his thoughts, the event made no sense. If they were trying to rob him, the whole exercise was misdirected. It seemed to have been an attempt on his life, intended to stop him in his tracks rather than rob him, or why would the gunman have kept firing; after there was no chance of taking anything from him? It only made sense in relation to Ngami.

He restarted his journey, still badly on edge, and decided that he would stop at a friend's pub.

Jeffrey, the pub's owner, had moved to South Africa from Malawi, many years earlier, to take advantage of the higher wages paid there. He and Peter had worked together for a unique mining company. A miniature industrial kingdom set on the western edge of the Witwatersrand, and covering a vast area. They had both started there as trainees; doing practical work on site and attending technical universities on a part time basis. Jeffery in mining and Peter in mechanical and electrical engineering. The training had been good by any standard. A mining empire had been built on the shoulders of the company's 'graduates'.

As Peter walked into the pub he looked around at the quality of the fittings and thought how well Jeffery had done in his move from a successful mining engineer to owning the pub.

Jeffrey was sitting on his own when Peter arrived; he had been thinking how much greener Malawi was and how tired he was of South Africa and its violence.

He came from a place near a mountain called M'lanje. The view of which, from the hills at Limbe, is one of the most beautiful in Africa. The sentinel stands about two thousand meters above the surrounding plain, with beautiful green farms at its base. It looked its most impressive when black rolling clouds come in from the East coast, to swallow all but the highest peaks. They would stop at the mountain, swirl around its base, and then sweep up to the peak.

Jeffery's move from the mining company, to buy a house and the pub in the expensive area of Santon, had been achieved by his accepting a generous redundancy package.

He and his wife had been happy there; but, after she had died of cancer, six months earlier, he had begun to lose interest in the successful venture. She had, in a way, been the pub's spirit, always there, a support and a companion. She'd made sure of the tidiness and character of the pub, almost without seeming to do so. He looked around and thought the proud establishment was beginning to look tired.

In the days when Peter and Jeffrey had worked together, Jeffery had done most of the talking, enlivening their work.

As Peter sat down in the air-conditioned comfort of the bar, Jeffrey smiled warmly at him and asked how he was.

"I've just had the closest shave of my life."

"What happened?"

"I was forced to stop at a green light, outside our office building, by someone walking into the road. The light changed to red and another man attacked the car."

"He jumped on it?" Jeffrey asked with wide eyes.

"No man."

"Seems a bit odd attacking a car?"

"He used a steel frame to break the window, but luckily I'd seen him and was accelerating."

"That's not what you said."

"Come on Jeffrey, I was nearly killed."

"You should be more careful."

"Jeffrey. I was nearly killed."

"I heard you the first time Peter, but I don't like thinking about it. I'm sick of the whole mess. This city is getting too dangerous," Jeffrey said.

"South Africa has always been dangerous, but it's also a dynamic place, going forward into a future, that we can all help build."

"Too dynamic for me. I don't feel like the future here, too many people and too much crime."

"I think this might be something more. I've an odd feeling that the attack might relate to the project in Botswana that I've just taken on."

"Attacked for taking on a project?"

"The attack was somehow unexplainable."

"This violence is just too hard to deal with, I've decided I'm going to sell up and move back to Malawi."

"Why so suddenly?" Peter asked.

"Some idiot was in here, a moment ago, telling me I was under his protection, asking how I would compensate him."

"This morning?"

"He's just left."

"Hell."

"Yes, that's about what it is. It's in the air; theft and violence are becoming a way of life, in the streets and in businesses. I never go out anymore. I'm virtually a prisoner, and, now I'm expected to be afraid in here too."

"Is it any better in Malawi?"

"Not such huge concentrations of people."

"We'd never manage without you."

"You would, and, as I've said, it's time to for me go. I'm tired of this city. Anyhow tell me about the project in Botswana."

Peter explained the problems of Ngami.

"Shite Peter, if the attack was deliberate it won't be the last attempt."

"I did think about that but it seems unlikely."

"Unlikely be damned. If someone is capable of bankrupting the significant people you describe, they are capable of stopping one person like you; in any way that they choose. You should stay with me until you go."

The gentle Malawian turned to serve another customer before Peter could reply.

As he waited, Peter realized Jeffery was right; and, when he returned, asked if he could spend the weekend with him.

Anders was furious when he heard that Peter had vanished. He phoned van Zyl; and, after abruptly greeting him, said, "You pride yourselves on your ability to get things done and you lose the one bastard who can finish me off?"

"I don't know what could have happened, I'm sorry."

"Sorry won't fix this bloody problem, he can't be allowed to get that site review done. He'll be much more difficult to deal with once he's there."

"I'll make sure he doesn't get there. We've got his house under close surveillance."

"I bloody well hope so."

13

On Sunday, the aircraft, carrying Rebecca Rosslynn to finish Anders' technical effort to shut Ngami, flew toward a huge bank of cumuli nimbus clouds, black and blue with every shade of white.

The inexperienced pilot called the control tower to check the weather report and asked if he should divert.

The person that he spoke to, told him the storm was not as bad as it looked.

They flew straight into one of the worst storms of the season.

It met the aircraft like a challenger in a boxing ring and seemed able to toss the aircraft around effortlessly.

Despite his lack of experience the pilot had been through several of the highveld's thunderstorms, which are a daily occurrence in the summer. They had been gentle compared to this maelstrom. Almost paralyzed by fear he alternated between cursing the weather bureau for failing to provide accurate reports and saying barely remembered prayers.

The dark indigo caverns through which the plane was flying looked immense, seeming as though they could, not only crush the aircraft, but moved into positions that would enable them to do so. The clouds seemed to boil, and continuous seeming lightning caused the scene to change colors, so that the swirling vortices took on multiple shades of; purple, white, grey and yellow.

The confusion presented by the storm matched Rebecca's inner turmoil. She had a bad feeling about Ngami, and now this. She had never dreamt that there would be any real danger in flying to the site.

Suddenly the plane started falling. The drop felt certain to take them back to earth but was checked, with a sickening lurch. The engines whined and the aircraft struggled to regain altitude.

Rebecca's stomach felt as though it had been left behind, she was terrified. The emptiness of her life hung over her like an invisible cloud.

At last, looking out of the window, she saw some bright crowns among the peaks piled high above the aircraft. Seemingly impossibly high havens. Then, as suddenly as with the onset of the storm, the aircraft broke free from the swirling nightmare, to continue smoothly on, to its destination.

Rebecca felt as she had once done after agreeing to go white water rafting. An experience that she never intended repeating.

They landed a half hour behind schedule and she made her shaky way to the terminal building with the rest of the passengers.

The afternoon was further dragged out by a long delay at customs.

Gerry Heldebron, the Ngami general manager met her with a warm greeting, when, at last, she staggered out from customs with her luggage.

He introduced himself with a European charm he reserved for people who mattered to him.

Looking as ruffled as she felt, she described how the aircraft had been tossed about by the storm, feeling almost childishly relieved at having survived the experience.

Heldebron listened and seemed to understand. He asked if she had been sick.

"No, thank goodness."

"The storms over the highveld are legendary, I've experienced a few, but what you've just gone through sounds worse than most. Sadly it never reached us. We haven't had much rain for years now. A storm would be very welcome here."

"Did you stop off on your way from Australia?" he asked as he helped with her luggage.

No, I didn't sleep much on the flights either, she answered as she climbed into his vehicle.

On the way to the hotel, he explained the generalities of the site and the project.

After they arrived Heldebron turned to talk to someone, in the foyer, as Rebecca was registering and she was again forced to wait. This time for almost thirty minutes, and her hopes about his attitude began to fade.

At last he strode across to where she was standing and said. "Sorry for that delay, why don't you get cleaned up before we talk?"

Rebecca tried not to show her feelings, wondering why he could not understand her simple need for sleep,

"Okay Gerry, I'll see you back here in half an hour or so?" she answered.

"Fine," he said and turned to stride back out through the foyer door.

Heldebron returned to have dinner with her after she had showered and changed.

He provided her with more information on the project while they ate and some explanation of what he was expecting from her.

She produced a folder from her brief case and showed him how she intended going about the assignment.

"I've arranged for Willers to work with you, he's in charge of security and has a technical background."

"Perhaps someone from a more operational role might be better?"

"No, I can't give you anyone else," he said and told her that Anders had specifically asked him to use Willers, explaining that the security chief knew the workings of the different departments and was completely familiar with the technical side of the operation.

"If that's what you want then I'm sure it'll be fine."

"It will be. He's very intelligent, a former air force captain, and he has a degree in electrical engineering."

"Okay we'll leave it at that," said Rebecca, not mentioning a concern she felt at the element of control that someone like Willers could represent.

14

By convincing Peter that he should not return to his home in Sandton, Jeffery almost certainly saved his friend's life.

Together they went and bought Peter the basics that he would need for the trip to Botswana, and a lightweight suitcase.

For the rest of the weekend Peter helped in the pub.

On Monday morning, Peter took a different flight to the one on which he had been booked, to make sure he stayed off any antagonist's radar.

The storm, that had nearly finished Rebecca's assignment, before it began, the previous day, had disappeared by the time Peter left Johannesburg.

On the flight he looked out on the colorful land between the highveld and Ngami as they flew north. The colors of the countryside, with its many outcrops of reddish rock, were accentuated by the orange and gold of the early morning sun.

During the near perfect flight, Peter became increasing aware that Ngami was now as important to him as it was to the de Bruins and Charles' tribe, so that, although the flight North to Ngami was short, it was as serious a leap as Peter had ever made.

James De Bruin had emailed several reports related to the project over the weekend and, as he skimmed through these on the flight, his sense of danger increased. He sighed regularly, put his hand to his forehead, and untidied his thinning sandy hair.

The reports indicated a situation that was far worse than Peter had thought it would or should be, from what he knew of the plant's design. Without needing to see the works, or anyone there, he could safely conclude that operation and maintenance of the Ngami plant was unacceptably bad.

The flight attendant drew him back from his concerns when she asked, "Coffee, sir?"

"Yes, please."

She had noticed Peter as he came aboard and had thought he seemed interesting. She wondered what he did for a living and asked if he was going to Ngami on business, as she poured the coffee.

"Yes, I am," he said vaguely. He accepted the coffee, put it on the table and she wandered off to attend to her other duties.

Having been brought back to reality he watched her as he took his first sip of the coffee.

Her graceful walk, back to the front of the aircraft made Peter think about his wife, Christine, in Sydney, and that the barriers to their getting together were increasing.

He closed his eyes thinking of their good times together and then dozed for a few minutes, to be woken by the pilot announcing that they were approaching Ngami.

Conversation slowed as the aircraft made its descent.

The glow of the morning sun accentuated the size of the approaching trees and kopjes. There was a slight bump as they touched down and the bushveld rushed past the windows, less attractive from up close than it had been from the air.

The pilot taxied to the small terminal building, where there was a short wait as stairs were rolled into position.

Eventually the flight attendant opened the aircraft's passenger door and they disembarked into a hot morning.

Peter struggled down the stairs to the runway, concentrating on not losing his step with his cumbersome load of briefcase, jacket and laptop. He and the rest of the passengers then walked, in groups, and separately, across the sealed runway to a concrete path, that led from the tarred surface to the terminal.

Small, neatly pruned, red bougainvillea formed a border on either edge of the concrete pathway, that led to the building. Outwards, from the bougainvillea, a fragile looking lawn stretched toward hedges of hakea, that were in line with the terminal building's walls.

A fly screened door led into the neat and functional building. There was a bench that formed the customs counter, a frosted glass wall, and no air conditioning.

Peter could see people in the area beyond the counter through doorways and windows in the wall. One of them was watching him surreptitiously and moved out of sight when Peter looked directly at him. He felt a chill of apprehension at what such close attention could mean. In South Africa such close attention often preceded robbery, but he knew that this was most unlikely in Botswana. He put the thoughts aside and turned to look for the baggage trolley.

The waiting area grew hotter. Passengers fretted and children began misbehaving. Eventually two trolleys of stacked luggage were wheeled through the door from the landing field.

Peter found his bag and carried it to the customs queue. The wait there seemed extraordinarily long. When he eventually got to the counter, the officer asked him a few desultory questions before allowing him to walk through the official gateway to Botswana.

In the combined arrivals and departure hall, he hired a car and left the building to find the vehicle in the unsealed parking lot. It looked too small and flimsy. He decided to insist on a four-wheel drive and went back to the hire company.

After a short delay the replacement was agreed.

The company representative changed the paper work and gave Peter the keys for a four wheel drive.

He walked back out into the heat and climbed into the vehicle, started it, opened the windows and turned the air-conditioning to maximum.

The short trip through dry bush, seemingly untouched by civilization, brought him to the relatively new and attractive company town. The more traditional village of Ngami was concealed, on the opposite side of a dry creek, by a fairly dense stand of mostly small, bushy trees.

The architecture of the solidly built company village gave Peter a feeling of being in one of the older parts of the Cape. He drove straight to the hotel, confirmed his booking, went to his room, dumped his case on the floor, and returned to the vehicle, to drive to the Ngami plant.

Van Zyl had arranged for Peter to be killed as he left the airport. The small flimsy car he had been allocated was a part of this plan. A heavy truck, had been set up to 'accidentally' crush the small vehicle as he passed through the car park exit.

When the expected car had not emerged thirty minutes after most of the people had left the airport the driver of the truck phoned van Zyl to ask what he should do.

He was told to return to base.

The short journey from the village to the plant spanned scenes that could have belonged to different centuries.

Peter was in unspoiled bushveld within minutes of leaving the village.

A small herd of dainty impala crossed the road on the way. He stopped and watched until they had disappeared into the bush.

Fifteen minutes after leaving the hotel he arrived at the smelter. The bush where the plant was situated had been cleared. Its stack reached high into the sky, trickling a small plume of smoke.

Peter left his vehicle in the visitor's car park, a sealed section of land next to the plant, that was enclosed by a galvanised mesh fence, and topped with coiled razor wire.

He parked and walked to the gatehouse, to be admitted to the plant's similarly enclosed area.

The office block, built as an annex to the main facility was stark and grey. He felt as though he was entering some sort of prison.

No one was at the long reception desk, which divided the foyer into two parts.

Peter walked across the immaculate space, past the desk and up the stairs behind it, to the third floor where, the security guard had explained, Heldebron, the general manager's office was located.

A woman, who looked as though she had seen more than her share of life, was waiting for him at the top of the stairwell.

Looking down at Peter as he came up the stairs she felt sorry for him. She thought that he looked a nice enough person, like many she had known, in her life in South Africa, somehow different to the international people she usually encountered in Ngami. She thought he probably played rugby as he seemed a bit big and clumsy for soccer.

Her face was heavily lined, grey coloured and matched by her mousy hair. Her appearance and dress blended with the colourless building. She greeted Peter with a surprisingly warm smile and introduced herself as Marie the general manager's personal assistant.

He smiled back and explained what he was doing there.

She told him that she would advise Heldebron of his arrival, and asked which part of South Africa he came from, as they walked down the Spartan looking passageway.

Peter said he had been born in Rustenburg.

She replied that she had many good memories of the district.

Marie's life was linked to Ngami because her husband owned and ran the international school in the village. She wished she could somehow escape. Her husband was not an outdoors person of any kind. He was a thin, and, she now thought, mean looking man. Sadly she could not remember when he had been anything else. She had married him because he had seemed clever, wealthy and sophisticated and made more money than many entrepreneurs. She now knew that she was not the main interest in his life. Her father's farm, which she would inherit, was what held his attention.

When Peter spoke, his soft South African accent made her feel more homesick than usual, and made her long for her childhood near Nelspruit. The difference between Peter and the usual people she dealt with at Ngami was hard to define. She thought that perhaps the international people, who were generally products of the globalisation of mining, were perhaps quicker and less homely. She hoped that Peter was prepared for what she thought would be in store for him. He was not the first to have been sent to solve the problems at the site but she had heard that he was intended to be the last.

Having been asked to bring Peter into Heldebron's office when he arrived, she did so, showed him a seat, wished him well, and then left.

Heldebron sitting at the end of the extensive office, writing at a small table, behind and to the left of a large desk grunted an acknowledgement of Peter's presence seeming to be closed off, in a smoke filled world of his own.

Peter waited.

Heldebron sometimes held the pipe in his hand, and then, sometimes, clenched it between his teeth, as he wrote.

The pipe tobacco smelled nutty and pleasant to Peter, who had recently given up smoking. He was reminded of an early suggestion, made to him when he had joined McNeil associates, that he carry a pipe and put it in his mouth and clench it in his teeth, as Heldebron was doing, whenever he felt the urge to speak too quickly. A habit he had still not fully controlled.

The minutes moved on and tobacco smoke remained all that reached out from the corner.

The general manager put the pipe down occasionally and shuffled through the papers in front of him.

Peter glanced around the sparsely furnished office and noticed that it stretched across the width of the building. It had two windows, one smaller, behind Heldebron's desk, and one that ran for much of the length of the wall, against which Heldebron's work table was situated. Three doors were located in the wall that faced Heldebron's desk. The one at the end of the office, opposite where Heldebron was sitting led to the personal assistant's office. He thought that the middle door that had remained closed would connect directly to the passageway. The third led to what Peter was to discover was a conference room. The office walls were the same dreary cream colour as the stairwell and passage. The large window had a view of the undeveloped bushland that surrounded the plant. A photograph of the GVN managing director stared down from the wall facing the large window.

Peter's unease increased by the minute, he tried looking out of the window at the bush beyond the cleared area, thinking of how much it was like where he had grown up, although drier. And, of how he had struggled toward the role he was now playing, an eternity away from the simple hard working and rewarding life of a farmer.

His childhood had been isolated, but interesting and filled with adventure, spent largely on his grandfather's farm where he had learned to appreciate the land, its people and its complexities. His boyhood, among the people of the Northern district, black and white had been different to that of most South Africans, at that time. His grandfather had believed that doing the work yourself was the best way to learn its value and had made sure that Peter had worked side by side with the farm workers.

Peter had learned to gain respect for himself from the them as a result of this experience. He thought, as he stood and waited, that he had never lost that skill. It helped immensely when dealing with ineffective management.

His education had been at an inexpensive private boys school, paid for by an aunt, who believed such a formation was essential. He had been bored by school but had managed to scrape a pass each year. Training as a technician had followed the years in high school. He had then obtained an initial degree in computer science part time, and a postgraduate degree in engineering.

As his career had progressed, he had managed to gain a reputation as a skilled achiever of genuine results, even though he had little time for, or understanding of, people like Heldebron.

At last, to Peter's relief, Heldebron acknowledged his presence, saying, "Well Peter, now that's finished, I can deal with you."

"Good morning, Mr. Heldebron," Peter answered in what he was sure was too tense a tone. He tried desperately to ignore the aggression in Heldebron's voice. His insecurity, never far from the surface, was something he sometimes struggled to conceal.

"So the wonder child is my problem now, hey?" Heldebron continued.

"I'm not sure that I would put the work de Bruin wants done in those terms. I'm here to help you."

"So, what's it that makes you think you're good enough for fixing my place?" Heldebron asked, staring malevolently at Peter from behind thick bifocal glasses. His eyes, dark and shadowed, had an air of menace about them. His accent was perhaps central or northern European and broken.

Peter thought he looked a bit like a gnome from a fairy story. He had been told that Heldebron had never learned to speak English, or Afrikaans, or any other language of the multi-cultured southern parts of Africa fluently, although he had been there for more than twenty years. While languages were not Heldebron's strength, it also seemed to Peter that the man was lacking in the ability to conduct a civil conversation. The gnome-like man's hair was nearly completely grey, and formed a partial monk's tonsure around the polished dome of his head. The skin on his face and bald head was the same colour as his nicotine stained fingers. His chin showed traces of grey stubble.

Before Peter could answer the aggressive question, Heldebron continued to speak, subjecting him to a long monologue, on how difficult the general manager's life and career had been, ending with the sorrowful comment. "Yes, Peter, when I was your age, I was an engineer in a transport division of the army and then had to join industry as an artisan then work my way up; until I gained this position after years of frustration."

"I've been sent to help you." Peter answered warily. He had also been told by McNeil that Heldebron had a reputation for working his way up at the expense of anyone and everyone.

There was an apologetic knock and Marie entered the office, through the conference room door.

"Mr. Heldebron, the security people are here," she said awkwardly. "I explained that you were busy but they insisted that I should interrupt."

"I'll be back in a few minutes," Heldebron snapped as he stood and walked to the conference room door.

The silence was broken when Heldebron shouted, loudly enough to be heard clearly through the closed door. "As I said yesterday, the game's changing, now he's here we're very exposed. We're being put into a bad position. This whole thing is too exposed."

Peter thought of getting closer to the door, decided not to and sat for a few minutes wondering how on earth he would achieve anything in such a negative environment.

Eventually Heldebron bustled back into his office, looking even less friendly.

The unpleasant man then spoke abruptly to Peter, who had turned in his chair to face him. "Look, something serious has come up, so you go and see what's happening in the plant. I'll talk to you again tomorrow."

He picked up the papers he had been working on and walked out through the door into the personal assistant's office.

Peter said, to Heldebron's departing back, that he did not have time to spend walking aimlessly around the plant. He stood up and walked through the middle doorway, out of the office, into the passageway, past the personal assistant's office, ignoring the backs of Heldebron and Marie who were standing in front of her desk. He was not at all sure what to do and decided, as he walked, that he could not accept the approach

Heldebron had adopted. He checked his stride and turned back toward the personal assistant's office.

Marie and Heldebron seemed to be engrossed in the papers the manager had taken from the office, and which he was laying out on her desk. Peter hesitated at the door for a few moments then said. "Mr. Heldebron."

"Now what is it?" Heldebron answered rudely.

"I wanted to make sure you really want to cancel the arrangements."

"I never said I wanted to cancel anything."

"You certainly didn't seem interested in what I'm doing and I can't achieve anything if the people out there think I'm being pushed aside."

"Peter, you academics think that the world, and everyone in it, should stop for you. I've told you I don't have time to help you now. Please find something useful to do until I'm finished with this."

"Mr. Heldebron I'm not an academic, my qualifications were obtained part time. I have much the same experience as you."

Heldebron hesitated. "Peter I haven't got time at the moment."

"In that case I must go back to South Africa."

Heldebron, realizing that this would solve part of their problem, was tempted to agree, but knew it would put him in the worst possible light. He needed Peter to fail not be patently stopped by himself.

"Peter, you seem to want to have your hand held, like a child."

"That's not the situation at all. This review will be a waste of time if I go wandering around uncertainly. The people in administration and the plant will know you're not co-operating. So, Mr. Heldebron, either you get this work up and running this morning, or it's cancelled.

Now if Marie can show me where the canteen is, I'll wait there until you are ready for me."

"You do as you please Peter. I've told you that I've got too much else on my hands to spend more time with you today." Heldebron said and turned back toward the desk.

As Marie led Peter from her office, she said, "He's a bully Peter, don't give way and he'll back off."

Peter thanked her and followed her directions to the canteen, bought a cup of coffee and found an empty table.

After finishing the coffee he waited a few minutes and decided to return to the hotel.

He left the canteen, phoned Marie, told her he was going to wait at the hotel, and asked her to explain to Heldebron that if his work was not cleared properly he would leave on the afternoon flight.

"Good Peter, I'll see you soon."

An hour after Peter left the plant, following Heldebron's nasty 'welcome', the security superintendent arrived at the hotel with the necessary documentation for him to start his work.

The tall blond and lithely built man introduced himself as John Willers.

Peter thought he carried himself like someone from a military background.

Willers asked Peter if he needed an introduction to the operations.

Peter explained that he was familiar with the site and operation having worked there before.

"I think you should come along to the introductory presentation I'm giving the Australian. It would save time if you were there too."

"Okay then, let's go."

"I hear you've been here before, so I suppose you know a bit about the problems?"

"It seemed to be fine when I was last here."

"Must have been some time ago."

"It was a few years ago."

"You'll notice a deterioration then."

"So I've been told.

15

Having spent a restful night in the Ngami hotel. Rebecca arrived in Heldebron's office at ten in the morning, not long after Peter. She was met at reception and shown to the office and a comfortable leather chair facing the window.

Heldebron sat down with her and asked, "Is the hotel OK?"

"Yes, thanks, the room's very comfortable." She answered warmly, she had been warned by Wes Wilson, the South African head of Binnett, not to expect too much civility from Heldebron, but, despite the general manager's inconsiderateness the previous day, was still feeling more than satisfied with her treatment since her arrival.

Heldebron briefly expanded on the previous evening's conversation, asking her to save detailed questions for Willers. He then explained that he would like a synopsis of her report at the end of the assignment and that Willers would provide him with a daily commentary on her progress.

The overwhelming smell of pipe smoke and tobacco, that pervaded the office, made Rebecca feel slightly sick. She asked when she would meet Willers.

"Whenever you're ready."

"Now would be fine," she replied.

He phoned Willers and said, "John can you come into my office please?"

A few minutes later, Willers walked into the office, accompanied by Peter.

Heldebron introduced them to Rebecca.

Peter nodded politely and Willers shook her hand, not really militaristically, but somehow giving her an impression of authority or even of power.

She noticed that he was a thin hard man in his early thirties; his face tanned and finely chiseled, his blond hair seemed bleached, perhaps by the sun. His neatly trimmed mustache should have completed the appearance of striking good looks; but for some reason there was something waif-like about him, something that made him easy to forget.

She thought Peter Connor looked a few years older than Willers. He had a similar complexion, but was much more heavily built than the security superintendent.

Heldebron did not ask the two men to sit down.

"John, I have a lot to attend to this morning. Would you mind looking after our guests?"

"Certainly Mr. Heldebron," Willers replied, almost, but not quite, clicking his heels.

Before she left, Rebecca asked if Heldebron could arrange a meeting to introduce her to the work force.

Willers answered for the general manager and said that this had been arranged and would take place the following morning at nine.

The three left the general manager's office together; Willers leading the way to a conference room a few doors down. He strode to the head of the long table that occupied most of the room and picked up the remote control saying, "I'll show you the problems and give you a picture of the plant at the same time," and switched the projector on.

The screen filled with a colored image of a ladle pouring molten metal. The background was a beautiful, typically Botswanan, evening sky that was shaded from dark orange through mauve to dark purple. A floodlit overhead crane could be seen holding the ladle. The photograph was captioned 'Ngami Production'.

He sat down opposite Rebecca, allowing her enough time to absorb the scene depicted in the photograph, and said. "Unfortunately this process is not as continuous as it has to be, if Ngami is to survive."

Peter was sitting on the opposite side of the table to Rebecca, nearer to the projector, out of Willers' line of sight.

He watched Willers with interest, although seeming waif like, there was something unusually steely about the man.

Willers paused before saying. "There are several problem areas and you'll see a slide for each of these."

He then went through ten slides, each detailing a set of difficulties within a different area of the plant.

"John I'm experienced but I'm not keeping up with you here. Could you step back a bit and explain each function of the Ngami operation?" Rebecca commented after he had summarized what he had shown them.

He nodded, "Okay Rebecca, I've got another presentation that will help you see a more detailed picture of what is happening here and where it fits," and walked out of the conference room, leaving them with the view of the ladle and the evening sky.

Willers returned shortly with another set of slides.

The first of which was a line diagram. Showing:

'Mine - Crushers - Mills - Concentrator - Drying plant - Smelter'

"The ore is mined in an underground operation that uses traditional drill and blast narrow tabular reef mining methods."

"Drill and blast but what's narrow tubes got to do with anything?"

"Not tubes, tabular, I thought you knew about a similar operation?"

"Similar in that nickel was involved. It was an open cut operation. I've never had anything to do with underground mines."

"Jeeze, we mine platinum, nickel is a bye-product, I don't understand how you are going to pick all this up in the time you've got."

"Okay we can come back to narrow tabular mining if we need to."

"So, a standard breast mining layout is used. The orebody dips at 20° and there are six panels. Strike gullies are inclined at 10° above strike. Dip gullies handle the ore transported via the strike gullies to the three ore-passes, which are fitted with radial-door control chutes. Ore is then transported to the main shaft ore passes, by battery powered locomotives pulling spans of eight hoppers."

"So the reef slopes at 20 degrees, removal of the ore from the stopes is fairly normal for underground mining of narrow seams and battery locomotives and winches are the place where failures are most likely to occur?" Peter said.

"That's about it."

Scrapers are used to clean the stopes. Broken ore is transported to a conventional ore-pass system, with separate rock handling facilities for reef, and waste. The underground workings are accessed from a twin shaft system. Backfill is placed in sixty-five percent of the mined out reef areas. Between sixty and seventy percent of all panels are being backfilled concurrently with the advancing faces."

I can understand most of that, can I have a copy of your notes?" said Rebecca.

"Certainly. Shall we carry on?"

"Yes, thanks."

"Next we have the hoists, that bring the ore to surface."

"For most presentations this is something we'd skip over, quickly. There are losses here though. They take the ore from the underground operation to surface and are also used to transport men and materials. There are two for the vertical shaft and only one for the incline shaft."

"Incline, so the ore was an outcrop?" asked Peter.

"Yes the orebody starts on the surface.

The first shaft follows this down and the vertical shaft meets the reef further down its slope."

"You said you normally would skip over this part?"

"For an introductory presentation, as to production losses, it is an area where we've had quite a few problems."

"I see," said Rebecca.

"The rock from the mine is reduced in size by crushing, then fed to the mills where it is further broken down. The concentrator separates the ore rich product from the waste and this ore rich product is then dried, before being pneumatically conveyed to the smelter. The set of technical problems I first showed you start with the drier and continue into the smelting process."

"Right John thanks for that. I'm with you now."

"How about you Peter?"

"Why is there no mention of problems in the concentrator area?"

"There are problems there but the worst fluctuations are in the areas I covered," Willers mumbled.

"I wonder how we could achieve anything if we skipped half of the plant."

Willers looked away. "So let's look at them," he continued.

The next slide showed a large jaw crusher under the heading. Willers then showed them a number of heavy objects that had jammed the jaw crusher and had caused serious delays.

Three rotary mills were shown in the next slide.

The concentrator doesn't really includes the crushers and the mills from an organizational point of view," Willers said vaguely, and went on, "but the cyclones, the thickeners and the flotation cells are grouped under the heading of concentrator, since concentration of the metal bearing ore takes place in them. The notes will show you how many delays we've had in that area."

"Many?" asked Peter.

"Yes, far too many. There are problems with the drier," he said and showed them a diagram taken from his original presentation. "You can see how the drier injects damp concentrate into a stream of heated air. There are multiple cases of the drive mechanism failing. Another weakness in the drier area is that the interlock system, which is electronic and controls air temperature and flow; relative to feed flow, and moisture content of the concentrate, has been replaced and the new design was not properly commissioned."

"Why would anyone do work like that and not commission it properly?" asked Rebecca.

Willers explained how a project, to replace the control system had been badly managed and that the documentation of what was done was incomplete.

"Sounds ridiculous to me," said Rebecca.

"Like everything else here, a series of mistakes have added up to cause disasters."

The presentation continued, showing difficulties in the concentrate conveying system, which also involved control problems.

"And," Willers said, "the smelter has many problems that we cannot seem to get a handle on. The smelter feed, the furnace lining, the precipitators, the waste heat boiler, the exhaust fans, and the acid plant all have weaknesses that seem to be getting worse."

By the time he had finished they both had a much better perspective of why Ngami was not producing what it should.

Finally Willers handed each of them a summary of his presentation, a map of the site marked with the key problem areas, and a set of data relevant to the plant and its support structure.

Rebecca thanked him. "John, that was very useful. I must say what you've described seems to be a straightforward set of technical faults which have happened so often they are now impossible to repair?"

"That's about it Rebecca," he replied, "there's not enough ability to get the problems solved."

"If they've recruited and can still get good people here, which is what we've been told, why is there no one that can do the work?"

"That's a question that I think you will need to address in your investigation."

"You've no opinion?"

"I think it might be better if you answer it through your enquiries."

"So it's nothing to do with the problem?"

"I can't answer your question simply, Rebecca."

"Okay, I'll summarize what you've said today and use it as the introduction to the report. The details will come out as we go."

"Sounds like what we want," he replied, "I've arranged a company Land Cruiser, Rebecca. You can use it in areas where hired vehicles are not allowed. Here are the keys. I've parked it next to the manager's space in the place marked Head Office, it's beige and the license plate number is on the key ring."

He ignored Peter.

"Thanks," she replied. "How about accommodation in the individual plants?"

"Each area has arranged an office, so you can conduct interviews, they'll have phones and computer connections in them. If you can coordinate your activities so you are not contending for resources it would be a big help."

"That sounds fine, thanks John," said Rebecca.

"If you need anything else, please don't hesitate to ask, my office is three doors down, to the left. I've arranged for you to meet Brett Halliday first and will take you there."

Peter had been amazed by the omissions and horrified at the amount of work that seemed to have been allowed to get out of control; and, particularly worrying for him, was the way Willers had provided them with incomplete information.

Peter said to their departing backs. "I'll see you there."

Peter phoned de Bruin and told him his initial impressions.

"You said you thought the design was okay?" de Bruin answered.

"This is not design, this is poor management, or more accurately complete neglect.

"I wonder why we didn't fully realize that before? Its hard to see how so much could have been discussed about improving and trying to improve when the operation was actually falling into neglect."

"You knew it wasn't producing. It's hard to say any more at this stage. Something must certainly have been very wrong with the way the project was being controlled."

"Controlled? Managed, which is it?"

"I'm saying controlled quite deliberately. When things go wrong in any situation and someone tries to do something, good bad or plain foolish, it's a control effort. No control effort and no correction. In a machine that would mean a lack of feedback without which there can be no control. If management has any purpose at all it should be to ensure that control systems exist. Sometimes applying however well meaning flavor of the month approaches cause common sense to go out the window. That might be what's happened here."

"I understood you were an engineer not a management expert."

"Some management experts come from a marketing background and that makes them expert at what?"

"Images, I suppose."

"Or, at creating them. What I concentrate on relates more to 'engineering' management, of people and plants, to achieve results."

"Seems a fine point."

"Perhaps but short sightedness is very much a part of our perhaps 'over-marketed systems and methods', to an extent that any chance of steady progress is lost in the flurry."

"That does describe what's happened in Ngami. On another subject, have you heard anything from my brother?"

"No, I haven't."

"I hope he's okay."

"Do you want me to do anything?" asked Peter.

"I don't think there's much you can do, but thanks for the offer."

16

Peter, John and Rebecca met again in Brett Halliday's office and the effort taken to include Peter was again minimal. Brett then took them for a tour of the problem areas. On their way back he showed Rebecca an office, which he said, she could use for her work in the complex and left her there with Willers.

He asked Peter if he would mind sharing his office.

Peter accepted, having no other choice. Since James de Bruin had suggested that if he needed someone in the Ngami management structure to confide in, he should use Brett Halliday, this was not an additional worry to the badly frustrated engineer.

"So Peter, what do you think?" said the plant manager once they were seated.

"I'm not at all happy with the exercise Brett," Peter answered and started to describe his concerns about Heldebron's attitude and about what Willers had said after they got to Brett's office.

Brett acknowledged his comment vaguely, shaking his head as he did so and stood to walk through the doorway, signaling Peter to follow him. Once away from the office he said. "I think my conversations are being monitored in there so please be careful what you say when you're in the office."

"Surely not?"

"Unfortunately I'm right, and another thing you need to be careful what you say on any of the company's phones and cell phones, the same applies."

"A bit crazy?"

"It's a fact nevertheless."

"Anyhow, back to your meeting with Heldebron. If I didn't know he was as cunning as they come I'd think he was completely mad. They will make things as difficult for you as they can and there isn't anything I can do about it, except to try to listen to your problems and advise you on how to survive."

"I expected difficulties, but the main worry that I have is that the way Willers described the plant's problems they'll not need to try too hard to prove the plant is a failure."

"Why?"

"The presentation Willers gave Rebecca showed it to be in a terrible state."

"Can I see it?"

"It's in the office."

They went back and Peter handed the presentation to Brett.

Brett looked through it and his face changed as he did so. The ends of his mouth were drooping more than usual by the time he had finished. He looked as though he had tasted something very sour.

He signaled Peter back out onto the veranda.

"Peter this isn't accurate."

"I intend checking what he's said."

"So you have a plan B?"

"No, I think we should work the way Willers laid things out. If we lose the pattern, we'll lose the fight."

"How would you normally start an exercise like this?"

"The introduction Willers gave us would be fairly typical. I then check the actual situation."

"How?"

"The design and process criteria, with the flow diagrams are as good a place as any, then I just keep walking the plant, checking all the way through, I use individual knowledge all the time. By asking people what they think, I gain twice, they become involved and I gain from their filtering systems, good bad and indifferent."

"What if they don't give you an accurate picture?"

"This would be the fourth furnace type exercise I've done and I've worked on the design and construction as well as operated four or five concentrator and several smelter operations. I also had a hand in the commissioning of this one. I don't know everything but I can pick up inaccuracies."

"So what's next here?"

"I'd like to start my work in the planning department."

Brett agreed and took Peter to the plant planning office and organized for him to be allowed access to the files.

Before leaving the engineer, he invited him to dinner that evening.

Peter returned to the hotel at he end of the long day, showered, and drove to Brett's house. He was met by Claire, Brett's wife.

She greeted him with a firm handshake and said, "Welcome to Botswana, Peter, I hope you like it here."

He explained that he had worked on the project in its early days and that he had enjoyed working in Botswana.

She led him into the house, which was very comfortable, even by the high standards of the wealthier people of South Africa. The doors were made from some attractive heavy timber, which Peter could not identify. The floor was slate, a dark variety, with bronze, gold, and green veins woven through the nearly black background. Lightly shaded Persian rugs partially covered the slate. The lounge was furnished with soft cream leather chairs, a mahogany coffee table, marble lamp stands, and paintings of Africa. Full-length windows looked out onto a floodlit pool.

Gentle Celtic music came from a sound system that Peter could not see. An aroma of spices and barbecuing meat drifted through the room and mixed with a scent of frangipani. He could hear water splashing and presumed there was some sort of fountain off to the side of the pool. A French door led into a side garden in which the unique silhouette of aloes could be seen in the light from the veranda. There were trees in the background, these faded into the darkness.

A man clad in white and wearing a red fez served them drinks and bite-sized snacks.

These were followed by a pleasant meal.

When Peter mentioned how comfortable their home was, Claire said. "It belongs to the company Peter, and if that fails we'll be back where we started."

They spent most of the evening talking about the poor state of the operation, the people involved, and how the village and its people would be affected by the impending closure.

The human cost of shutting the plant would clearly be high, with hundreds of jobs, in the mine and on the plant, on the line, and many more in the town and subindustries.

Eventually, when the conversation slowed, Peter thanked them for the evening and stood to leave.

Claire wished him well as they said goodbye, adding, "Good luck Peter, you're holding many people's dreams in your hands."

"Thanks Clare." He replied.

"Peter," Brett said, as they walked toward the garden gate, "Perhaps you should use tomorrow morning to do some reading, rather than walk unsupported into what could easily involve them trying to discredit you in some way. We've got to attend Rebecca's first meeting in the morning and I'll pick you up at about eight thirty."

Peter agreed and walked towards his vehicle, climbed into it and drove back to the hotel thinking over the pleasant evening, and that it was odd that Bret seemed to have done little to correct the mess the plant was in. Two weeks would pass quickly though and there was a lot for him to think about, and solve on his own.

As he drove up to the hotel he thought it looked Spanish. It's white walls were flood lit. The tropical gardens were shadows in the night.

The scent of the bush and blossoms blended pleasantly with that of wood smoke. Peter passed through the shrubbery on a crunchy footpath to the front door. He found that it was locked but could see the night porter through the glass door and rang the bell.

There was a noise in the bushes to his left, and he thought he saw something move. His neck prickled.

He nervously rung the night bell again.

The porter stumbled out of his chair and asked Peter, through an intercom, for his name and room number. Once satisfied that Peter was a guest, the gray haired man released the door lock electronically, and Peter was able to make his way toward his room, down the passage to the left of the reception desk, through a door into the courtyard, on which several rooms formed a closed in square periphery, with a garden at its center. He was again assailed by the scents of the African night.

Once in his room, the pleasant fragrance of the courtyard was replaced by smell of insect spray, reminding him of holidays he had spent in the Kruger National Park, as a child.

The nervousness he had felt while waiting for the porter remained with him.

17

The meeting to introduce Rebecca was held in the Ngami recreation hall. There were not many empty seats and an air of expectancy filled the venue.

The hall, like much of the village, was built in a modernized Cape Dutch style, to a very high standard. It was a double brick structure with a roof that was tiled in terra cotta. It looked as though it would still be standing in a hundred years.

Heldebron introduced Rebecca as having a unique set of skills and extensive international experience. He said her review was critical to the integrity of their livelihoods and that this was a final effort to see if it was possible to rescue the project, because ongoing uncertainty was likely to leave it in limbo financially.

Peter was not mentioned

Rebecca spoke clearly about her background and plans for examining the project. She explained that problems in an organization are systemic and could not be changed by management without commitment and learning at all levels in an organization then said, "So systems are what we need to address."

"We know what systems are," said someone.

"Of course you do. Perhaps because they're a good way to define things?"

"So they're going to use your opinion to confirm the project is a failure?" asked another of the participants.

Heldebron answered for her, "Uncertainty is more dangerous than a correct view of the situation. Rebecca's international knowledge and direct engineering experience will put the situation we face into a valid perspective."

"So we'll first spend time defining the objectives of what we're doing," said Rebecca.

"Where are we headed now?" asked Whitehead, the maintenance superintendent, cynically. "We've done all this before."

"We're headed exactly where we're supposed to go, looking at production capability and potential. In our search for a strategy to address the systems problems, there are three key criteria: *Suitability (will it work?), Feasibility (is it practical?), and Acceptability (will what we do be made to work?)*'

She showed this on a screen as she spoke, then continued, "Now lets look at systems thinking. The idea of the learning organization is developed from systems thinking. Systems thinking has four parts; systems thinking, personal mastery, mental models, shared vision and team learning. These must be apparent at the same time in an operation for it to be a learning organization. If some of these characteristics are missing then the organization is not a learning organization and will not move to where it needs to go."

"All of them fall short here," said Whitehead, "So does that prove we're going nowhere, or is the lack of production enough of a proof?"

"That's the issue. Let's look at them one at a time. The commitment by an individual to this process of learning is known as personal mastery."

"Like Kung Fu." Said a tall young man with pork chops mustache and huge glasses.

Rebecca looked annoyed and continued, "The workforce can learn more quickly in a learning organization. A learning organization is a summation of individual learning. There needs to be a way for individual learning to be transferred into organizational learning, so we have, 'Mental Models', individuals' perspectives of organizations are called mental models. These with shared vision, which is something that creates a common identity to focus energy for learning. Transitory goals are very unhelpful on their own and term goals need to be set that will be intrinsic with the overall approach a company intends following."

There was no comment from the group, all of whom had heard this story before.

"Is this reasonable?"

A few heads nodded.

"The accumulation of individual learning constitutes team learning. Learning organizations have structures that enable team learning.'

"There are negative sides to his stuff too you know?" said Whitehead.

Rebecca nodded, "That's what we're here to look at. Even within a learning organization, problems can stall the process of learning or cause it to regress. Most of them come from an organization not fully embracing all the necessary facets."

"Definitely not embraced here," said someone.

"That could very well prove what the lack of production indicates. Once these problems can be identified, work can begin on improving them."

"Already failed here," came the comment.

"Some organizations find it hard to embrace personal mastery because the idea is intangible and the benefits cannot be quantified, personal mastery can even be seen as a threat to the organization and this threat can be real. If people don't engage with a shared vision, personal interest, can be, and is used to advance their own objectives."

"Rebecca we are nearing the end of our tether here, not starting out on a new mission. This stuff is all very well but we've seen it before," said Brett Halliday.

Rebecca nodded. "I know and that's exactly the point. Is a solution possible? The management think not. We still need to start at a finite point."

"A lot of this stuff is common sense which has been so badly mishandled here that if anything like it is seen as a threat," Brett replied.

"I think that's the point GVN are making," said Rebecca.

At this stage, Peter, as well as most of the audience, felt that the end was in sight, whatever happened. His uncertainty about his chances of succeeding had increased steadily throughout the presentation. If he were sidelined now anything he said or tried to achieve would seem irrelevant.

Nothing improved for him as the event progressed.

Near the end of the meeting, his phone buzzed on silent. It was Ben. He went outside to answer.

"Good to have you on site," the geologist said, after their preliminary greetings.

"I think it's all over," Peter said and told Ben what had been happening.

"So you are virtually cut out?"

"Yes, and this Binnett person knows exactly what she is talking about."

"Hang on Peter, I'll see what I can do. Phone me when the meeting's over. I'll stay here where there is a signal. I'll talk to Charles now, about putting your position right."

Ben sent a message to Charles, saying, "Peter says he's being sidelined. Can you do anything that will help him?"

Charles replied, "They haven't mentioned him, I had decided to step in at the end and make sure he's not excluded."

When Peter was back in his seat he heard Rebecca saying, "So the lack of any possible path forward will then establish the need to close and we'll ensure you receive generous redundancy packages. "

She then went on to explain how she would show them her conclusions at the end of the three-week period, and said that the same presentation would be made to the World Bank, in Johannesburg, on the Monday after they left site.

Charles Obenta stood up when Rebecca finished, thanked her and said, clearly and firmly, "Rebecca has been employed to close the site. Peter Connor, who many of you know, has been engaged for a technical review, specifically intended to prove the potential of the project. His effort will be independent of Rebecca's work."

There was a strong a positive reaction to this.

The meeting then closed.

Peter went outside and phoned Ben to tell him Charles had ensured his inclusion.

"Everything we have depends on your work Peter, thank you."

Brett moved to Willer's side as Rebecca thoughtfully strolled off toward the refreshment table.

"So how did you think that went?" Brett asked.

"Good, she certainly knows what she's doing."

"Connor should at least be working in some kind of step with her shouldn't he?

"You don't want them working hand in glove?" asked Willers.

"No of course not but we must have some degree of cooperation. They can't walk round saying the same thing or contradicting each other and wasting people's time. We've got enough trouble here as things are."

"Of course," this was not what he had intended, but since Brett Halliday was the most senior person on site after Heldebron, he agreed.

They arranged to get Peter and Rebecca to have joint meetings on a regular basis and that the two consultants should discuss their initial plans with Willers and Halliday the next day, over a working lunch in the conference room, to lay out a rough program for the coming weeks.

Charles walked from the venue with Brett and asked him what he thought about the way Rebecca's presentation had gone.

"She's exactly right of course, we have done all this and it just doesn't hang together," said Brett. "Nothing here hangs together. I for instance can't get anything to fall into place and I really have done my best throughout the time I've been here."

"Let's hope Peter can do something. If she's right though, the project would seem to be as hopeless as we have been told it is."

"I must say I've had about enough."

"What are you going to do?"

"I'm not sure, but going down with the ship is not a very intelligent way of doing things in the real world."

"Try to hang in with us Brett."

"I will, but I do have to face reality."

After Charles had left, Brett drove Peter to the plant. On the way he told him that he would arrange for him to meet the engineering manager, Stone, that afternoon.

Peter thanked him.

Brett then went on to explain how Stone had failed because the individual departments, who handled their internal work processes themselves, would not cooperate with him.

"Why have someone in the engineering role then?" Peter asked.

"I don't know, for legal reasons I suppose."

"What does Stone do, if no one takes any notice of him?"

"Craig reports directly to Gerry Heldebron and answers for the plant's functionality, through weak lines of communication."

"So he answers for the problems but can't get anything done?"

"A process based approach is supposed to create better teamwork."

"Sounds a bit haphazard," said Peter wondering at why someone as competent, as Brett clearly was, would put up with an organization so obviously flawed.

"Ideally suited to Ngami you mean?"

"It sounds terrible."

"That's about it. So back to Stone. Theoretically, they should ask him for advice."

"Why would they, if there are weak lines of communication?"

"It doesn't work because he needs to be a better salesman, or so the last lot of consultants told us."

"If he was a salesman he wouldn't be sitting out here would he?"

"One of our problems is that we're drowning in bullshit from consultants." Brett answered irritably as he swung the Land Cruiser into a parking spot that was marked for him.

Peter felt alienated by the criticism of consultants and did not respond. Brett's negative attitude was a contradiction that he wished he could understand, he was critically important if Peter was to achieve anything. And, although Brett was trusted by de Bruin, he seemed almost disinterested at times. In his bad moments he seemed as ineffective as he had explained that Stone was.

Peter spent the rest of the day reviewing the planning systems and examining the statistics related to the operation, quietly and methodically building on his knowledge of the operation and its shortfalls. He found a number of anomalies that would allow him to fast track his efforts in the days ahead.

Stone, the engineering manager, never arrived to speak to him.

Willers' contact kept a close watch on him. He had been told to advise the security superintendent of everything Peter said, did or looked at.

Willers reported to Van Zyl about what had happened at the meeting. He told him that Rebecca and Heldebron had set a standard that would make it very difficult for Peter.

"They nearly had him out of the running with their effort. Had Charles Obenta not stepped in at the end of the meeting we would have had nothing left to do but shut the place down."

"I'll tell Jack. So far so good. So, in summary, Peter Connor is looking like less of a problem."

"I think the Australian woman, with the efforts of Heldebron will floor Peter Connor."

"That's what we want."

"I'll keep a close watch on things and do what I can to support her efforts."

Jack Anders was more than pleased when he heard from van Zyl.

The news of the leap in progress, made by the success of Rebecca's meeting, toward his objective of declaring the project a failure, meant that he was one step closer to joining the ranks of the truly rich.

He thanked van Zyl and asked him to keep the pressure on Connor, saying, "I don't want him to be given the slightest bit of a chance to succeed. Block him in every way you can."

"I realize that Jack, don't worry, we'll make certain that he won't achieve anything."

18

Brett, Peter, John Willers and Rebecca met the next day for lunch. The frosty atmosphere had not been displaced. Peter walked straight to the selection of tasty looking snack foods that had been laid out on one of the side tables, helped himself, and took his plate of finger food to the conference table. He met Rebecca's eye as he sat down.

"That looks a healthy helping Peter?" she said half smiling as she moved toward the table to get something for herself, then arrived back at the conference table with an even bigger helping.

"You've got room to talk," Peter said.

Both Brett and Willers expressed a few points about priorities and logistics and then asked if the two consultants had anything to add. Rebecca said she had thought about what was important common ground and asked Peter if he would mind going through her plans with her, to make sure they were on the same wavelength in what they were investigating.

Peter agreed and Brett and Willers both decided to stay.

Rebecca fitted a flash memory card to the presentation computer and began to describe her intended approach.

"As I've said, systems are what we need to address," she said.

"Like the young guy said, I've a reasonable idea what a system is." Peter said cautiously, regretting his agreement to working cooperatively.

"I'm sure you do, but keeping a consistent set of descriptions of what we're doing will mean we don't get lost."

"Okay Rebecca, we couldn't agree more on that point," he answered.

"Systems thinking is important because it allows us to stand back from events and see what the basic drivers are."

Peter nodded.

"Once we understand the drivers we can develop strategies that enable us to close the gaps."

"How will you do that?"

"By modifying the system where necessary, or changing it completely."

"So what will the goals be and which gaps are you going to close?"

She turned back to the white board and wrote.

'All systems are variable'

"That's a bit like saying a clock goes tick tock." said Brett wearily.

Rebecca looked irritable but did not answer.

"I presume that in looking at the reliability you'll document the systems behind each outcome in the plant and then list problems with subsystems that cause the problems?" she asked Peter.

Peter nodded.

"Good because that's where I need to go, we need to examine each of the subsystems behind the problems carefully, to see what can be done about them. We need to understand the factors influencing them, down to the finest detail, if we're going to present anything that can be proved."

"So the eventual idea is to redesign the systems when necessary?"

"Not exactly. There is another part we need to agree on. Optimizing one part of a system in isolation can often be detrimental and even catastrophic for the whole system. The next step is to fully analyze the set of problems." Rebecca continued. "First we separate them into two types, those that result from the way the system was designed and those that result from single occurrences or events which are not built into the system."

"Single occurrences?"

"A failure or production loss that has occurred as a result of a random event, such as a human failure."

"Right Rebecca but I am conscious of time more than anything else.

"I'd like to stick with one agenda Peter."

"Of course, you're right Peter," said Brett.

Willers made no comment.

"We have to be sure of not setting up isolated solutions," Rebecca said.

"Of course."

"But, you're not happy with my overall approach?"

"Yes, I am Rebecca, it's the basis of all my work."

"As I've said repeatedly, we've been through this learning organization stuff with Binnett before," commented Brett.

"That's why we can use it to see whether the problems here can be fixed."

"It's supposed to generate commitment and it did not."

"Would anyone else like any more to eat?" interrupted Willers, "And please help yourselves to fruit and coffee.

They had coffee while Willers explained that he thought they should follow their own agendas for the actual review.

"Where do you intend to start?" Brett asked when they were settled back in his office.

"Systems, as Rebecca explained, are a good way to define things but in an exercise like this they provide a chance to do what GVN want. In some cases, such studies provide a reason to use dozens of consultants to retrain the workforce, which is sometimes a necessary exercise, but not always. What I've got is an approach I developed as a means of working through complex exercises, it is based on systems thinking."

"I see," said Brett looking skeptical, "I'm not the one you are going to have to convince, we've a World Bank meeting in a few weeks.

"Yep I know but Rebecca is going to win hands down if we don't fully fit with what she's saying. The difficulty with any exercise like this is that different concepts are merged blended and confused. You really do need to provide a baseline for knowing the actual conditions."

"Interesting but a bit of a play on words?"

"Exactly and that is the main point."

"A play on words?"

"When teams of consultants set out to do something it has to be sold."

"I suppose so."

"What is being sold is what the 'Improvement' methodology that company has available, it is often applied by large teams of people, who sometimes are not ideally suited to what they are doing."

"That's certainly what we've had here, dozens of them."

Brett was sitting at a chair against the wall. He looked away from Peter, down at the floor, with his hands clenched in front of him. Clearly worried. "Anyhow, carry on Peter, you're the one they've trusted to address this, so let's see how we go. What do you want to do?"

"I'd like to talk to as many people as possible." Peter replied.

"How many?"

"I'll need a valid sample size of answers, about thirty for each system checked."

"Okay. But, you might frighten them into total withdrawal, they're already half way there."

"I won't, I've done this before."

"When do you want to start?"

"Could you send an introductory letter out today?

"Have you got something I could use?"

Peter took a letter from the folder he had brought with him and they amended it to what they thought would be the most suitable format.

"I'll get that typed Peter and we'll send it out this afternoon. You can start the interviewing process tomorrow morning."

"What time would be best?"

"Probably seven. Would that be too early for you?

"No that'll be fine."

"Where do you want them to come from?"

"Choose about ten or so critical problem areas based on what we've spoken about after Willers' summary from right across the site and a good cross section of the related work force and management structure."

"Problems areas I've spoken about?"

"That's right. You should be close to exact. Another separate exercise can be set up later to prioritize the plant if we need it."

"It won't be perfect."

"Close though, we need to go fast, I know the plant myself don't forget. We can go over it before you start if you like."

"No, you're right, it should be pretty close to the actual needs; I'll go with my instincts. I'll arrange a series of groups, starting at seven. How long will you need for each session?"

"An hour for each should be enough, and a thirty minute break for me to summarize the results."

"What time do you want to finish?"

"When does the afternoon shift start?"

"At three."

"I'll stop at two and start again at four. Then we can start talking to the afternoon shift, I'll finish at seven in the evening."

"That's a long day."

"I don't have much time and I'd like to finish collecting the information about what they have to say as soon as possible. Any gaps can be used to walk through the plant. I'll also develop a list of statistics that I want, as I go, and might ask you if you can get them ready while I'm busy with the interviews."

"That's great Peter, now if you'll excuse me, I've got to get back to my normal routines for an hour or two. I'll see you later."

Brett met up with him later in the day, and told him he had made all the arrangements for the meetings and gave him a list of people he would be seeing.

Peter and Rebecca met again at the hotel that evening, where they had a pleasant dinner, during which they discussed aspects of Australia that Peter was keen to know about.

Rebecca had enjoyed Peter's company during the evening and for that matter had been impressed during the lunchtime discussion.

As she drifted off to sleep that evening she thought she would have to be careful not to become too friendly with the unaffected South African, who was quite unlike the fast talking people she more often had to deal with on assignments.

19

Peter held to a torturous schedule throughout the following days, managing to ignore Rebecca's high profile, and priority treatment. He used every spare moment, between interviews, to research the commentaries, to get out into the plant, and to examine theories of his own.

During these plant walks, he repeatedly saw why the production from the operation was only a quarter of what it should have been. It shut down regularly.

On one occasion, he watched as luckless fitters entered the hot gassy precipitator units, masked and covered in acid proofed overalls.

The skilled workers had to clear the precipitator plates by standing in the narrow spaces between the plates, hitting and chipping at the slag that clung to the long narrow metal strips. Their expressions clearly showed their stress and how much they would rather be anywhere but doing this thankless job.

As the work progressed Brett had arrived.

Peter commented that he had never heard of precipitators, designed to remove dust particles as they were, collecting slag.

"And all we're fixing is systems thinking," said Brett smiling lopsidedly.

Then when the plant was supposedly operating, between start ups and shut downs, there were long periods of instability.

Throughout Peter's efforts Willers kept track of what he was doing by spying on him in one way or another.

Anders was not keen to hurt Peter in any way during his work on site, because it would certainly create a massive police intervention.

However as Willers' reporting grew more urgent, Anders asked on the second Monday, "So Rebecca's not in control?"

"She'll end up with a recommendation that represents an impossible task and we'll have what we want, but, he knows what he is doing, and from what I can see, more about what she's doing than she does herself. He's building a subset of things that will be effective and I think he might just end up with a working solution."

"Can't be allowed. He must be stopped."

"As you keep saying, that will not be simple here. Botswana has a small population and is very well run. Everything is in the open."

"I'll arrange things."

Willers did not answer.

The next morning Peter went for what had become a regular walk with Brett, using the time as an opportunity to talk, without too much danger of being listened to.

"You seem to be getting there," Brett said as they walked.

"The progress I'm making is good."

"The de Bruins and Charles with his people should be delighted. I'm a bit surprised you've met so little direct opposition."

"Yes, perhaps the incidents in South Africa were just normal South African violence," Peter said as they reached the bottom of a small kopje.

Before Brett could answer a shot rang out and a bullet nicked Peter's shoulder. It would have hit him in the chest if he had not been moving to the left to avoid standing on a loose rock.

The two men dived for cover behind one of the huge boulders that formed the kopje.

A second bullet ricochet off the rock.

They heard a rock clatter higher up the kopje.

Peter looked at Brett questioningly.

The lithe Englishman said, "We can't wait here, let's go after him," and leaped from behind the rock; and, in a zig zag pattern, raced up the little hill from behind one boulder to the next, yelling at the top of his voice.

The would be assassin had been told to get clear immediatcly, his movement, to get away, had caused the rock to clatter down from where he was hiding. Brett's charge was thus unseen, but was heard. The man stumbled around the kopje, toward where he had left his vehicle. Scratched by thorn trees and bleeding, he was moving like someone possessed.

Brett caught up with him at the vehicle and tackled him in the half-light.

The assailant was screaming himself by then. Terrified by the effort, by his failure, and worse by the unexpected retaliation. He had been told to avoid injuring Brett at all costs but knew he had to get away. He jumped up and hit Brett with the rifle.

Brett fell.

The frantic man threw his rifle into his vehicle and dived in after it, to be gone by the time Peter arrived.

He found Brett groggily pulling himself to his feet.

"Are you okay?" He asked.

"My head's a bit sore but I'll survive. I feel ten years younger from that little venture."

"Hell but you're fit." Peter said. "Where did you get the yelling from?"

"Tough upbringing."

"Who was it, did you see?"

"Not properly."

They discussed calling the police and decided that they did not want any delay in the already shaky campaign to rectify the smelter so they went to see Charles Obenta and explained what had happened.

The tribal leader shook his head and said. "At least neither of you was badly hurt. You didn't recognize him?"

"I don't know who he was but I'm pretty sore," Peter answered. "I suspect that he would not have stopped for a breath of fresh air until he got to the Zimbabwe border. The way Brett frightened him, I almost felt sorry for him."

Charles sent them to the hospital to have their injuries seen to and arranged a full time guard for Peter, then phoned James de Bruin, and told him what had happened.

"Is he going to carry on?" asked de Bruin.

"He didn't seem terribly put out, he seems to work himself into a bit of a trance and keep going no matter what. And he apparently does not have much more he needs to do."

"And the injury?"

"The injury is just a scratch, luckily, the doctor put a few stitches in it and Peter seems to be quite okay."

"Hell I have no idea what to do, it's impossible to be fair and keep going to achieve our own ends. I almost wonder if the only choice is that we should give up?"

"No I don't think so. I asked him and he said he definitely wants to complete the exercise. They only seem to have annoyed him, it's as though, in his mind, he is their target rather than us. He says he's being paid a great deal and seems to be enjoying himself, as though it's some sort of a game. I think he's got personal problems and the stress helps him to forget his own life."

"I suppose we should be grateful for that. Perhaps you could talk to him about what's worrying him?"

"I've tried. He doesn't seem to want to talk about what's wrong."

Anders received the news with anything but equanimity.

"The person I used was as good as we have here," van Zyl answered irritably, "all this is happening in a very well run country, there's a very real limit on what can be done, and get away with here, and you're the one who keeps saying we must not go too far out on a limb."

Anders knew his long time associate was right and said so, adding, "It's just that we are so close to getting what we want that one unimportant person should stop us seems ridiculous."

"Calm down Jack, he's got a long road ahead of him we'll deal with him. If the shooting exercise had been successful we might very well have had the roof fall in on us. Connors is good but Rebecca has the inside track. Heldebron is right, getting that place moving with the current set up, really is going to be impossible."

"We just have so much at stake."

Heldebron went to see Willers when he heard about the attack and was told the security superintendent knew nothing about it.

"Oh?" said Heldebron and left Willers without making any further comment.

They were both in the same awkward position, not knowing about, and not wanting to be involved in, anything like this attack, but also frightened by their exclusion.

Peter worked fast.

The bodyguard that Charles arranged stayed with him, and he minimized the time during which he was exposed. He reached the point of his review that he was looking for on the second Wednesday after he had arrived at the Ngami site.

He showed a summary, of why he thought the plant could reach full production, in a reasonable time, to; Willers, Craig Stone, Brett Halliday, Heldebron, Charles Obenta, and Rebecca.

They listened to what he had to say without interruption; then Heldebron asked him for details.

Peter explained that a detailed report would be presented to the World Bank meeting.

Heldebron was not sure he could grasp what Peter was saying and said his responsibility and interest meant that he needed the full report before it was published.

Peter apologized but pointed out that his three week time frame was not complete and said he had given the agreed presentation. He explained that the detailed report could only be submitted when it was finished.

He left the site and went back to the hotel, where he worked for a while in his room on a draft. Then putting this aside, he looked out of the hotel room's window into the gardens. Deciding to have dinner he walked toward the restaurant. As he rounded the corner on the veranda, he nearly bumped into the startlingly attractive flight attendant from his flight to Ngami.

"Oh hello," he said awkwardly, "Anita?"

"Hello Peter, how's your work on site going?"

"Pretty well finished," he said wondering how she knew his name. He supposed that most people in the village were discussing his role.

"You going to dinner?"

"I am."

"Mind if I join you?" she asked, looking demure.

"Not at all," he answered.

"Are you here for much longer?" she asked.

"I'm leaving tomorrow. I didn't know you stayed overnight."

"The aircraft had a technical problem and we have to wait for a part to arrive from Johannesburg."

"How long will that take?"

"The part should be here tomorrow."

Dinner took longer than usual and, as they made their way to their rooms, Peter tried, half-heartedly, to think of an excuse to get away.

Anita walked close to him, talking about her experiences on the flights to Botswana.

Heldebron was waiting for Peter in the foyer. Barely acknowledging Anita, he addressed Peter as though they were still in the office. "Peter there's something I need to clear up.'

"What, Gerry?"

"Can you spare me a moment?"

Anita waved to Peter over the shoulder of Heldebron.

Peter, both disappointed and somehow relieved, followed Heldebron into the lounge.

The ensuing discussion took several hours.

It was past midnight when they finished.

When he got back to his hotel room Peter found a note from Anita under the door, thanking him for the pleasant evening and saying she hoped they would meet again soon.

Heldebron contacted Anders the next morning and said that he thought that Peter might have a basis for getting the plant into full production.

"What about the Binnett effort?"

"It's very intricate and well done but he might have enough knowledge to fulfill some critical aspects of its expectations."

"If he gets the chance."

"You'll be controlling the meeting."

"I can't let him get there."

20

As the reviews of Peter and Rebecca progressed, Ben's hopes for his exploration had grown steadily higher. He worked at drawing parallels between his knowledge of the Ngami ore deposits, to investigate all aspects of the potential of any find within the area selected. The folds in the ore-bearing reef made it possible to conclude that there was more than one ore-body. He needed to know which if any of them was what they needed.

Both he and Rob were hot, tired, and were feeling the strain of the long period away from civilization.

The urgency of ensuring the ore was claimed drove Ben; but Rob had almost reached the end of his tether. He was looking bedraggled, having several days' growth of untidy facial hair adding to his decrepit appearance.

Ben looked slightly better.

When they stopped to make camp, on the same Wednesday evening that Peter met Heldebron in the Ngami hotel to provide an explanation of what he had found, Ben chatted away to Rob trying to pull him out of his lethargy, "I think we're pretty well there Rob," he said as cheerfully.

"I sure hope so," said Rob feeling utterly frustrated, but trying to draw strength from Ben's assurances that progress was being made, he continued doing his best to keep things moving in any way he could.

"I'll be back in an hour or so."

Ben found the platinum where he expected it, in a flat area that was divided by a small ridge and gully near the carefully selected campsite, took a systematic set of samples and walked briskly back to where Rob had set up their camp and got ready for their evening meal.

Ben's jaunty pace and cheerful expression told the story before he spoke.

"How did you go?" Rob asked.

"I've found what I need."

"Enough to save the operation?"

"I'm sure it will, it follows the geological structure I expected. The problem is that there are a number of folds and it's easy to get the wrong idea with the deposit. Of course we will have to drill and quantify it properly but now we just need to register the claim," Ben answered.

They spoke about the work that had to be done to register the company's interest. The claim had to be made on behalf of the company, which meant that they would have to return to the Ngami to follow the correct procedures.

The next morning, awakened before dawn, by the sounds of morning, Ben stepped out of the tent and looking up, saw a beautiful male Kudu walking out from the bush.

The statuesque antelope stood perfectly still, for a moment, head held high, curling horns reaching up to the canopy of a fig tree, its fine head was accentuated by the horns, its graceful ears, and the mane that hung from its neck completed the classical picture of a Kudu, that's often used to epitomize the beauty of Africa's wildlife.

The Kudu watched Ben for several seconds, then walked quietly toward the water hole, stopped, looked at him again before spreading its front legs slightly, so that it could drink from the pool between them, seemingly unafraid of him. It finished drinking, looked at him again, its huge brown eyes deciding for a second time that he did not represent danger, and then it strode peacefully back into the bush.

They cooked breakfast as the sun rose through the dusty African sky, as hunters had done for thousands of years. He completed the sampling he had planned and marked the claim.

As Ben and Rob were marking the claim, on Thursday morning, van Breda, the mine manager, greeted Peter warmly and waved him to a chair.

He answered Peter's questions about the mine and its ore reserves without hesitation and showed Peter how the mine was in a precarious state, and told him why it was running short of ore.

"That means if we improve the smelter performance the mine will be an impossible bottle-neck?"

"Yes."

Peter shook his head, "That's a disaster."

"Heldebron knows the situation."

Peter asked if he could see the mining machinery workshops. They walked around these and he was shown an impressive array of equipment, but was surprised to see that the area looked neglected and untidy.

When they had finished their tour Peter thanked the mine manager and went to see the chief geologist.

Ngami's chief geologist, Itzaak Bierman, was defensive when Peter asked about the company's plans.

This was reasonable since geology is an area where confidentiality is important, but there was something more than natural caution in Bierman's manner. His knowledge and ability was, Peter had heard from Brett, without equal, so he persevered, but did not gain much from the interview.

After Ben finished marking the claim they returned to their Francistown office, unloaded the equipment and briefly discussed their successful venture with the receptionist at their office.

Van Zyl recorded their conversation.

The receptionist asked if they had seen the unusual water hole that she had once told Rob about.

He replied that they had and that they had thought it was most attractive sight.

"Did you swim there?" she asked looking mischievous.

"Of course." Said Ben.

Ben then phoned Charles Obenta and said that he'd be back on site the next morning.

Charles spent some time filling him in on his perspective of the reviews by Peter and Rebecca.

Peter and Charles had been playing golf when Ben phoned, protected by several of Charles' most trusted people. The holes on the course were laid out through the kopjes and bush country around the Ngami village. Their erratic journey around the nine holes was overseen, with seeming great interest, by a troop of baboons perched on the kopjes. They barked encouragement from their rocky, vantage points. Peter could almost imagine they were thinking his efforts were more interesting than many they had seen.

After the call, Charles said, "It was Ben, he's getting back tomorrow morning," he said to Peter.

"Did he find what he was looking for?"

"He says he did and has the samples and information with him."

Peter repeated van Breda's commentary about the mine running out of ore and Charles said that neither he nor James de Bruin were officially aware of a major problem with ore reserves.

He explained that Ben's efforts were initiated at the same time he had asked for Peter's help and were aimed at supplementing the ore reserves.

They arranged to meet the next morning and Peter returned to the hotel as the evening sun began to color the landscape.

Although Charles had asked him to stay away from exposed spots he decided to have a beer on the veranda of the hotel, and sat, for a while, at one of the simple tables, looking out over the valley with its kopjes and bush and clumps of baobabs.

The setting sun enhanced the golden color on the bushes, trees and kopjes for a while and then they were swallowed by the dusk.

A waiter asked if he could get him anything to eat and Peter ordered dinner. He ate slowly, thinking of the work he had to do at Springvale and not liking the prospect of returning there or of doing similar work elsewhere. Whatever McNeil's plans for him involved, he thought that if all he could look forward to was unending "management consulting" exercises like the one at Springvale, he should jump at the opportunity that Ngami might present.

He fell asleep that evening looking forward to seeing Ben de Bruin the next morning, not only because of their friendship, but also because of his concern about the ore problems. They seemed, from what he could gather, to be far more serious than Charles Obenta and James de Bruin realized.

Ben and Rob discussed their route from Francistown to Ngami and eventually decided back roads would be their safest option. They had a pleasant dinner at Jamieson's house.

They set out for Ngami the next day before dawn, on their way to their disastrous clash with the vehicular assassin on the banks of the dried river.

21

Ben, half dozing and withdrawn from his agony, was jerked to full consciousness by his phone ringing. He had it in his hand, wedged between his body, his hand and the seat. He struggled to hold onto it, trying desperately pick up the call.

The blood had dried somewhat and he succeeded in doing so, to find the caller was Charles Obenta.

"Ben, where are you?" Charles asked.

"Charles," he gasped, "we've been forced off the road."

"Who by? Where are you? Are you hurt?"

"I'm badly hurt and I think Rob might be dead, he doesn't seem to be breathing."

"Oh hell, Ben! What's happened?"

Ben explained that they had taken the back route from Francistown to Ngami to ensure their anonymity and safety, and that someone had somehow followed them and forced them off the road.

"Where are you?"

Ben explained.

"Right I'll be there in about ten minutes."

"You'll need to move Charles, I'm loosing blood and whoever forced us off the road is still close."

"You say Rob's dead?"

"I think so, he's so terribly still. I can't reach him." Ben gasped. "Also I've given my diary and samples to a young boy and sent him for help. They are our lifeline Charles we must get them from the boy."

"Which boy?"

"He said his name was Joseph and that he looks after cattle."

"Hang on Ben, I'll get there as soon as I can."

Charles turned to Peter, "Ben's hurt come on let's go."

They ran to Charles' vehicle and set out to find Ben.

After the call Ben sighed and slipped into unconsciousness again. This time the dreams were more fleeting, he felt warm, and the pain was subsiding. He floated near death, dreaming of the boy to whom he had given the case; and again about his own boyhood on their farm, and many happy days with the children of the farm village. There had never been a racial aspect to those adventures, he had, at that time, been confused by the grown up apartheid world.

Other images floated like clouds, coming and going, of the farm village, of a terrorist attack by people who had tried to turn the villagers against the family. Several people had been hurt in the raid. Police reservists from the town had been brought in to support the family.

The subsequent and tragic hunt for the perpetrators floated through his mind. The group tracking the terrorists had stopped on the brow of one of the blue hills that overlooked his family farm. They looked back, down at the farmhouse, far below, separated from the neat village by several acres of Douglas fir, enclosed by two continuous rows of red, white and pink flowering gums.

In his dream, Ben thought he could smell diesel fuel, through a warm and beautiful golden mist.

In the dream, two shots rang out across the valley and one of the group fell to the ground.

It had been Ben's first experience of the violence that wracked the continent.

James, his brother, had been first to the man's side, trying to revive him.

He had failed.

While Ben was speaking to Charles, Albrecht, the driver of the reinforced vehicle, was still waiting for Joseph, from where he planned to shoot the boy and recover the samples, but Joseph failed to appear. After a few minutes he phoned for instructions.

"If you're sure the boy has gone another way, get out of there but first make sure the geologists can't tell any tales."

"And the boy?"

"If I don't hear back from you that you've got him, I'll arrange for him to be hunted down by the people we've got in the village."

Albrecht waited for another few minutes and decided the boy must have gone some other way. He went back to his vehicle, turned it and drove back to the site of the smash, and climbed down to Ben's Land Rover. Realizing that it was too unsteady to hold his weight. He did not try to get to the window to see if the occupants were dead, he did not intend risking his own life. Firing blindly into the vehicle would not guarantee anything, so he climbed back to the Land Cruiser, unloaded his spare can of fuel, then slowly and carefully climbed back down to a point on an overhanging rock from which he could throw the fuel onto the Land Rover. He poured the fuel, making sure it got into the cabin and then splashed the rest over the outside of the vehicle, being careful to keep it off his own clothes.

He put the can down, took his cigarette lighter out of his pocket and stepped back to light the fuel. Then realising he might be caught in the explosion, took the can back to his Land Cruiser to make something he could light and throw onto the smashed vehicle from a safe distance.

He fashioned a torch from a stick, some string and papers when he got to the vehicle. He doused these in the remains of the fuel, climbed back down the cliff, along a ledge from which he thought he could safely throw the torch onto the Land Rover, took the lighter out of his pocket, and tried to set fire to the makeshift torch.

A storm that was brewing had darkened the sky and the increasingly strong wind was enough to extinguish the lighter flame. He tried, again and again, but the lighter kept going out. At last he managed to shelter the flame by first putting the makeshift torch on the ground and then covering the lighter's flame with one hand, while working the lighter with the other hand. He sighed with relief as he did so, thinking of his upcoming flight out of Africa, tens of thousands of dollars richer. This was his last contract in Southern Africa. He would be free to continue his profession elsewhere in the world under another alias.

Charles and Peter had driven as quickly as was possible through the village and were approaching the crash site as Albrecht was trying to light the makeshift torch.

Charles barely checked the vehicle's pace on the rough winding road until he saw the heavily reinforced vehicle parked where he was expecting to find Ben.

He stopped, took his hunting rifle from a rack behind the rear seat and they walked over the rise.

They saw Albrecht as they went over the rise.

Charles looked through his telescopic sight at the scene.

Albrecht had by then put the torch down to shelter the lighter flame. He leaned forward and lit the torch.

Charles did not hesitate he aimed carefully through the telescopic sight and squeezed the trigger twice.

Both bullets hit Albrecht and he dropped like a sparrow shot off the branches of a tree, to tumble down the cliff face, leaving the torch where it lay burning.

They scrambled down toward Ben's vehicle. Charles arrived first and stamped out the flames of the torch that lay where Albrecht had dropped it.

Peter, who was by far the heavier of two men, applied his weight to the back of the vehicle and Charles climbed cautiously onto the smashed Land Rover.

Ben was unconscious.

Charles managed to get the door of the vehicle open and tried to free the injured man, who was breathing very shallowly. The vehicle rocked precariously. He crept back and made his way up to the Land Cruiser where he quickly located the long rope he carried. He tied one end of this to a tree near the crashed vehicle and the other to Ben's Land Rover.

Peter's weight and the rope were enough to allow Charles to free Ben. He carried him to safety and then climbed back into the vehicle to check on Rob, who he sadly realized was past human help.

Charles asked Peter to take Ben to the Ngami hospital.

"What are you going to do?" Peter asked.

"Find the boy with the case."

"On your own?"

"I don't have a choice."

"I'll come back and help you."

"You've a plane to catch."

"Not now, I'll go on tomorrow morning's flight."

"These are my people, I'll be okay. I can get a lift from the police. I have to call them anyway," said Charles as he loosened the rope. He had fetched an axe from the Land Cruiser and they fashioned a stretcher using the rope and two trimmed straight branches, they cut from the bush.

"You don't know who to trust any more than I do, Charles," Peter said as they carried Ben to the vehicle.

"I think the majority are trustworthy enough, but of course it's those who I don't know about that are the worry."

"Phone me when you're on your way back," Charles said as they lifted Ben into the back of the vehicle.

"How do you know where he went?"

"I'm guessing that he went down and toward the village. He'd have known the person who forced them off the road was up here."

"I'll be back after I get Ben into the hospital," Peter said.

As Peter buckled Ben in, the geologist regained consciousness for long enough to greet Peter and ask what was happening at the site.

Peter explained what he had found during the review.

"That's sounds good Peter. Thank you," Ben said and smiled faintly, before slipping back into a coma.

Peter started the vehicle, turned it around in several motions, due to the encroaching trees and rocks, and headed for Ngami.

Looking back through the rear view mirror he saw Charles disappearing toward the ravine, his hunting rifle slung over his shoulder, talking into his cell phone.

Charles phoned the police as Peter left, and then James de Bruin.

The police said they would have someone contact him.

James de Bruin was overwhelmed; he asked Charles if he could call him back, then sat staring out the window of his home office in the farmhouse. Now, Ben, his only brother, was close to death, consumed by Ngami.

Because of the rough track, Peter's journey with the badly injured Ben, to the hospital, took what felt like an eternity. He had contacted the hospital on the way in and told them that Ben had been badly hurt, describing his injuries to the hospital superintendent, so Ben was met at the emergency entrance. Fortunately the hospital staff were familiar with the severe injuries which happen all too often in mines and wheeled him straight into the theatre.

After twenty minutes or so, the surgeon came out to tell Peter that Ben would probably be okay. He contacted James de Bruin and explain that there seemed to be every chance that his brother would recover.

James asked if Ben was safe in the hospital.

Peter told him that Charles had arranged for a protective tribal guard to be with the injured man.

22

Joseph's birth had never been recorded, he was thought to be between twelve and was fourteen years old but looked younger.

Despite his size, he could run faster and for longer distances than anyone he knew.

When he heard the four-wheel drive start and follow in the direction he was heading, he stopped and crept behind the overhanging cliff face, where he waited until the engine noise had passed overhead.

He then crossed the dry riverbed, and climbed the opposite bank, to run on, at a slight angle to the river. Eventually his pounding feet brought him to a crest of another cliff in a bend of the same river.

The warmth of the day and the exercise had made him hot, so he stood for a while in the shade, with the breeze cooling him. Looking toward the village of Ngami, listening for sounds of pursuit, he could see a small plume of smoke from the smelter, near the village, drifting toward largely uninhabited lands on the East bank, slightly dispelling the image of an unspoilt wilderness or perhaps accentuating it.

He thought it looked quite beautiful in the morning sun.

The slight plume showed the direction of the prevailing winds. Rain was approaching and Joseph could see thunderclouds building fast. As he watched, the trickle from the stack faded as it regularly did, indicating the huge metallurgical marvel had stopped producing.

At the time of Joseph's flight, the wide river consisted mainly of sand, pebbles and a few rocky outcrops. Bush covered the land between the riverbed and the cliff's base.

Flat-topped Acacia trees with sharp white thorns, called 'wag n' bietjie's' in Afrikaans, roughly 'wait a moment' in English, slowed Joseph as he climbed down to a cave entrance that was sheltered by a clump of the Mopani trees.

The Mopani tree with its unusual butterfly shaped leaves is a relative of the beautiful pink "Bauhinia Elegans", found in tropical gardens around the world. The local version is home to a traditional delicacy, the Mopani worm, that provides a valuable and tasty complement to the people's diet.

In a minute or so Joseph was inside the cave that he used as a secret retreat and a storage place for his few treasures. He sat down for a moment and tried to gather his thoughts. He wanted to help the man in the wrecked vehicle but he could not think of any quick way to contact anyone.

In the part of the cave that was lit by the sky he opened the case, the latches were strong and made from solid metal. They clicked open like no case he had ever seen. There were several rocks in numbered plastic bags. He noticed that some of these exactly matched samples in his own quite extensive collection. There was also a diary, with notes and sketches, an old knife, and some money.

He counted the money. There were more than a hundred 50 Pula notes, easily the largest sum he had ever seen. He sat back and thought what he might do with such a sum. The knife was beautiful too. Then he thought of the man's anxious face. He put the case with the rocks it contained on a shelf, next to where he sat. He hid the diary, money and knife far back in the cave, in a dry spot, with his collection of rocks, and a few books he had collected at negligible cost, from people in Ngami selling up when they were about to return to the countries they came from.

He could not see how he could help the man in the crashed Land Rover. He thought restlessly of his own sorry background. His father had died five years before, and Joseph's sole occupation was caring for his mother's few cattle. His family were not fully accepted by the clan. He was not sure why, perhaps it was because of the closeness of his bushman ancestry, or perhaps because they were so poor. He desperately wanted to break away from the village life to become like the people he had seen in films, in cities, happy, well dressed and excited, driving beautiful clean cars on sealed roads through huge green trees and living in amazing houses. For a moment he dreamed. The money presented a possible key to an escape.

The baying of dogs pulled him from his reverie. He could not decide what to do; there was the injured man to think of, but the cattle had to be cared for before anything else. So he set out to return to the herd, quickly concealing the access path to the cave using cow manure which should, he thought, keep the dogs from the cave. He knew this would mean the group following him would get closer, but he was sure he could outdistance any man or boy. The dogs were not a danger if they stayed with whoever was managing them; but since this was not guaranteed, he took a rocky route that would be difficult for dogs to follow.

He worried as he ran; about the cattle, the man he had promised to help, the case, and how to get help.

He decided it would be better to go home, from there he would send one of his brothers to care for the cattle. Changing direction, he loped along bare footed, his oversized ragged coat flapping like a broken sail. His handed down oversized shorts stayed up in defiance of gravity. His pace would have done a much more mature or even professional long distance runner credit.

Luckily for Joseph large drops of rain began to fall.

The group of five men from the village that had been sent to find Joseph were delinquents who had originally left the village to go to South Africa. There, they had drifted into the ways of the criminal elements in Johannesburg, before having to return to Botswana to escape the police. They were not popular and were largely ignored by the good people who made up most of the village's population. However they could not be completely rejected because they were a part of the people's families and everyone hoped that they would soon settle down.

They had been dropped off near the crashed vehicle and had made their way down to the to river and then used the dogs to follow the boy, along its course.

Charles, after contacting the police, had started his search at the base of the cliff below the smashed Land Rover. He was a highly skilled tracker and easily followed Joseph's footprints in the riverbed. The trail to the cave was more difficult, there he had to rely on finding the damage done to the bush. He found the sample case in the cave without much difficulty. He then called Peter. After he was assured that Ben was stable, he asked Peter to get back to pick him up. "Please hurry Peter, I can hear baying dogs, probably looking for the boy, but I'm not too keen on being caught on my own."

"I'll be there as quickly as I can," Peter said and ran from the hospital, back to Charles' Land Cruiser.

As the Land Cruiser hurtled out of the hospital emergency area, he just missed a shabby old car that was meandering along, on the wrong side of the road, and drove as fast as he could on the track, to where he had left Charles.

The group following Joseph saw Charles as he returned across the river. They left their dogs with one of the men and followed the agile clan leader with great care. They knew him and were aware of his importance and his ability to use the rifle he was carrying. They were also not certain about whether he had anything to do with Joseph, or the crash.

Charles climbed quickly through the increasingly heavy rain to where he had asked Peter to meet him and was relieved to see his Land Cruiser when he got there. He climbed into the vehicle and settled back in the seat, saying, "I'm pleased you were here a group of men are right behind me."

As Peter turned the vehicle, he saw the men come around the corner and drove off.

"Who were they?" asked Peter.

"I don't know. They might be after the boy, I'd like to find him but can't think how."

"What's happened to the police?" Peter asked.

"I don't know. I've phoned them, I know the officer in charge, and he said someone was on their way."

"Surely with someone dead?"

"Police can be bought Peter."

"But, you're...?"

"There's more going on here than I can deal with Peter."

Peter turned on the wipers as they drove off. They muddied the window so he had to use the windscreen washer.

The group of men saw Charles get into the vehicle and watched it disappear before returning to the search for Joseph.

Joseph had heard the dogs stop and was pleased to gain some distance. Still trying to make his way along the higher ground, away from the actual track, jumping from protruding rock to rock, he slipped and fell, hurting his head badly. He managed to get up and kept running.

Peter and Charles visited Ben in hospital after they got back to the village. They found he was still unconscious but stable.

Charles gave Peter the sample case to take with him to Cape Town and walked with him to his vehicle.

There was still time to catch the evening flight.

Peter drove straight to the airport. Once there he phoned Ken Lavers, a friend, and asked if he could spend the weekend with him.

Ken agreed.

Peter then phoned James de Bruin to say he would be in Cape Town with the samples that evening.

Ben was also taken to the airport, in an ambulance, to be flown out in the same flight as Peter. Charles accompanied him, in the back of the spotless and professional looking vehicle.

On the short journey Ben regained consciousness for a few moments and recognized Charles. "The boy, the case?" he murmured.

"I've got the case."

"Oh thank heavens, there are two... ," he mumbled and then closed his eyes before he drifted off into another dream of making the most important discovery. In it his grandfather was busily congratulating him.

He woke again while he was loaded onto the aircraft, smiled weakly at Charles thanked him and drifted back into his dreams.

The police had finally arrived at the crash scene, long after Charles had left. They found the Land Rover with Rob Jamieson's body in it, but the Land Cruiser and its driver had gone.

This was duly reported to Charles and he was told the investigation would remain on the police books, but as an accident, because there was no concrete evidence of anything else having happened.

Charles silently and slowly shook his head as he put the phone down. At least the boy had not been found dead, which is what he had been half expecting.

James de Bruin met Peter at Cape Town's airport at eight thirty in the evening. He greeted him warmly and asked how he was. He listened with interest to Peter's summary of the work and then asked if Peter knew anything more about his brother Ben.

"He's still unconscious."

"Do you think he will be okay?"

"They said he would be. I know they took him to Johannesburg on the same flight as I left on. Have you spoken to the dead man's wife?"

"I have, but there's so little to say. He apparently went of his own accord because he was worried about Ben. I'm going to the funeral."

"Have you heard from the police?"

"No. I don't like dealing with them myself and Charles will let me know as soon as they find anything."

He gratefully accepted the sample case, asked Peter about the smelter and, after listening to his brief summary, said he was looking forward to his full report.

"I'll be at the farm early on Monday morning."

James said a meeting in Cape Town would be a better idea, so that it would be more convenient for the other directors of the de Bruin organization to hear what Peter had to say.

Peter agreed and after parting, hired a car to drive to Hout Bay to his friends', the Lavers, apartment.

23

At the de Bruin board meeting on Monday James met Peter at reception and asked how his brother was.

Peter told him that Ben had recovered consciousness and was having trouble remembering what had happened.

"What an absolute nightmare this has turned into, no way forward and no way back."

"I don't suppose life is ever that easy, but you sure are meeting some stiff opposition to your efforts."

James shook his head, "Well Peter, I seem to keep saying it, but thank you for your efforts, they are certainly more than we should have expected," then led Peter into the boardroom.

The board members watched the powerful looking man for any sign of weakness, dressed formally and yet seemingly out of place in the sophisticated environment, his input was critical to all of them in one way or another. They saw none. Although Peter was not as accomplished a speaker as they were used to, his grasp of the subject matter was impressive. He explained Rebecca's perspective that nothing would work in the Ngami situation and showed why he thought that he could do better than she was saying was the case.

His final slide gave them a summary of how he would make the project fully productive and profitable.

"What you are showing is not some individual or system solution but a number of interrelated problems?"

"That's right, some seem quite obvious but what's happening is that they are getting lost in a mass of confusion."

"I can't see how we've allowed such an important investment to deteriorate to such an extent." One of the directors said quietly.

"They've employed people with the best possible backgrounds to solve the problems," answered de Bruin defensively.

"The people there feel there is no hope of getting the plant working. It's hard to believe how such a negative outlook has developed without some outside assistance," Peter said.

"The people there have got every reason to work toward developing their futures," said de Bruin.

Peter shook his head, but did not reply.

He concluded the presentation by saying. "What I've proposed here would take six months to implement, if handled properly, and would ensure the project reaches full production within two months. Profitability would only be achieved six months after the longer period."

"Would you be prepared to implement the plan?" asked de Bruin sitting back in the chair.

"I've got to think about that," he answered.

"We'd pay you at the same rate as we have done for this assignment."

"I still have to think about it."

De Bruin said he understood Peter's hesitation and asked him to keep the offer in mind. He then concluded the meeting, saying, "Thanks Peter we'll look forward to getting your written report.

He was silent while Peter packed his equipment away, and then said, "Thank you again for going to Ngami, Peter. You've given us much more of a chance than we had before."

Peter nodded and thanked him before leaving.

One of the directors reported the content of Peter's report to Jack Anders.

"You say his work would satisfy you as an accountant?"

"It's well put together."

"Will it satisfy the World Bank?"

"I don't know anything about the technology, but it looks good. You will need to be sure that the case for closure is watertight."

Peter, having some time to spare, decided to visit the Kirstenbosch Gardens set on the inland slopes of the Table Mountain.

He was followed. His ability to stop Anders and his associate in Francistown from making billions having been confirmed by the informer from the de Bruin board had made his existence too much of a threat. There was no conscience involved and the key players did not have the slightest interest in Peter's future or existence. The only questionable point had been whether his disappearance at such a critical stage would provide a bigger check on their plans than facing the report he made using Rebecca's skill and the recommendations of her report.

As Peter strolled through the lower parts of the huge and beautiful botanic gardens, he was distracted by the memory of his family, who had been with him when he was last there.

Eventually he made his way up the complex web of paths that led up the slopes of the mountain, enjoying the huge variety of seemingly color coordinated plants that formed the border between the paths, lawns, groups of trees and natural rock formations. The path steepened steadily leading into one of the natural forests that occupy the valleys on the mountainside.

He stopped for a rest at the top of a trickling waterfall in one of the valleys. There was a long drop from the smallish level area, where he paused next to a single bench that had been provided there. He looked back in the direction from which he had come and caught a glimpse of sunlight reflected from within a bush and rock formation to his right. His heart checked. He thought of running, but forced himself to remain calm, hesitated and then walked deliberately toward the rocks.

After Peter had left the de Bruin board meeting, James de Bruin sat in silence for a few minutes, then said, "We have to get him there if we're to survive."

"I don't like your chances" the gray haired man on his left replied. "He's not going to drop a his career with McNeil to go to Botswana for a few months work."

"It's a pity there isn't anything else we could get him to do when he's finished."

"Knowing he can help and not getting him there isn't going to be much use."

"I suppose we have to deal with one thing at a time, we have what we wanted from him. I'll keep in touch with him. I'm sure he'd like to take the work, but he's naturally worried. It's a pity we're not bigger. It won't help to ask McNeil. I really don't think McNeil can do anything that GVN doesn't approve of. If Peter starts improving something while working at Ngami, when GVN want it shut down, they could make things very difficult for McNeil."

"Are you going to wait until the World Bank meeting to talk to Anders about what he's said?" asked one of the directors.

"No, this information is enough to put Anders under a lot more pressure. I'll send him and his cousin a copy of the summary."

"Why involve the cousin?" one of the directors asked.

"I've known him for years and helped him when he was younger. He's a very straightforward sort of a bloke. I'm not sure of the politics but the cousin owns a large portion of the company's stock."

"I thought it was a publicly listed company. Anders would have a contract as managing director and the support of their board. A shareholder is still a shareholder in that case, even if he's a major share holder."

"I know but I have to open every door I can."

"When will we get Connor's written report?"

"In the next day or so."

After the others had left, de Bruin took a fax sheet out of the stationery drawer and wrote a brief note to Jack Anders with a copy to his cousin Michael. He asked his personal assistant if she could type it and send it as a fax, with the synopsis of the report that Peter had given him, to the Anders cousins.

As Peter forced himself toward where he'd seen the glint of the cell phone, he was certain that turning his back on danger in a remote spot like this was an invitation to anyone wanting to rob or otherwise harm him.

The person waiting near Peter, was startled by his quarry's sudden move toward him. It was not where he wanted Peter. He had intended to finish Peter off by pushing the him over the railing.

The assassin knew he had to move. He stepped casually out onto the pathway, fiddling with his trousers, pretending to be embarrassed, excused himself, and walked on up toward Peter.

When the man brushed past him Peter sighed with relief and turned back to head past the bench and down through the park to the car.

The man spun as Peter got behind him and grabbed Peter's arm. He was big and powerful.

The gravel pathway was slippery and Peter heard the movement, then saw the man moving out of the corner of his eye. A very accomplished rugby player in his day, he dropped below the outstretched arm, to grasp the collar of the man's coat on either side of his head. He then dropped backwards and swung the man over his head as he had done dozens of times on the rugby field. The man sailed over his head, over the railing, and crashed down the cliff with a pitiful wail.

Peter stood, looked around, brushed himself off and headed back down as fast as he could, using a different path, to make his way back to the Lavers' apartment.

No one followed him.

He drove quickly to the Lavers and did not think that he was followed.

Ken was not home when he got there so he told the story to Jess Lavers with whom he had once worked.

"Should you call the police?" she asked.

"It could end up delaying my departure to the World Bank meeting."

"I suppose so but perhaps you were seen."

"No, there was no one about."

Always a good listener, she had then led him through his options for taking the work while getting him a glass of wine and some savories that she had prepared in readiness for his visit.

"Sound like there's a hell of lot at stake Peter?" she asked.

"More than I've ever dealt with."

"Perhaps you should stick with it to the end, you might change their lives and yours. You might be able to achieve something more than you've ever imagined you could."

He realized she was right. "You mean more than the initial consulting fees?"

"Yes, it sounds like there's a mountain of work needing to be done in one way or another. You could employ others to help and charge their work on at a premium"

"That's true but I've always preferred to work on my own though."

"Yes, and probably annoyed those responsible for generating fees."

"They do seem a bit edgy at times."

Jess smiled and told him they had invited a friend of theirs to dinner, who knew a great deal about independent consulting, to advise Peter.

He discussed the attempt on his life in the gardens with Ken when he got back and they decided that involving the, sadly, sometimes dishonest, police in the incident might provide the de Bruin's enemies with another opportunity.

At dinner the Lavers' friend Dave told Peter how he had accepted a similar assignment, to the one Peter might be asked to take, and had built it into the university position that he now held, and went on to explain that he still did consulting work. He provided more information about what he thought about the real prospects and dangers, of working on one's own as an expert, then asked Peter why he was so concerned about working on his own.

"For one thing, in a competitive market, the big firms have names that speak for themselves, for another, so many so called consultants spend most of their time writing procedures, which is really what I did in my first job. Not very interesting."

"Big firms do have reputations, but that is not always what people need," said Dave, "and procedures are important."

"The other worry is that after the work finishes there, I could end up as just another voice in the wilderness, having to take whatever silly job that I could get, or worse, having to pay someone for work."

"There is a need for people who can be brought in from outside who are not tied to big name firms, to solve real problems though."

"I don't see why."

"For one thing, large consultancies have extended networks that can pass information on as easily as they provide it. Companies often have problems they don't want others to know about, and in such situations they need someone they can trust, just as the de Bruins need you now."

"I must say," said Peter, "some things about McNeil are worrying."

"What do you mean?" asked Ken.

"McNeil has talked about the prospects I have with his firm, but you can so easily become a scape goat at any time. Then there is the pressure to load each job with as many people as possible. Something that goes against my sense of being there to help the client."

"It's hard for someone like me to comment, it could happen on your own just as easily. You could, as easily, be recruited and used as a scape goat as being employed to be the driving force in an improvement program and you would not always be able to tell what was planned. And regarding the loading, companies do need fees to survive."

"That's my worry."

"There will be work you will need to be able to avoid," said Ken, "and the main problem, that I see is that the career McNeil talks about might not ever happen."

"Why?" asked Peter.

"Whatever you may have been led to believe, most key positions in McNeil's firm are held by people who he knows from elsewhere, like school."

"I suppose that's true, but that would apply to almost work wouldn't it?"

"Yes, but the offer from de Bruin is a good chance to use your knowledge of high technology, machinery, and management to analyze the problems, and correct the organizational aspects of the project. You would also make enough money to allow you some flexibility in deciding what to do next."

"Deciding what to do next while being at a loose end does not appeal to me though. Anyhow there is still a very big barrier in the way of the re-financing of Ngami being approved."

"What's that?" asked Dave.

Peter explained Binnett's report on Ngami.

"If Binnett say the place has not got the organizational competence to succeed it will be an almost impossible barrier for you to deal with Peter."

"I can see that."

"No organization means that nothing anyone says will improve the production. It's hardly rocket science. And, from what you say, this Rebecca is eminently qualified to make such a comment. It's not something you're going to easily have put aside at the World Bank level."

"Isn't your plan perhaps too idealistic Peter?" interjected Ken.

Peter hesitated, "There might be a few details that Rebecca has missed."

Ken looked at him oddly, "Is that a hope or a fact?"

Peter shrugged, "Perhaps a bit of a hope, but I am fairly confident of my facts."

"Confidence will not raise your credibility though. You do not have the credibility of Binnett."

24

Joseph's terrible day continued as he loped away from the group of men that had been sent to deal with him, after Ben had been forced from the road.

The intensity of the rain increased until he could barely see where he was going.

Fortunately neither could the group following him, and their dogs lost Joseph's scent.

He ran on until he reached his mother's house; wet, holding back tears and bleeding, he almost fell as his mother opened the door for him.

"Joseph my baby, what has happened?" she cried.

He explained as she cleaned him up.

Her life had been hard enough. She could not understand his situation. The last thing she wanted was to lose Joseph, or for him to be hurt. He was one of the best of her children. Suppressing her tears, she washed the nasty gash in his head and covered it as well as she could, with Joseph sitting on a stool.

She asked what had happened and he explained.

"What of the cattle," she asked.

"I don't know, I was afraid to return to them."

"We know which cattle are ours, are there any others nearby?"

"I never saw any."

"I'll send your brother to collect them, but you need to get out of here before these people come looking for you."

"They will know it is one of us by the cattle."

"Not if they are moved quickly," she said and left to give instructions to the children who hadn't noticed Joseph's return and were playing nearby.

Eventually he left her, when the rain had stopped. She was crying softly as she wished him well. She said that it would be better if she did not know where he was going.

He hugged her, said goodbye, and headed for the country where he knew the tribe of Bushmen, to whom he was related, lived.

He went by way of the cave where he had hidden the money and the notes and saw with horror that the case he had been trusted with was gone. He turned fearfully and headed for where he had hidden the diary, money and knife. They had not been moved so he wrapped them carefully in some plastic bags he had stored in the cave, and headed for the inaccessible country in which his relatives lived, taking the valuables with him.

That night he slept fitfully on a rocky ledge of another cave, and in the morning hid Ben's treasures in the second cave then set out to circle the area where the Bushmen existed, as their ancestors had done, for longer than anyone had managed to determine with accuracy. It is thought that they were directly descendant from the original inhabitants of Africa.

His Bushmen relatives found him on the third day of his search and welcomed him warmly. They tended the nasty cut, telling him, as they did so, that he was very lucky that he had survived such a fall. They thought, indeed, that he might be especially blessed.

Joseph listened politely to the small people, but thought, despite their wisdom, that it was more likely that he was especially cursed.

The little people had little or no reason to communicate with the village. They were however able to find out about the men that had been asking after Joseph and discovered that the same group were regularly meeting with a leading member of the clan, Charles Obenta's cousin, and with members of Andselc security. They brought this information to Joseph and sat together with him in the shade of a Baobab discussing the odd affair.

Joseph had no idea what to make of the situation and together they decided that his best bet was to stay out of sight. So he hunted, trekked, ate, and slept with the tribe for long enough to recover from his head injury. During this time they discussed things he could do.

Among their suggestions was one that he should be taken in as a member of their group.

Joseph knew that he could never really be a full member of the tribe and that he was probably a bit of a burden, which could easily become an irritation. He said that he had an aunt who lived in Ngami and would ask her to take him in for a while.

The little people thought this would be too obvious, so they formulated an alternative plan. They organized for him to move to the Ngami village and stay there with someone that they trusted.

So Joseph moved back to the village and there helped the family with their small herd of cattle, staying largely out of sight.

The family was called Kolwane and they lived in a pleasant part of the village in a six-roomed house. Mr. Kolwane had a good position with the Ngami project management and his children were all away at boarding schools, something most people could only dream about.

Joseph's first meal with the couple was his first at a dining room table and he was very awkward. Mma Kolwane had to show him how to eat in the white person's way and he was most embarrassed.

His embarrassment was counterbalanced by his enjoyment of the newfound luxury. He was overwhelmed by the difference between his own home and theirs, there were four bedrooms, a bathroom and a kitchen. The floor was made from polished stone and wood.

Then amongst all the other luxuries there were the Kolwane's clothes, they were like ones he only dreamed about.

25

Heldebron asked Rebecca to meet with them and explained their concern about Peter's progress and the explanation he had been given by him before he left for Cape Town.

After telling Anders about the potential of Peter's work, he had discussed this with Willers and had asked the security superintendent for his views. They concluded that what Peter had in mind could definitely provide a means to recovering the capability of the site.

"There's very little for me to prove, this place can't survive the way it's working now," Rebecca said to Willers and Heldebron after listening to their point of view.

"What about Connor's opinion?" said Heldebron.

"Time and money would be needed for Ngami to change or improve in any way. This has clearly been tried, and equally clearly has failed, so there's no economic case for any change or improvement effort," she said, and added that she fully accepted Peter's case but equated it to the original potential that had never been fulfilled, largely through lack of competence of one form or another.

"We cannot have him provide a solution."

"Someone saying he can do something is not sound economics Gerry. We're going to talk to the World Bank, not a hopeful bunch of optimists he does not have anything going for but a personal competence. That's not enough in view of the reality here."

Her review complete, her 'office' was filled with piles of carefully sorted and indexed paper. She spent an additional two hours after the two men had left, running through a trial of the presentation of her findings. Once she was happy with its standard she packed her documents into portable files and made her way back to the hotel for dinner.

Peter arrived back in Ngami on the Friday morning of her site presentation. He was met by Brett Halliday at the airport, and went with him to the project offices.

Rebecca's presentation was planned to take two hours, it was not intended to provide any surprises. The people concerned had been interviewed individually or in small groups before the meeting, and had agreed with everything she was planning to show them.

Rebecca stood in front of the assembly on Friday morning and reintroduced herself to the audience, for the benefit of anyone who might not know her, and repeated her objectives.

She then went on to show them her findings: One slide per problem area. Each problem carefully analyzed in terms of the systems on which it depended.

The audience had been asked to comment on the findings during her opening, and to comment on the analysis.

The impressive woman's personality captivated the group.

Rebecca' work was faultless and she showed the difficulty that would be faced in any attempt to solve the complex set of problems.

Her conclusion to the presentation consisted of another four slides. Suddenly she realized that she was losing control as she started to work her way through these, if she could not speed things up and the point of the meeting would be lost.

A discussion about what she had said started among segments of the audience. She tried to regain the attention of the group but failed.

The interruption went on for several minutes, so she turned the projector off and stood facing the audience.

The noise abated.

Whitehead, the maintenance superintendent, rose to his feet cleared his throat theatrically and looked at Rebecca without saying a word.

He waited until there was silence in the hall then said, "Ms. Rosslynn I'm getting a strong impression that you are going to give us another learning system."

Rebecca said, "Mr. Whitehead, you saw and agreed with this very slide two days ago. I'm saying that such an approach is the only way forward and that this probably will not work."

"I agreed to what you were saying then, but as you were presenting the information up there, and during the discussion we've been having here, I fully realized what you were leading up to."

She turned the projector back on and put up another slide, showing the problem areas again and addressed the audience. "Do you agree that these are the problem areas?"

Whitehead answered for them. "Yes, of course. You're saying we've got problems, that's quite obvious as we told you about them, but you're leading into some or other prescriptive system. We don't need more procedures to address problems, we need action."

"If you would give me time that's what I'm saying."

Heldebron interrupted. "Rebecca, I think that's enough for now, each of the points you have covered has already been addressed in other initiatives and nothing has worked and nothing more is likely to work."

"Yes, and that's exactly what I'm saying."

Peter noticed that heads were nodding but some people were also looking put off, or perhaps frightened.

"This reaction has proved what you're saying,. Thank you Rebecca. We'll look forward to your written report," said Heldebron.

She quietly closed the meeting.

The result could not have been better from Heldebron's point of view. Rebecca had handled the effort perfectly; she had done what they wanted her to do, presented the solution and stated that she did not think it would work. The effort to derail her commentary by the disaffected work force, her loss of control and the subsequent confusion made her or any other improvement effort look hopeless.

Brett Halliday and Peter left the meeting together.

"That did not help," said Brett.

"I must admit I'm glad this place is not my investment."

"It will be if you gain acceptance of your claim that you know how to improve the place."

"I'm not at all sure I want to do that."

"Without you, Rebecca is right, I don't think there is any chance of anything improving here."

Peter did not reply.

They parted, agreeing to go together to the World Bank meeting.

Heldebron informed Jack Anders of the outcome and drove smugly to the golf club, where he had arranged to play nine holes with an associate from the business community.

When Peter got back to Johannesburg after Rebecca's presentation, he was met by his friend Jeffery at the airport and they went to see Ben de Bruin.

Peter asked Ben how he was feeling once they were settled.

Ben said he was improving but still could not remember what had happened to him. "There is something though Peter; I think I found something that was very exciting, I'm dreaming about my family in the Cape and then it gets mixed up with this huge opportunity."

"What though?"

"I can't bloody well remember."

"You can't remember the samples?"

"Not in the context that you are expecting me to, no it's just a blank. I remember the case had to get to Charles and my brother and there was something else very important but that's all, I can't remember the rest, it's an awful feeling."

"Is it about the furnace?"

"No something about opportunity. There is something that you need to know though, about the furnace, that I learned at the dinner with the Rileys. There was a technician at the dinner who has a farm, he had a practical sounding idea about the instability."

"I've some ideas about that myself but I'll talk to him."

As they were about to go Peter said, "I think you should try to make it to this World Bank meeting yourself Ben. It's going to rely on credibility and James knows very little about the technology. I don't want to be caught out on geology or mining."

"I've been thinking the same thing, I'm getting more mobile now, and if I get there before everyone else and can be sitting I'll not stand out too much."

"I'll take you to the meeting," said Jeffery.

"Okay, see you on Monday."

26

The wealth that lay at the heart of GVN, and Johannesburg, came from one of the richest and most famous gold deposits in the world. GVN's part in the build up of this fortune was on show in every aspect of the corporation's boardroom.

When Peter and Brett arrived for the meeting with the World Bank, the room was almost full. Ben was already there, sitting facing the window, talking to Jeffrey.

James de Bruin, who had been waiting for them, moved to greet them.

Peter was surprised at how much older he looked in the dark business suit he was wearing. He then looked away from James into the penetrating stare of Jack Anders.

The managing director's dark eyes were partially concealed by glasses with fine golden frames. They seemed somehow to be sunken into his head. He was immaculately clothed. His perfectly fitted suit looked as though it was starched.

If Peter could have read the polished executive's mind he would have been more nervous than he already was.

As James spoke to Brett, about the funeral of Jamieson, that had been held the day before, Peter walked around the room, looking at the expensively framed photographs, of the city's past, that lined some of the walls. All showing some aspect of GVN's part in the city's development. His attention was drawn by the view through the windows, that made up most of one wall of the room. The boardroom was thirty stories above the streets of Johannesburg and looked out over what was known in many African dialects as "Egoli" the golden place. He thought that he was probably standing where some of the most important people in the world had stood before him. It gave him a sense of being part of history.

Jack Anders moved to near the head of the mahogany table and asked the assembly to take their seats.

Peter noticed, from their name tags, that the three people seated opposite him were from the World Bank. Smith, the bank's key representative was the one closest to him. They looked, to him, like he would have imagined bankers should look, stern and perfectly dressed.

Michael Anders who had been asked, by James de Bruin, to be at the meeting, as a personal favor, joined the Cape farmer as they made their way to their places at the table. Michael was more casually dressed than most people there. Although he wore a suit, it was not dark and was made from some sort of tweed. He was very tall, almost a head taller than de Bruin. His tanned smiling face accentuated the drawn appearance of the Cape farmer

Michael had been puzzled, or more accurately irritated, about the Ngami situation ever since the first communication from de Bruin about the problems there. He would rather not have had to worry about it. However he was not only there at James de Bruin's request, Botswana held an important place in his plans for the future.

Michael was the heir to the Anders fortune. William, the great grandfather of Michael and Jack Anders, had founded GVN at the beginning of the twentieth century. He had developed an ability to optimise the effectiveness of mines on the fast developing Witwatersrand. Skilfully arranging mergers of small mines, he had recruited exceptional managers to run these, and had ensured that his company had prospered. William's son Adrian had carried on the tradition. Albert, Jack Anders' uncle and Michael Anders' father, had been the third member of the family to control GVN. Albert had been a man of great integrity, whose efforts, to help people less fortunate than himself, had made most South Africans familiar with his name and face.

A tragedy had provided Jack with his first big opportunity.

Albert's wife and two of their three children had been killed in an aircraft that had been shot down in Zimbabwe. His youngest child Michael, a one-year-old boy at the time, had somehow survived. He had been thrown clear of the aircraft, as it crashed into the bush, and had been found by a patrol that had seen the plane's destruction. Albert had then progressively lost interest in life, and in his only remaining child, Michael.

The withdrawal of his father's interest had meant that he had grown up with little support other than money. The corporation had progressively been passed into the hands of its exceptional managers. Jack had taken advantage of the gap left by Albert, and had used his uncle's unhappiness to his own advantage. He had worked hard, become close to Albert, and been made managing director.

Michael now in his thirties had degrees from Cambridge and Harvard. He had been trained in the company's operations throughout Africa and in other countries. Until recently, he had been managing a subsidiary of GVN's in New Caledonia, a thousand or so kilometres North East of Australia.

The World Bank meeting started on time with Michael Anders sitting nearly opposite Jack, his attention fixed on the papers in front of him.

Looking briefly at Michael, Jack opened the meeting by explaining the reason it had been called and by reviewing the agenda. He then asked Smith from the World Bank to summarize the bank's perspective.

Smith explained that the four-year period of the project's loan was up and that its renewal depended on the project's viability, which the bank had been led to believe was not looking promising. He went on to say that they were expecting that, at the conclusion of the meeting, there would be a final decision about the project's future.

Jack thanked him and introduced Rebecca, describing her achievements and qualifications. He explained that she had been engaged by GVN because of her international knowledge of similar projects.

Rebecca was more formally dressed than Peter had ever seen her.

She went ahead with her commentary on the status of the project, looking very professional.

She explained the plant's very degraded state, the complete lack of buy in by the people on site of any of the initiatives that had been attempted, and said there was an overall lack of organizational competence to run or repair the plant.

James de Bruin watched Jack Anders and Heldebron during this commentary, and thought, cynically, that it must surely be as obvious to Michael, as it was to him, that such direct criticism would not normally be acceptable to people as powerful as these.

There seemed little doubt that her argument was sound.

Jack thanked Rebecca and introduced Peter. Explaining that the engineer had been recruited to investigate the potential of Ngami from a technical perspective.

Peter connected his laptop to the projector and explained his findings. He said that he agreed with Rebecca's conclusion, then provided details of solutions, showing that there were ways to solve subsets and combinations of the problems, providing financial models and technical facts.

He waited a few moments, as Rebecca looked like she might interrupt, then put up a slide showing a time line of what he thought should be done. It showed full production within two months and profitability within six.

"All the work Rebecca mentions does not have to be done at the same time. She is absolutely right that the management of the exercise is critical. By close attention to the right detail, and understanding the priorities it can be saved. Technically the greatest danger is the furnace itself; if it fails then Rebecca's scenario is exactly right. Managerially there's a question of support and prioritization. Rebecca has shown that these are abysmal. There's a reason why nothing is falling into place, one that I found surprising. Binnett have routinely, to 'improve the systems,' got rid of too many competent people. This has saved money and justified the cost of employing the firm, which has made a fortune from the work, and, what that's done is create a huge undercurrent of fear, especially of Binnett."

Rebecca was stunned. "They've employed extra people, they've had teams of metallurgists and engineers in there looking at specific problem and they haven't solved anything."

"They've had their ranks severely reduced as well."

"If they could not achieve what they were supposed to do they did not deserve to be paid the large salaries and bonuses that are paid to the people there."

"No argument there Rebecca, but the fact remains that the whole site is now frightened silly of Binnett and your management approach."

Jack interrupted, "Peter you are confirming the potential that the project presents and always has presented, or we would not have been involved. You have shown, as did Rebecca, that the output is not reliable because of the poor attitude there. The fear you talk about is part of the poor performance that Binnett have helped us deal with."

"You seem to be missing the most important point Connor has made. He says that the problems involved in specific elements can be fixed with less effort than Rebecca is implying, he's given you a possibility of full production within two months. You surely need to consider that," interjected James de Bruin.

Rebecca, who had been watching James as he made his point, glanced at Jack Anders, and was surprised to see him watching Michael with what seemed to be contempt.

Michael's concentration remained on the papers in front of him.

Jack's normally urbane facade quickly replaced the look of contempt and he said, "James, we agree, it just isn't possible with the people we have. The plant is incapable of full production as it now stands and however good Peter's program may appear it cannot replace a totally flawed plant and organization." The polished mahogany table and the elegant trappings in the boardroom accentuated Jack Anders' air of authority. "Its off line now," he concluded.

There was a moment of silence.

"Critical spares were not reordered because the person responsible was made redundant by Binnett's last effort," said Peter.

Neither Jack nor Rebecca had any answer to this.

Michael Anders cleared his throat and said. "So you want to close the project down regardless of what Connor says? And, on a different plane, I thought the main basis of this systems thinking approach, that has supposedly been applied there, at great cost, was that it moved away from fear as a motivator? How is it that they have pushed systems thinking while frightening everyone to death? There's something wrong here Jack. Could you put that timeline of yours up again please Mister Connor," said Michael.

Peter turned the projector on and scrolled forward to the slide showing the timeline.

Michael's quick uptake settled Jack's thoughts. He and Heldebron, had gained personally from the consulting work. He could not allow Michael to find out about this. He needed to redirect the meeting.

Michael was sitting forward in his chair looking at the timeline, his tall powerful frame accentuating his interest.

Jack said, "Of course we've got to be clear about what we're doing. We want to avoid collateral damage if we can."

Michael relaxed slightly but was still clearly involved and was about to say something else.

Jack then said, in a quiet, controlled tone of voice, "Mr. Smith we'd like you to take account of the points raised in Connor's report, and allow us one more chance to get production stabilized. If you would extend the finance for another four months, we could, try to use Connor's plan to bring production up."

"That seems reasonable," said Smith.

Jack glanced at Michael, who nodded, and no longer looked as though he would take over the proceedings.

Smith, the representative of the World Bank cleared his throat. "So we can decide the future of the project in four month's time. Say seventeen weeks?"

Anders agreed.

"If the combined efforts of Rosslynn and Connor cannot prove that the project is capable of maintaining its design production in four months, finances will be terminated, and I think that covers our agenda for today,"

Peter walked out of the boardroom with de Bruin, who asked him, as they stood waiting for the lift, whether considering his positive contribution to the results of the meeting, he had decided that he would carry out the work.

"I'd like to have a little more time to think about it James. That meeting was not a vote of confidence in the project. Michael Anders put enough pressure on Jack to extend things and Jack's request to Smith seemed very much to me to be only a gesture. His own agenda won't have changed."

"You did seem to be talking about yourself in there, if you're not there, we are still in trouble with a lack of the right skills to correct the problem."

"I'll be very vulnerable, with Jack and Rebecca in control."

"You don't think you can manage?"

"Oh, I do. But, the effort will be undermined."

"The minute you think its hopeless you can leave with our support."

"Will I have a contract with you?"

"Peter, I don't want to put you in an impossible situation. The work we'd ask from you would not be intended to make you responsible for an impossible rescue. I'll have the contract worded to protect you and make sure you are paid a very substantial fee, no matter what the outcome is."

"That sounds very fair, thank you, but I still need some time to think about it, that's all. I'll contact you by Friday. Will that be okay?"

"Peter you're being a stick in the mud engineer," said Ben who had joined them with Jeffery.

Peter looked awkwardly at the younger de Bruin.

"You're playing silly buggers, we need you desperately, look at it as an opportunity for the future."

"Well Ben," Peter began awkwardly.

"Not well at all, come on man let's hear the decision."

"I'll let you know in the morning. I'm sure it'll be okay though."

"Sounds good Peter,"

"I must be sure I'm not leaping into something I'll regret for the rest of my life." He had seen the cold fury Jack Anders had felt as he made his points, and had felt, looking at Heldebron that the general manager had been further discomforted. He could not believe they would give in at that stage and was certain that they would use any means at their disposal to prevent the project succeeding.

After Peter had left, de Bruin contacted McNeil and explained what had happened.

"There's not much I can do about it James," said McNeil. "I'll talk to him again, but from what you say he sounds committed. He's cautious, and that's what will make him the one you need, the one that will get the results in the difficult conditions that you're working with."

"I suppose we are heading in the right direction."

"How is Ben?"

"Very weak but he's here, his recent memory hasn't come back yet."

"Hell what an experience, I hope he gets better soon."

"The doctors say it's only a matter of time, something will jog it and he'll be okay."

"How long is it now since he was hurt?"

"About a week."

"All we can do is hope and pray. I'll call you when I hear from Peter."

James took his brother to the clinic after the World Bank meeting. They were delighted about the progress Peter had made, but spoke regretfully about the funeral of Rob Jamieson that he had attended on the Sunday. It had been a nightmare.

"If only he hadn't come back with me," said Ben.

"It is terrible."

"Now we're putting Connor at serious risk."

"I can't see what else to do without giving up."

Peter and Brett made their way from the building talking about what had happened in the meeting.

"That was a great effort in there Peter, I think you may have saved the day."

"Jack Anders was pushed to the conclusion by his cousin."

"We only needed that push and you provided it. He could not ignore your comment about the bad atmosphere having been created by Binnett themselves. Did you see Jack Anders' face when you said it."

Peter smiled, "He looked a bit shaken didn't he?"

"And the rest, you've done a good job Peter."

"Thanks. I'm afraid of the exercise though."

"Of course and I don't suppose your close shaves have helped."

"No."

Peter decided his safest course would be to spend the night with Jeffery and took a cab with him to the pub. They discussed what Peter was going to do about the assignment over dinner.

"So Peter, what's it to be?" asked Jeffery.

"I need to talk to McNeil. There's no sense in walking into a hornet's nest without a clear path out and the right protection."

"They need you badly."

"They needed me badly years ago. They're on the edge of a precipice because they haven't employed the right people."

"Bit like any investment?"

"Not really."

"So the exercise is as hopeless as Rebecca says?"

"It's going to be very difficult to change things."

Out of a Southern African Furnace

Dr Thomas Bagot

Book 2

A Community in the Balance

27

Heldebron arrived back in Ngami on the afternoon of the World Bank meeting and went straight to his office.

Jack Anders phoned him shortly after he arrived, and asked if he needed help in blocking the planned improvement in a way that would not be seen as deliberate by the bank.

He answered he had not thought of anything specific that he could do to make the planned improvement as difficult as possible for both Rebecca and Peter, but that he was certain that he would be able to prevent any meaningful changes. "There will be no way that Peter Connor will achieve what he's talking about without me," he assured Jack.

"I'm going to stop Connor getting there, I'll tell McNeil, the principal of his firm that I'm going to cut back on their work, with us, if he allows Connor to go to Ngami. That should keep him clear of you."

"He was working on his own wasn't he?"

"On some kind of leave from them."

"I think he's supposed to come back on his own."

"That's just a front, as long as he has them to go back to, he'll be a problem. If I close the back door that'll stop him."

Heldebron sighed after putting the phone down, he wanted to leave the office, go home, and relax for a while, but problem followed problem.

When he eventually got home he found his wife asleep. He wished at times that she would support him more, but understood that his high pressure life excluded her more than it should.

As he put his two Alsatians out for the night his cell phone buzzed.

"The bloody smelter has burnt through the casing again," the voice on the phone rasped.

"I'll be there in ten minutes," he answered.

He drove listlessly to the plant, looking at the glow from the complex and problematic operation reflected in low clouds that blanketed the area. He wondered if this would be the end, the final failure, the one that that would shut the smelter permanently.

He drove on through the cleared area, in which the plant stood, flood lights glowing a fierce orange color.

Security guards snapped to attention as Heldebron's vehicle passed through the gates. He was a familiar figure and came on site at all hours.

He turned onto the haulage road and stopped near the furnace, got out and stood for a few moments, then walked the hundred or so meters to where a crew was working on a platform, about two stories above ground level.

The furnace formed a huge column that thrust through the access platforms into the deep dark sky. It presented a stark image of power that was lost on Heldebron.

The men working on the furnace casing were shouting instructions as material for the patch was passed up from the ground.

Occasional flames shot out at them through the hole in the casing, like tongues from hell.

Larger than most similar smelters, it was completely unique in the inconsistency of the way it was having to be fired. The variation caused its lining to be burned away more unevenly and more quickly than was manageable. Temporary patches were an ongoing part of the operation.

The men working on the furnace showed a lethargy that came from their frustration. They had to force themselves to keep working, driven by the dread of having to shut the furnace down for a complete reline and that would mean the end for the project.

Pieterse a grizzled South African expatriate was in charge of the repair team. When Heldebron walked up to him, he asked what the general manager thought of the situation. He was perfectly capable of carrying out the work without the advice of the highly stressed general manager but knew Heldebron had to be humored.

Heldebron answered at length, including a series of questions in the commentary.

Pieterse responded politely and patiently, until Heldebron was finished with his tirade on what he thought should be done.

Heldebron eventually turned back toward his vehicle.

Pieterse went to the repair gang supervisor and spoke to him, essentially repeating what he had already said, with some inclusions of the general manager's suggestions.

The gang leader then continued to do what he had been going to do in the first place.

Heldebron watched, like some malevolent bird of prey, his intense stare frightening the workers. He would have done them all a favor had he gone home to bed.

Brett Halliday was already on site, and having had a look at the furnace problem had wandered off, to the control room, to see the production statistics. When he saw Heldebron's Range Rover, from the control room window, parked where it should not have been, he sighed with frustration. Heldebron never seemed to understand that example was a more powerful form of leadership than pressure.

Brett walked back down and out of the building to the maintenance crew and asked Pieterse how the repairs were going.

Pieterse told him that Heldebron's advice giving session had wasted some of his personal time but that the work was going well. "The bloody man's mad, you know," he added, in a stage whisper.

Brett shook his head and walked over to the general manager.

Heldebron greeted him, but made no other comment. He was absorbed in plans about his future away from Ngami. He was thinking of his investments, about how much he had arranged to make from the mess that Ngami was in.

The patch was completed in record time and the furnace put back online.

Heldebron returned home, still planning his future, away from Ngami, certain that the erratic process was hopeless.

28

As he had told Heldebron he would, Jack Anders contacted McNeil, the principal of Peter's firm and expressed his annoyance at Peter's success at the critical World Bank meeting. He warned McNeil that he was likely to look very unfavorably at any future work arrangements with the McNeil firm if Peter returned to Ngami.

McNeil contacted Peter and asked him to see him.

When Peter arrived, he was told of the threat, by McNeil.

He answered, "So you're being forced to carry the can for Ngami?"

"There is no room for me to maneuver. The memory of your initial success will wear down in time but I don't think we can afford to have you working up there in any capacity now."

Peter was shattered, he nodded and stood to leave.

McNeil's weak sounding apology followed him from the office.

He spent the morning, thinking about what the news meant to him, and the de Bruin's.

He then phoned the de Bruins brothers, individually, and told them the position he was in.

Each in turn expressed desperation.

He said that he was going to site where he would tidy things up and then get clear.

They both said that, if he changed his mind, their offer would remain open.

He said he would make every effort to get the program moving effectively using Brett, as he finished off his efforts.

Peter cleared his business affairs in Johannesburg and then phoned Brett to explain what had happened and that he would be returning to Ngami to close off his work.

"That's bad news Peter."

"I'll make sure the platform for the improvements I foresee is in place.

"The sooner you get here then, the better, Peter. What do you need from me?"

"I'd like you to arrange for me to spend time in the smelter control room."

"What will you be doing?'

"I want to work with the operators and gauge their sense of priorities first hand. From the point of view of explaining what I am doing, to Anders and Heldebron, I need to confirm that the information in my report is accurate before putting it to bed."

"Okay Peter."

When Peter arrived back in Ngami, it was windy, dust being whipped into small low flying clouds. The countryside was, however, noticeably greener.

He was met in the arrivals area by a tall athletic looking man, in uniform and armed.

The guard introduced himself as Alwynn.

Charles had told him he would arrange for someone to be there to look after him and he was impressed.

A second officer, who was sitting in the back seat of the white land cruiser, also welcomed him.

Peter, feeling a bit like a character in a movie, climbed into the leather upholstered vehicle, that had been left running, so it would stay air-conditioned.

Willers met him in the conference room they had been using and he told the security superintendent he was spending a few days on site to finish off the work from the review and was then returning to Johannesburg to McNeil's.

Willers reported this to Anders who said that he should cooperate, and help Peter off site.

Peter spent the day in the control room with the operators and shift engineers, who he knew, and got on with, from his previous visit. By doing this he was able to experience each variation in the operating conditions himself.

In the days that followed, Peter's time was spent extensively in the heart of the operation, observing the furnace's erratic behavior, and in talking to the people involved.

He developed several strategies and discussed these with Brett Halliday.

As the aircraft carrying Rebecca and another consultant, a South African employee of Binnett Consulting, Cecil Baker, banked to land they noticed that the minuscule trace of exhaust fumes from the smelter stack was fading.

By the time they had disembarked the furnace had failed, and no stack discharge was visible.

Willers met them at the airport and Rebecca introduced him to Cecil. They drove silently to the site, parked, and were soon settled in the conference room

He wished them luck with the project and excused himself, saying he had something important to attend to in the plant.

"Not too enthusiastic," said Cecil after Willers' departure.

Heldebron arrived to welcome them and was more pleasant than the security superintendent. He asked if they needed anything.

Rebecca assured him that they were comfortable and enquired about the timing of the startup meeting.

"Marie has not been able to organize a time that's convenient for everyone concerned." Heldebron replied.

"Why is it a problem?" Rebecca asked warily. Willers' abruptness, and now no meeting, were barriers she'd met with on other sites when barriers were being raised.

"It's difficult getting everyone in one place at one time. We might be able to hold it on Friday and that will not delay the overall effect."

"I don't want my work to look like another Ngami muddle."

"Unfortunately the Ngami muddle is what I'm trying to manage. I'll do my best," Heldebron replied.

She asked if he knew when Connor was due on site.

"He got here last week. He'll be coming to see you soon, he's leaving you know," he said.

"What's happened?"

"His firm want him back in Johannesburg."

"He was working independently though, wasn't he?"

"Apparently he was only on leave from them,"

"That'll make things easier."

He nodded, wished them well, and left.

"That wasn't quite the welcome that I expected," said Rebecca to Baker.

"Not very helpful are they?"

"They're not expecting solutions, so perhaps we should just forget it and get on with preparing for the presentation."

Heldebron walked to the security office after seeing the Binnett consultants and found Willers at his desk.

"Is there any way you can get this conference going more quickly?" Heldebron asked. "I don't want these Binnett people sending back negative reports from day one."

"I can't get any support from maintenance or geology and the mining people are running around in a panic as usual."

"Please try to load her up with statistics or something. I'm sure that will help fill her empty time to her satisfaction."

"I'll try."

Rebecca's enforced idleness was broken by Peter's arrival. He strode purposefully into the conference room lifting the mood by his presence.

She introduced him to Baker, who then went to get himself a cup of coffee, he did not like Peter's straightforward manner. It made him feel uncomfortable.

Peter asked Rebecca if she had enjoyed her break.

She explained that she'd stayed in South Africa and had been trying to find out about the failure of her grandfather's company.

"What did you find?" he asked.

Pleased at having something else to talk about she told him the story of the growth and failure of the company.

"I met someone the other day before I came back here who spoke about being interested in industrial history in South Africa," Peter said.

"Who was that?"

"He's a successful consultant and a professor at Cape Town University, in the management school."

"He might be able to help, its not really something you can check on that easily."

"Why not contact him and ask?"

"I'll do that."

"Back to Ngami, I thought you should know what I'm doing."

"Have you managed to get much done?" she asked, wondering whether he had experienced the same negative attitude.

"McNeil has been threatened by Anders that if his involvement, remote or otherwise with Ngami is not stopped he'll loose all his work with GVN. So I am just tidying up before I go."

"What a strange place. So when do you leave?"

"As soon as I can."

"What have you still to do?"

"I've spent some time with the blokes in the control room confirming the commentary in my report on furnace failures."

"Have you managed to get anywhere?"

"It's going quite well."

"Well, can I show you how I'm going to work?"

"Sure, Rebecca."

She phoned Baker and Willers and asked each of them if he could join them.

Baker arrived within minutes with Willers.

She listed their responsibilities on one of the two white boards in the conference room.

They agreed to these without much difficulty.

Rebecca then went on to outline her approach.

"As you've heard me say before," she said, "systems are what we need to address."

Peter nodded, trying to contain his impatience.

"Now we're going to develop strategies that enable us to close the gaps."

"How Rebecca?"

"Your reliability studies have given us a good documentation about the actual drivers of the systems behind each outcome, so we need to list our actual approach to problematic subsystems with their root causes," she said.

"All this gets documented?"

Peter was thinking he was well out of this muddle. If he stayed he could end up being responsible for the failure of the program if he made any mistake in the bureaucratic role she was defining. She and Binnett would gain from his experience and be able to blame him for any errors that were made.

The main objective Peter said and stood to write on the whiteboard, *'Full production within two months and profitability within six months'*

"We will still need to isolate quick fixes from the need for major organizational or engineering changes," she said.

"That's okay, but the way you're planning to go is too complex and we don't have much time. Your approach is like painting by numbers. But first you're going to have to create the pattern. So how are you going to deal with the causes after you've found them?" said Peter feeling relieved at having set so much in motion that would not be affected by Rebecca's ponderous approach.

"The next step is to work out what must be done."

"Ye--s."

"Research shows that only fifteen percent of all causes of system variations can be ascribed to poor operations or special events. System causes account for eighty-five percent of problems. In such cases, redesign of systems is needed. We need to make sure we are working toward the full framework rather than bits and pieces here and there."

"It will take time."

"I heard you and would appreciate it if you would let me finish."

"Go on, Rebecca."

"Special events need to be carefully examined in a place like this, where people tend to be blamed too easily."

"Rebecca you don't need to do all that work to increase Ngami's production."

"It is necessary Peter. Isolated events are often more than they seem to be."

"And Ngami's history is one of ignoring the system and fixing problems in isolation? So the systems causes that were the real reason for the problem were never addressed?"

"Something like that."

"You are right on the mark there."

Peter knew the 'rightness' of her approach would be a problem as she moved toward solving the entire production problem from the highest possible level.

She stood looking at him, self-righteously, from her position next to the white board that was now covered with red writing that grew more faint toward its bottom edge.

Peter went to see Brett Halliday the first thing the next day.

Brett greeted him with his lop sided smile. "How are the consultants doing Peter?"

"Perhaps better than expected Brett but I've got a bad feeling about time."

"What are they doing?"

"Just going over the communications that they are planning. The program's on hold, while Heldebron arranges a general meeting."

"Is that going to affect the result?" Brett asked cynically.

"It could be very slow."

"I thought it might be."

"Nothing I've set up will conflict with what she's said and you've got key aspects moving fast."

"Your plan was accepted at the World Bank meeting. What are you going to do to keep it going?"

"You need to build on what I've done using Rebecca's process."

"So what's next?" Brett said with a look of frustration.

"We must talk to the support people that I've seen. Starting tomorrow morning."

"Good Peter, I'll arrange to start tomorrow, at seven again?"

"Yes, please, Brett."

"In between I'll need all the data I can get on failures, can I go ahead and draw this from the various departments?"

"I'll make sure you get all the cooperation you need."

"Thanks Brett."

Another storm's arrival was heralded by a pealing of thunder and what seemed to Peter to be an extraordinary amount of lightning.

He walked out of the office and across the barren ground that surrounded the office block. He managed to get into the driver's seat before the first heavy drops began to patter on the windscreen, turning the dust on it to mud. The rain was so heavy that he could not see enough to drive and had to wait for a few minutes. He then made his way carefully back to the main offices.

Rebecca was alone in the conference room when he got back.

"Have you heard any more from Heldebron?" he asked.

"His secretary phoned; they're still trying to get things going. The meeting won't be 'till Monday."

"Next week?"

"Yes, A bit ridiculous isn't it?"

"How much of what you showed me has Heldebron seen?"

"About the same as you."

Peter nodded and then said, "Well I'm going to report back what I found to the people in the smelter."

"We agreed we would have the general meeting first."

"This is just feedback to the people I spoke to during the review, I'll make sure we don't get away from your agenda. I've involved them from the start and need to give these blokes some thanks for their contributions, especially since I've said that I would."

"I suppose that's a reasonable."

"What are you planning to do in the mean time?"

"I don't know."

"Why don't you do some research into your grandfather's company?" Peter asked.

"What was the name of that man you suggested I contact?"

"I'll phone him, you would be able to get to Cape Town and back without too much trouble."

Peter phoned Dave Gabrielson and arranged for Rebecca to meet him where he was staying at his holiday cottage in Hermanus, a village near Cape Town.

Rebecca booked flights to Cape Town for Wednesday morning, to return to Ngami on Sunday.

She discussed the Cape with Peter and asked what she should try to see on the trip to Hermanus.

Peter suggested she hire a car and go from the Cape Town airport to Hermanus, spend two nights there. And then stop at Gordon's Bay on the way back. Spend a night in the Strand on the peninsula, South of Cape Town and then fly back to Ngami.

Rebecca made the bookings after discussing each hotcl with Peter.

As she did so, she wondered at Peter's pleasant, perhaps even fully cooperative, approach. He seemed to value her efforts. Contention, rudeness, go slows and most other forms of opposition she understood and could deal with, cooperation on the level shown by Peter was not something she had come across before. His attitude almost drew her toward working with him. If nothing else it was a relief after what seemed an almost stupid approach of the site management.

That afternoon she returned to the hotel and completed the planning of her journey using the Internet.

29

Rebecca found Hermanus to be lovely, small and interesting.

She made a circuit of the village, after driving there from Cape Town, went to the picturesque hotel, into which she had booked using Peter's advice, and the internet.

After she'd unpacked she drove to Dave's cottage, an attractive compact thatched home built in the Cape Dutch style, with gables, white walls and small paned colonial window frames. She guessed it would be about a hundred years old.

Dave's captivating smile, his dimpled cheeks and warm personality, were a relief in themselves.

They chatted about generalities for a while then Dave asked her about the chances of salvaging Ngami.

"It's really is a basket case Dave, I know Peter is competent but it's been allowed to slip into virtual chaos."

"I know Peter has put a lot into it and he's quite good."

"I don't think an army could salvage the place."

"Anyhow Rebecca, Peter asked me to help with your grandfather's company's history so let's stick to that."

She nodded.

"I'll briefly summarize what I've found."

Rebecca listened intently to what he had discovered

His discourse showed meticulous research and he needed quite some time to show her the information he'd managed to find about the losses that caused her grandfather's company to fail.

By late afternoon, he could see she was tired and suggested they meet again the next morning.

That evening, before dinner, Rebecca went for a walk along the well maintained waterfront path. It was bordered with native Cape flora and traversed the length of the village.

Winding from the harbor; between the sea cliffs and some very impressive homes, the path was bordered by a variety of Cape flora and in parts touched on the edges of the low sharp cliffs, that dropped down to the roughness of the Southern Indian Ocean.

Dave, the village and then this walk were so far removed from the Ngami situation that it was hard for her to envision the immensity of the responsibility she would have for shutting a huge project.

Dave met her for breakfast the next day. After enjoying croissants and coffee in the village, he went over additional details of what he had been able to reconstruct about the failure of her grandfather's company. The exposition showed a clear connection with GVN. His work had shown that someone in the corporation, if not the corporation itself, had definitely gained by her grandfather's loss.

"Are you planning to do anything specific about the failure of your grandfather's company Rebecca?" Dave asked when he had finished.

Her answer was indirect. She said that she had been very close to her grandparents because her mother had been away for a large part of her childhood. "We were nearly put on the street by the losses. It was horrible."

"Were you hoping to get any of the money back?"

"I very much doubt it would be possible, I suppose I would if I could."

"If you were almost robbed of your childhood?"

"It was painful."

When they had finished their second coffee he suggested that he follow up a particular lead he had uncovered. One that seemed to indicate a particularly odd aspect of GVN's involvement.

She agreed and they arranged to meet in Ngami when he came that way on a trip he had been planning with some visitors.

"You travel to Botswana regularly?" she asked not wanting to leave.

He explained that he often had people from other countries visit the University, which was internationally known for its standards, and that Botswana provided a unique opportunity for anyone wanting to experience traditional Africa.

"How do you get there?"

"I've a pilot's license so I fly there."

They then spoke for a while about Dave's plans to go to Australia, which led to his telling her about the death of his wife and child; a story so upsetting to him that she felt like crying herself.

The intensity of his grief excluded any other conversation on the subject of Australia.

They had lunch together at Rebecca's hotel and parted after she had thanked him for his help.

The road trip from the village back to Cape Town was spectacular, at first passing along the Indian Ocean, toward another fishing village; leading between sand dunes that had been reinforced by small shrubs imported from Australia. Turning away from the coast, it led across the Kleinrivier Mountains to Botrivier, and from there on up through plantations of pine interspersed with natural bush that looked like heather.

She thought that the partially misted mountains seemed a bit like Scotland. Leaving the main highway she explored Elgin, a wine and fruit producing area that Peter had told her was worth a short detour. Fresh air with a fragrance of the sea, pine and Cape heather helped to clear her mind.

There were several very picturesque farms along the way that made her wonder about the 'settlement' objective of her family who had once, she had heard, planned to farm in the Cape.

Another short detour from the direct road to Cape Town, after Sir Lowry's Pass, took her to the sheltered beaches of Gordon's Bay, where she had booked a night's accommodation. A short swim, in the clear, sheltered, unspoiled, blue sea, surprisingly cold water, a superb seafood dinner, two glasses of Cape chardonnay and a long night's sleep completed the day.

The next morning, after an early morning dip in the cool clear sea, she set out for Cape Town passing through Somerset West along the main coastal highway, to approach Cape Town through the Cape Flats. The huge area of temporary looking shacks that provided housing for hundreds of thousands of people on the Cape Flats made her more conscious of the true difference between success and failure in life. Thinking about the area's unpleasant reality brought her back to her concerns about Ngami, and what she was doing there. Why? she wondered, was she putting so much effort into impoverishing people. She would be better employed in trying to make her own fortune. The fact that her effort at Ngami was beginning to look like it might be helping enrich the same people who had been behind the loss of her family's wealth made the question more pointed.

The journey continued on, to take her along de Waal drive curving around and up the slopes of Table Mountain, bypassing central Cape Town and winding out into the city's beautiful suburbs along the Atlantic Coast. She found her hotel there, on the Strand. It was exceptional in its position, decor and food.

She explored Cape Town the next morning after a sensational breakfast. Not having been to the City since she was a child, she found it to be as beautiful as she had expected, but more interesting. Most fascinating was the age of the settlement, founded in 1652. Supposing she must have read this, or learned it in school, it struck her more forcefully during this visit because she had recently visited Britain and was still filled with those memories.

The facts were not new but not ever having thought much of the city in terms of world history, the realization that its founding in the seventeenth century was a long way back. Just after Queen Elizabeth the first, the times of Cromwell, really important times for Britain, and ones she had always felt were more significant and older than the Cape Colony. The Dutch population must, she thought, have remained nearly static in the intervening years or that of Britain must have expanded at a great rate.

The Castle of Good Hope was big, constructed in stone, and completed at the end of the seventeenth century. It would have been a significant historic monument in many parts of Europe. Knowing the famous parliament houses in Britain were only completed in the late nineteenth century put another large question mark on her image of the two country's histories.Rebecca left the Cape that afternoon feeling refreshed.

She didn't meet anyone she knew when she got back to Ngami, skipped dinner, and went to bed early, thinking about the presentation she intended making.

Thoughts about what else she could do kept drifting through her mind as she tried to plan the Ngami work. The prospect of the presentation felt more like an annoying distraction than it should have normally she was excited by an interesting start to an assignment.

On the day after her return from her journey, Rebecca arrived at the conference room looking tense.

Peter asked how her investigation had gone.

She looked at him sharply, was silent for a moment and then said, "There's a tie-up between the failure of my grandfather's company and GVN."

"They caused it?"

"Dave is following up some specifics but it looks like there was a connection."

"And that was?"

"There were a series of losses that are still unexplained and they or someone important there might be behind the family disaster?"

"Wow."

"It's a problem. Anyhow, I've asked Dave to check some aspects of what he's found and he'll be on site during the week with his results."

"On site?"

"He'll be on his way to Maun with some visitors."

Peter confirmed that her much-delayed kick-off meeting was scheduled for the next morning. He also mentioned that there had been some progress in the way the plant was performing, as a result of his close attention to the way the furnace was fired.

"Odd they could not do that themselves."

"Durning my training I learned how to fire some unstable boilers in a huge power plant and I learned a trick or two."

Later in the day, after organizing the resources for the much-delayed presentation, Peter and Rebecca had a long and energetic conversation about its format.

Their effort looked comfortable. To an uninitiated person they could have been long time associates.

30

As the exchange between Peter and Rebecca about the way forward progressed, Cecil Baker pretended to concentrate on what he was doing.

He was not impressed at their degree of cooperation and decided he should tell Heldebron what was happening.

He slipped away from the conference room, along the passageway, to Heldebron's office.

After a short wait he was shown in to see the general manager.

"So, Cecil, what is it you want."

"Gerry, Rebecca seems to be working hand in glove with Connor. Isn't he supposed to be going?"

"So, thats what's supposed to happen. He is going, so why the worry?"

"No, its more than that."

"Well, if they leave you out, interrupt."

"Gerry believe me this is not something we want. They're being too friendly."

"He'll be gone soon. Talk to her about it."

"I can't give her instructions myself. Could you talk to her?"

Heldebron sighed, "What's happened?"

Baker explained.

Heldebron was quiet for a few moments, and then said. "Get hold of her and I'll speak to her."

"Can you hang on for a minute?"

"I'll wait."

Baker went back to the conference room where Rebecca, Peter, and Willers were deep in discussion.

Baker interrupted them. "Rebecca could you spare me a few moments, Heldebron wants to speak to both of us."

"Of course Cecil," she answered, looking at him oddly.

She asked Cecil what the problem was, as they walked down the passage.

He told her Heldebron would explain.

She was coldly annoyed, but too controlled a person to answer any statement as blunt as this without having time to think about it, and its implication.

"What's happening now Rebecca, I believe you're working very closely with Connor?" asked Heldebron when she had settled into a chair facing the general manager's desk.

"What else am I supposed to do?"

"First Rebecca, you do understand that GVN has sunk as much money into Ngami as they feel appropriate, don't you?"

Rebecca was nervous as well as annoyed and did not answer.

"Rebecca are you with us?"

"Yes, Mr. Heldebron, I'm thinking about your question."

"Well?"

"I'm a competent professional in a major international consultancy and I'm running this assignment as well as I can. I'm not used to being called out of a conference by someone who I thought worked for me. Then being asked if I know what I'm doing, by the person that employed me. I'm out of my depth."

"I am sorry about my abruptness, but your attitude to Connor has got us worried."

"Oh? I've got the World Bank and the Botswana Government looking at the results of this work. I cannot afford to have them find any problem with my approach, so I'm a little concerned at how I should respond to your remarks," Rebecca replied.

"You don't have to say all that much Rebecca."

"I can't be seen to be doing a half hearted job and I'm not sure that I'm prepared to work that way."

It was Heldebron's chance to think twice. He was more concerned about her now than he had been at the start of the conversation. Her tone was completely wrong.

"Rebecca, we don't employ consultants to tell us how to wipe our noses. You took the assignment and you should be mature enough to know what we want done, how you present your approach is your concern, but we are not going to put up with you working against GVN."

"I'm well aware that you don't want to put more money into a dead project. If it were simply a matter of proving the project was dead I'm sure that we could do that, but an accepted report by Connor says that the project is viable. It has been distributed to all your shareholders. We cannot now simply be rude to Connor. I have to, at least, put up some kind of a show. We must complete the program properly and if, in the end, after doing our best, we cannot get the place working, then you'll have what you want."

"A show does not need Connor's approval."

"Quite honestly, I don't know what you expect. You are the one who messed up the start of my work.'"

"To an extent you are right Rebecca, and I don't want to have to talk to you like this, but I'm not interested in any 'ifs or buts' about what is going to happen here. We are paying you to do what we want."

Rebecca managed to maintain her professionalism. "Mr. Heldebron, I do appreciate that you are writing the cheques, but please allow me some credibility for knowing my job, or I'll have to ask my company to replace me on this assignment."

"You must run the situation as you see fit, but remember what I've said."

"I'll do my best," Rebecca answered and stood to return to the conference room. "Now I must get back to the others."

"Thanks Rebecca," Heldebron answered. "Cecil, I'd like a word with you, alone, for a minute, if you have the time."

"Certainly," Baker answered and thanked Rebecca as she walked out of the office and closed the door behind her.

"Are you happier with the situation now?" Heldebron asked.

"Not exactly, I'll let you know how things develop."

"You did the right thing, pulling in the reins, Cecil. Her attitude is wrong. I knew this part was going to be difficult, but we mustn't interfere with her approach. She does have a responsibility for the professionalism of what she does here and we need that credibility. I will speak to Wilson about her though."

"That sounds like a good idea Gerry, thanks for your help."

Rebecca was furious.

As she walked slowly back to the conference room, she tried to rationalize the situation, but could not see how she could manage her work in any way other than she was doing, even if she were totally committed to annihilation of the project, which she was beginning to think she was not. Equally and confusingly she had not intended to, nor did she wish to, work against the organization or Heldebron, but after Heldebron's commentary she realized that she had taken as much as she was prepared to accept from any client. She wondered again at the futility of her direction, her mind was clear as crystal about the work, but the objective was becoming as muddy as a pothole in a badly maintained road.

Heldebron reported the progress that was being made to Jack Anders and then phoned Wilson, the principal partner of Binnett's South African office.

Anders put the phone down and called McNeil, "I thought you said Connor was finished on Ngami?" he asked.

"He's just cleaning up loose ends."

Anders told McNeil about the call from Heldebron.

"I'll contact him, and tell him to get out of there," said McNeil.

John Willers and Peter were talking about something in the local paper when Rebecca got back to the conference room.

She resolutely put the difficult meeting to the back of her mind and said, "Peter, how improvements have been, and are being, implemented, is an important issue that needs clarification."

"You mean you want me to look at the documentation?"

"How the work is originated and so on."

"Okay."

"Some notes on planning are in this folder," Rebecca said and reached into the filing cabinet to produce a substantial file.

Peter glanced at the contents of the file and said he would go through them and contact the departments concerned.

Rebecca took another folder from her case, left the conference room and went for a longish walk to try to calm herself down.

Willers had not been concerned about what Rebecca was doing, however the look on her face as she had reentered the conference room after speaking to Heldebron was one of complete outrage. He guessed what had happened and was annoyed, so he had left the conference room and went to see Baker who he found standing on his own, in Willers' office, looking out of the window.

Baker turned toward Willers as he opened the door, as smug as an overfed, spoilt child.

"What happened to Rebecca?" Willers asked, as annoyed by the look on Baker's face as he had been by Rebecca's look of outrage.

Baker explained.

"I'd be a bit careful," Willers said.

"What do you mean?"

"She is not going to accept what you've done."

"She and Connor are getting too close."

"I think you are about to stuff this exercise completely, and not in the way GVN want," Willers said and left Baker looking a little less full of himself.

Willers left for home feeling dissatisfied with the exercise himself. He had not meant to be involved in anything as underhand as this was turning out to be when he had joined Andselc security. He wished, as he drove, that he had continued his pilot's career instead when he left the air force. This position, in a big security firm, had appeared to offer a more settled lifestyle, than an airline pilot's job, which had been his other alternative. The hints at having to be more flexible and adventurous had seemed exciting, ventures into the world of capitalism.

Peter received a call from McNeil while Willers and the GVN consultant were speaking, asking him to meet in Johannesburg, the next day, about dropping everything because Anders did not want him on site.

Peter phoned James and told him what was happening.

"Peter our offer is still open. I think those lot have to be faced by you, now. If you walk away you will at the very least regret it. At worst they will progressively destroy you."

"McNeil is a fair minded person though."

"Big money is the only thing he can consider Peter, he can't allow Jack Anders to shut him down, and make no mistake, Jack is capable of doing just that."

McNeil's decidedly frosty attitude at the next day's meeting, almost frightened Peter. He was given no room to manoeuvre or comment, it was as though shutters had come up in the man's mind. He was a different person.

"You've said you know and like de Bruin though," Peter tried.

"Liking and reality are often different issues Peter."

The clear need the deBruins had for his help, combined with Peter's feeling of detachment combined to make Peter's decision easier. He told McNeil he was leaving permanently.

"That is going to make my position difficult," said McNeil.

"I wish that were not the case, but intuitively I think I have no choice," answered Peter.

McNeil sighed and nodded, sadly, Peter thought, and they parted.

Peter emailed James de Bruin after the meeting, accepting the assignment in Ngami and asking if he could recruit Jeffery Nyasa.

De Bruin replied that it would suit them well if he did, as it would mean that Peter would be less vulnerable.

Peter phoned Jeffery and told him that he had obtained agreement for his help on the site, and asked, "How is the sale of the business going?"

"I've had two offers."

"That's going to fit perfectly."

"Let me know when you're ready for me. And, Peter be careful."

31

Shortly after his return Peter had phoned Charles Obenta to ask him if they could meet after work.

Charles agreed and arrived at about six in the evening. They found a quiet spot on the hotel's veranda and ordered two beers.

"So you've decided to stay Peter?"

"Yes," said Peter.

"That's very good news." Charles then asked what it was Peter needed to talk to him about.

"The furnace instability is being caused by ore quality as much as by control problems so the mine and geology must be checked."

"I know Ben is worried about reserves Peter, but he's said it's not the most pressing problem. Is this geological problem you're talking about something else?"

"The furnace needs to be fed with ore of the same general consistency or it 'flickers' and that causes unstable air flow and combustion conditions. We've enough trouble without worrying about that."

Charles said that the person responsible for the mining and geological departments, Bierman, was difficult. "I've never found him to be very approachable, he almost seems to avoid me," he continued.

"What about van Breda, the mine manager?"

"He reports to Bierman. He's okay, but he's apparently very vulnerable. He'll do his best but can't afford to swim against the tide," said Charles, "And, Ben de Bruin's much better, but not well enough to help."

"I believe it could take weeks or even months and longer for him to get it back, so our problem is how we check geological and mining aspects."

"Marnie Stone in geology might be okay. She's married to the engineering manager. I'll arrange a meeting with her. She's told me she's fed up with the way the site and geology are being run."

"I haven't spoken to Stone, he almost seems to be keeping out of my way."

"He's another misfit," said Charles.

"We really have to have somebody who is very competent and trustworthy in the mine," said Peter. He explained the agreement, with the de Bruins, for Jeffery Nyasa to help him, saying that, while this had not been what he had had in mind for Jeffery, it would fit his skills.

"Would he be able to check the mine and the geology."

"Yes, he's worked on exploration programs before and knows mining back to front."

"Can you get him up here quickly?"

"Yes, he's sold his business, so he's available now."

"I'll make any arrangements you need, just let me know what you want."

Rebecca started the much delayed presentation to the Ngami staff on what she and Peter were planning to achieve with a summary of the program to bring the plant up to full production, shown on an overhead screen.

The recalcitrant maintenance superintendent allowed her to finish then interjected, "Ms Rosslynn you still don't seem to understand that we don't have time for another river of words."

"We're here because GVN asked for us. The only question we need an answer to now is, 'Do you agree with the information that has gone up on that slide?'" said Cecil Baker.

"I agreed with it when I saw it, but you people need to understand that we don't want need another set of rhetorical nonsense."

Peter interrupted Whitehead, "Hang on Mr. Whitehead is this what we all agreed on?" and gave the meeting a brief technical summary of the problems.

"We've agreed and we all know what's wrong, but sitting here listening to this repetition is a waste of time."

Peter moved to the computer and showed them a list of technical solutions giving full credit to the people who had suggested them, and Whitehead nodded reluctantly as they were listed.

Peter then said, "In plain language you are up a creek without a paddle and you need help. We're not simply another set of consultants trying to lay blame somewhere or sell you a set of feel good procedures. We want to help ensure your future. The principles Rebecca used to analyze the inconsistency are a proven approach, which is essential to ensure that your problems are put out of the way."

Rebecca watched the sea of faces as Peter spoke, most were showing hope.

"Her work is intended to help you save your livelihoods so could you please let her to continue?" he finished.

Rebecca had decided how to deal with Whitehead while Peter was speaking. She looked right at him, and asked, "Mr. Whitehead you talked about rhetoric?" quietly.

"Yes, I did." Whitehead answered, smirking.

"It's a little difficult to hear you up here, Mr. Whitehead, could you speak up please."

Whitehead repeated his confirmation clearly.

"To get us going, Mr. Whitehead, would you mind explaining what you see as the most important thing you and the rest of the company's employees could be doing today?" she asked.

"Well," he replied, "I would have thought that that was fairly obvious. Producing what we are paid to produce."

"Thank you, Mr. Whitehead. Achieving full production is why we're here and in that case it would seem that you and I want the same thing?"

"Yes, but..."

She showed and read out, *'Performance Deficit must be addressed for Survival'*

"Can we agree on that Mr. Whitehead?"

"Of course."

"So we have a common vision on that point?"

"I suppose we do."

The next slide read, *'Ngami needs to reach full production.'*

Whitehead nodded.

She put up the third slide.

It read, *'Performance How?'*

She looked at Whitehead and said. "Am I correct in saying Mr. Whitehead, that preventing failures will enable the full production to be achieved?"

Whitehead nodded.

"Now," she asked. "If we're agreed on our direction, and why we're headed there, could we continue and try to reach some other conclusions about goals we can work toward?"

The next slide read, *'The Cost of not producing?'*

"In terms of a common vision this relates to your livelihoods. You and I want to see the plant, and with it, all of you, succeed," she said firmly. "We would like to use what you've told us individually to make real progress and as long as we're going forward I'll make sure the enforced redundancy program is put on hold."

There was a long silence.

"No more sackings?" said someone almost to themselves but loud enough to be heard by all in the quiet.

Willers and Heldebron exchanged annoyed glances. The program was supposed to be slipping sideways, Rebecca had not dropped the ball as she could easily have done.

Rebecca handed over to Peter who went ahead with a technical presentation related largely to reliability and risk assessment methods.

The initial problems at the presentation having been dealt with, the exercise had ended up as a pleasant and successful morning's work.

Charles Obenta telephoned de Bruin and told him the efforts of the consultants had been well received.

"I hope they don't get rid of her,' answered de Bruin.

"Surely they wouldn't?"

"I don't think they'll hesitate," de Bruin answered. "I'm not sure how, but they will. I really didn't think we would have such a positive contribution from her. Perhaps she has something else planned?"

"I'm not sure, Peter and Rebecca were working together."

Charles then went and found Peter to ask him what he thought of the day's work.

"A bit of a surprise."

"Is Rebecca working for the same result as you now?"

""She's very professional, they've been treating her badly, anyhow we must just hope for the best and carry on."

"Good work anyhow Peter," Charles said and left looking as pleased as he felt.

Baker had made his way from the meeting to report on its effect to the Binnett South African principal, Wilson.

"It's simply the start of the exercise Cecil. There's no reason to believe they can bring it up to full capacity in two months, but I will speak to Rebecca about this comment on redundancy. I don't know who authorized her to say anything about that."

The issue of the furnace itself dominated the consultants' work in the following days. The increasing rate of production resulted in more and more of the unstable periods.

32

The news of Rebecca's success worried Wilson more than he had indicated to Cecil Baker. He phoned her as soon as he had finished speaking to Baker and asked what had happened.

"I gave them a review of our approach. I introduced what we're doing in exactly the way we discussed," she said, wondering where he had got his information.

"What about the redundancy program our proposal to them specifically mentions it as a source of benefits?"

"The redundancy program was used, at the world bank meeting, to show that the project was failing because of bad management. Michael Anderson emphasized that."

"The bottom line Rebecca, is that you know failure is what GVN want and from what I've heard you've now provided a platform for real improvement. They can do us a lot of harm Rebecca. Without their business this year we would have to halve our work force."

"You've told me that and it certainly is a worry."

"Our clients don't want another revival, we discussed that. You need to do what you have just finished doing in Australia. That project in Ngami has more problems than the one in Australia. GVN simply want it shut down, and your job is to do what clients want."

"I don't know how to answer that one. There were other people at the meeting in Johannesburg, that agreed to put Connor's ideas to the test, and we have some kind of professional duty to perform."

"Of course Rebecca, but this is not black and white and I'm really beginning to wonder if you know what you're doing."

"I am fully aware of what I'm doing. What do you want me to do, Wes?"

"All that's needed there is a reasonable effort, and you've turned it into a crusade."

"You could not possibly call my efforts a crusade. Connor is a very competent engineer who is driving the improvements, I can't stop him."

"If I have any more complaints from these people I'm not sure how I'll handle them. If you'll just make the basic effort, knowing that the plant cannot be salvaged because of poor management, we'll be fine."

"Part of the problem, Wes, is that you said that this was a basket case. Now you seem to think I'm here being paid to sabotage a huge working entity, because you have no other clients."

"It's hardly anything but a basket case. It has only produced a quarter of what it should have, and its four years into its life."

"I'm doing my job, I can't sit here and do nothing. Can you please leave me to do the work in my own way?"

"Rebecca we accepted the assignment to close the place, now you're working hand in glove with an engineer who looks like he might pull it back from the brink. We're not being paid to do that."

"The world Bank might be surprised at that definition of why they've provided the ongoing funding. In fact I analyzed the situation perfectly, there was no way that what I've said can be faulted, Ngami is a basket case, or more accurately has been reduced to a basket case over four years, I've proved that. Peter has also done some very effective work. That's got nothing to do with me."

Rebecca's world had been turned upside down by Ngami. If she walked off it would end her career; if she stayed she could not fulfill Wilson's expectations in any way she could think of. She went back to the hotel and lay on the bed trying to work out what to do.

The problem with morale was something she had helped with, but it was a few moments of lost control that had put her on her back foot. She had simply recovered control of the meeting. If only the interruption by Whitehead had been handled by Heldebron, but then she supposed he'd orchestrated it.

She eventually phoned the Australian principal partner and explained what had happened.

He suggested she try to conform.

"Its not a case of conforming Chris, they're hell bent on shutting something that's capacity is improving."

"How did that happen?"

"Connor has used our systems basis before but has a fine tuned version which works more efficiently."

"Sounds like they have this Connor to thank for that?"

"That's it."

"I don't know what you should do."

"I'll keep going but I think realistically you should expect me back there at very short notice."

"That doesn't sound good."

"It's not."

"I'm sure you'll do your best Rebecca, thanks for letting me know what's happening and good luck, it sounds like you'll need it."

Rebecca had been forced from a state of confusion to actual fear about the future. Talking to the Australian principal partner had helped her in a way, but having put her fears into words had made them more real.

As she returned to her room that evening she felt the empty loneliness again. She wished she could work out what she really wanted.

Dave Gabrielson arrived in Ngami late on Thursday afternoon, on his way to Maun and the Okavango Delta with his European guests. He'd phoned Rebecca to confirm their dinner date, to talk to her about his latest findings in the investigation into the failure of her grandfather's company.

The enthusiastic young agent of the car hire company at the airport remembered him because of his personality and because professors were not all that common.

He had spoken casually about the weather and she had drawn him into a more general conversation asking him about his latest reason for visiting Ngami.

He told her that he was going to see Rebecca Rosslynn.

This clearly appealed to her, and she went on to explain the consultant's place in the village saying that Rebecca was important to all their futures.

He replied that he knew about the program.

"She's most attractive you know?"

"Yes," he agreed, "I've met her."

"Do you know that the work they are doing will get full production there?" The hire company representative, like everyone else in the town, was only too aware that closure of the project was imminent.

"That's good news," he answered politely.

"Rebecca Rosslynn is very competent, perhaps a bit lonely?"

Dave smiled, the dimples on his cheeks making the smile seem special, his sadness though seemed more obvious through the smile. "I don't know about that."

Dave still loved his wife and their child who had been killed, two years before, when a speeding taxi had driven through a red light into the side of their car. They had died instantaneously, or so the doctors had said.

Smiling brightly, with perfect white teeth lighting up her face, the car hire representative pointed to where he would find the vehicle."

Dave smiled as he took the keys, thinking how the young woman was so typical of the nicest aspects of Africa, and especially Botswana. He thanked her, picked up his bag and walked slowly across the car park to the beige Toyota Land Cruiser that she had pointed out.

He slowly drove his guests to the hotel, while explaining the project and the district.

It was a beautiful evening, the white walls of the hotel were reflecting pink tinges from the evening sun when they arrived.

He was thinking, as he spoke to his visitors, of how unspoiled and unassuming Botswana still was. It was a country he loved, the dryness made green special, rain a treasure, and every plant that was well tended seemed to grow better than anywhere else. The scents coming from the hotel's gardens and the comfortably warm air made the evening a uniquely African experience.

He made sure his guests were comfortably settled, and then went to find Rebecca.

Rebecca saw him as he walked into the hotel's lounge and smiled. She thought the medium sized, quiet man, with tints of gray in his hair and beard, seemed relaxed and fit. Although a little overweight his smile lit up his face.

Dave asked how her work was going.

"I'm not winning, I'm afraid."

"Bad is it?"

"The work is going brilliantly, unfortunately that's not what the clients want."

"How is that?"

"The production is improving, driven largely by Connor's efforts and GVN want it closed."

"I can imagine what you feel like and certainly can't advise you on what to do. Perhaps look for something else, but there's hardly time for that."

"No, I've phoned the Australian principal, he knows I'm in a situation that's not of my making."

"What's he like?"

"Not very human, but competent."

"I'm sure I can find something for you in South Africa if you need to look for another position."

"Leave it for now, I'll see how it goes, but thanks all the same."

He explained that he had traced most of the information she needed and that it confirmed the involvement by GVN in the failure of her grandfather's company.

"Of course business is always complex and there's absolutely nothing I've found so far that indicates anything illegal."

"A bit like Ngami, then?"

"It could be, but we don't know that," Dave said.

"Do you feel you've covered everything?"

"No, but perhaps it would be better not to know anymore? What I'm finding is presenting a possibility of there being something unpleasant and related in some way to your client here."

"I don't know, perhaps we could leave it at that. It's not as if the knowledge will change anything."

They changed the subject and talked about common interests.

They were the last to leave the dining room that evening and went for a walk in the gardens of the hotel. The evening was one of the most pleasant either of them had experienced in some time. Eventually parting reluctantly in the foyer, they headed for their separate rooms, both thinking of the many things they had in common and feeling a little less alone in their complex worlds.

During the evening Dave had said that he would be leaving on his tour at daybreak and asked if he could call her.

Rebecca agreed and went to bed wondering if there might not be some way to recover her grandfather's fortune.

Her interest in Dave had also grown with the meeting. Aside of his warm nature, he seemed somehow stronger than he had when they first met.

33

Wilson phoned Rebecca on Friday to ask her to return to Johannesburg, for a Saturday morning meeting.

She booked an early flight and met Wilson at ten on Saturday in the Binnett offices. He again outlined the reasons that GVN were not happy with her efforts.

"Wes," she replied, "it sounds as though they want me to break the terms of reference,"

"That's not the case, they have never wanted to prove the plant's capability."

"What do you think I should have done? Gone out and pulled the switches."

Wilson's unemotional face showed a trace of outrage. "Look Rebecca, the simple fact is that we get more than half our work from GVN. I can't let you get something going that the managing director has said is a basket case. I simply can't afford to allow you to carry on the way you have been doing."

"That's settled then," she said, as she stood up, impatiently, and added, " I'll leave for Australia as soon as I can get myself booked on a flight," and walked out of Wilson's office.

After the meeting Rebecca called Dave Gabrielson, Peter, and Cecil Baker, individually, to explain that she was leaving and that Cecil Baker was taking over her work.

Peter immediately contacted James de Bruin and told him Rebecca had been taken off the project.

"Where has she gone?" de Bruin asked.

"Back to Australia."

"Surely not."

"I'm afraid so."

"What affect will that have?"

"It won't help, but production is improving, and we're heading in the right direction with work practices. She has made a measurable difference by her attitude or perhaps I should say, leadership, and the place needs a sense of direction to ensure its future."

"So what are you going to do?"

"Stick to the technical aspects. We have gained a huge advantage in credibility by our success, and that will certainly help."

"Will that be enough?"

"If the workers get to think she was removed because the project is worthless we'll have a problem."

James asked if Peter could meet him and his fellow directors in Cape Town.

After arriving there late on Saturday evening, Peter took a taxi to the Vineyard Hotel in Constantia, an exclusive suburb on the landward side of Table Mountain. Developed around a colonial home, set in a small established vineyard with several acres of gardens facing Table Mountain, the hotel is deservedly well regarded by most of its guests.

He was tired when he arrived, so after dropping his cases he ate dinner, and then went to sleep.

He dressed the next morning, decided he needed some exercise, and walked quietly out into the gardens between the hotel and Table Mountain. They seemed to lead up toward the slopes of the mountain.

Walking toward the towering landmark he reached a fair sized stream that had been concealed from the hotel's window by trees. He could not find a way across and wandered back toward the main hotel building, the part that used to be the house, and found the hotel's pool. The water looked inviting and he decided to go for a swim instead of walking.

De Bruin and the other directors arrived at nine. They had been provided with a continental breakfast, from a buffet, and by the time Peter got there, they were sitting with their choices of food and drinks around the oval conference table.

De Bruin greeted Peter.

"Hi James, how are you?" answered Peter.

"That depends on what you say about the departure of the Australian consultant, I don't know whether to protest or go out and celebrate. Trying to communicate when the communications might be bugged is driving me mad."

"From what we had heard, Rebecca's departure should be an advantage?" said one of the participants.

"It's worked out quite differently, she turned herself into what the depressed employees were hoping for," answered Peter.

"So everything depends on her," asked one of the directors.

"Not at all," Peter said and went on to explain what he had done to improve production.

"So what is it that she's doing?"

Peter gave them an idea of Rebecca's effective approach saying that the reason her departure presented a danger was that the work force would think that her withdrawal signaled the last ditch effort was being shelved, and this would accentuate the loss of her personal drive.

"Seems unbelievable."

"It is and it isn't. Don't forget she's internationally recognized for her ability to deal with problem projects. She does shut things down when they don't work but she has turned a few around."

"So what happened when you had so much trouble with her?"

"She wasn't employed to improve the place, she was there to confirm the lack of capability."

"Now she's doing the opposite?"

"No, I am, she has simply shown a sense of responsibility and we're working together."

"Can you achieve the same results without her contribution?"

"People implement changes, and their effort has to be good. Her capturing their imaginations and then going will tend to contribute to their worst fears."

"Sounds hopeless," said another of the directors.

"No, not hopeless. My work is going well, but many of the problems are caused by sloppy attitude."

"Can we do anything to help?"

"You should try to get Rebecca back. Can you perhaps hire her yourself, on a contract like I am?"

"It would contravene normal agreements to an extent that would land us on the losing side in court."

"Then if I were you I would put every bit of pressure you can on GVN to get her back."

"I'll get our lawyers involved, and make sure both Jack and Michael Anders are told we are going to sue them, for trying to block the recovery of the project, by taking her off site," said de Bruin.

"It's hard to see that a firm that size will be told what to do by us. They've done as they please so far."

"The heir Michael Anders is a very straightforward. He's the one I have to get through to."

34

Michael Anders read his copy of the email he had received from de Bruin's lawyers threatening to sue them, over their mismanagement of the critical improvement effort in Ngami. He printed it and walked resolutely into Jack's office to say, "Jack, I've just been sent a copy of a very legalistic email about Ngami. I've told you that I don't want problems there. What's happened to this woman you were so pleased about a week ago?"

"Yes, I've seen it and been in touch with them. Problems with the woman and the manager on site, Michael, I'll fix it don't worry."

Michael who was still baffled by the succession of problems that were originating from the Ngami project shook his head, "I'd like to think so but as I've tried to explain, on several occasions now, I'm working on other investments in Botswana and I don't want any blow up there to get in the way of what I'm doing," he said, then turned and left the office.

Once Michael had gone, Jack phoned Wilson and asked him to get Rebecca back to Ngami.

"Jack, she was in conflict with your agenda there, we agreed she would go."

"I want the project out of the way without problems and major scenes, not the woman, I wanted her doing what we've paid you to do, attempt an improvement, then confirm the poor performance cannot be addressed. I did not want her to walk away," Jack said sharply.

"Sorry Jack. I've had a terrible few days."

"We don't employ you to listen to your complaints, Wes, please just get her back. The de Bruins are going to sue us if we don't."

Wilson got off the phone feeling desperate. Jack Anders feeding him work using a mutually beneficial arrangements had been an easy way to make money. GVN, as he'd told Rebecca, was now his main client.

He phoned Chris Bain, head of Binnett's in Australia.

Chris listened to what Wilson wanted and then asked him if he could phone back when Rebecca was with him.

After the phone call from Wilson he asked his assistant to contact Rebecca.

Rebecca was in the building and walked into Chris Bain's office within minutes.

Chris repeated the request that she should return to Ngami.

"No way in the world. They haven't got a shred of decency among the lot of them. I've already explained what happened."

"I thought that would be your answer. I'll phone him," he said and dialed Wilson's number.

Rebecca told Wilson she did not intend getting re-involved with Ngami and reminded him of what had happened.

"Perhaps you've got someone else who could hold the situation under control? I'll try to stall for a day but if you can work something out it really will help," said Wilson.

Chris said he would get back to him.

He turned to Rebecca, after Wilson had hung up and asked her what she thought they could do.

"As you know Wilson was hard to deal with."

"You did say that, but more than half his work is coming from GVN. You did have a few problems there yourself."

"I don't like the way I was treated at any level."

"Still we are Binnett and if he goes belly-up we're all in serious trouble, Rebecca."

"I've got to think about it Chris can I get back to you."

"Of course."

Rebecca decided to go for a walk, and made her way out of her office building down to the arcade that ran below the building, thinking she would have a cup of coffee in one of Sydney's many attractive coffee shops.

This did not work. The arcades seemed filled with women like her, dressed in suits. Its strong Catholic past felt like an inverted convent. No smell of incense, only of coffee. No atmosphere of spirituality, only of wealth and power. Stifled by the atmosphere, that usually cheered her, she changed her mind about the coffee and strode on, her head thrust forward looking down rather than in front of her, into the streets, toward Circular Quay, where she found an empty bench where she sat for a while, watching the ferries come and go on the twinkling harbor with its bridge as a backdrop.

She decided that she could not afford to endanger her career, went back to her office and packed up for the day.

The next day she took a long walk along the beach near her home, soaking up the beauty of the Pacific. The rising sun turned the clouds on the horizon to multi hued reds and gold, and were reflected in part by a rough sea, that reflected her inner turmoil.

She decided to ask her friend and associate Ed Chalmers to go to Ngami in her place and phoned Chris Bain.

"If he were interested it might work, but he's general manager of his company," he replied.

She explained that Ed's role as general manager was not currently demanding because the expansion that he had initiated was completed and nothing was planned for the rest of the year.

"Sounds good, can you find out if he would go?"

"There's one problem, he's quite blunt, not a marketing type of person."

"I don't know much about him."

"Ed was made general manager of Genting Resources when he was thirty-eight when the company owned two small mines. He's improved the mines' productivity and obtained leases on ore bodies that were not rich enough for operations with large overheads and managed the startup of the mines on the leases."

"Impressive stuff."

"It is, and Genting Resources is now worth nearly three times more than it was."

"They couldn't object to that resume could they?" said Chris.

"If he can get there quickly we can imply that I'm needed elsewhere."

"Okay can you talk to him?"

35

The day after returning from the Cape meeting with the de Bruin board, Peter sat alone in the Ngami conference room that they were using as a makeshift office, looking unseeingly at the pile of production loss data he had in front of him. A complete solution, he felt sure, was somewhere in the accumulation.

There were failure details of many kind detailed in the lists. High unstable gas velocities caused partially combusted slag to be carried through the furnace into the waste heat boiler and on down the exhaust train. Many waste heat boiler tube failures were caused by uneven heat patterns. The induced draft fans collected it next causing vibration problems. And then it collected on the precipitators. The slag's uneven settling through the chain of equipment was as unpredictable as the furnace. Then the continuous cooling of the acid removal equipment, during shutdowns and other varying furnace conditions, caused acid erosion.

Brett Halliday arrived in the smelter office shortly after Peter, and greeted him cheerfully, "Morning Peter. What's the matter? You look stressed."

"I'm a bit more than stressed," Peter said. "Rebecca's gone back to Australia."

"What on earth for?" Brett asked, his face showing his amazement.

"She wouldn't say."

"Well in some ways good bloody riddance."

"She did a good job at the kick off meeting."

"I wouldn't trust her or anyone else from Binnett."

Peter shook his head and they worked on in silence.

During Peter's search through the statistics and reports, he found a pattern, some common factors.

They discussed these and decided to use the next period of furnace instability to run tests on ways of stabilizing production control.

As luck would have it the control room phoned Brett while they were talking, to tell him the furnace had become unstable again.

"This is as good a chance as any to test a control solution," he said to Peter, after explaining the call.

"Okay Brett, tell them to cut the feed to the bin until the process stabilizes and then run the feeder slowly and continuously. I'll be there in about ten minutes. Can you make sure Andrew is there as well?"

Brett passed on the message and left for the furnace.

Peter finished his coffee and followed Brett to the car park.

When Peter got to the furnace control room, Brett, said, "We've reduced the feed and the furnace has steadied."

"We need to empty the bin. How long will it take?"

"I'll work it out, if you'll give me a few minutes."

Peter turned to Whitehead, who he had phoned on his way to the smelter, and they walked to a table with the drawings Whitehead had brought with him. They spent twenty minutes going over what Peter wanted done and then parted.

"I suppose we won't meet even our minimal target for the week," remarked van Breda, who had arrived shortly after Peter.

"We haven't dropped too low yet."

"Will we have to shut the furnace down again?"

"We're not shutting the furnace down. We'll cut feed to it for the time we're planning to work on the feeder, but that will need only thirty minutes at the most."

"Oh."

"The bad news is that if what we're trying out works, we'll have to repeat the exercise at short regular intervals until the changes are made more permanent during the shutdown."

"What's happening now?"

"We're emptying the bin before we adjust the feeder. Brett is working out how long that will take."

Andrew Riley entered the control room while they were talking and walked to where Peter and van Breda were standing, looking worried. His red hair seemed appropriate as it protruded in bright tufts from below the dusty white of his helmet.

"Peter there are a few things I need to check with you, if you have a few moments."

Peter rubbed his forehead, leaving a streak of dust. "Sure, what is it?" he said, wondering why Whitehead, the maintenance superintendent, was not attending to whatever it was that Riley was concerned about.

Riley led Peter to the bound set of drawings that Whitehead had left on the table in the corner of the control room and paged through them to find one that showed a cross section of the feeder.

Peter, after listening to Riley's concerns, explained what he wanted done about settings and tolerances, and then asked, "How are your people doing?"

"Not too happy, I'm afraid."

"We're going to have to repeat the exercise again, every few days."

"They won't like it," Riley answered. "They might refuse."

Outside the cabin, in a dimly lit spot, a man from Francistown, called Nelson employed by van Zyl and working under cover for the smelter, was watching Peter's every move.

After the adjustments were completed the furnace production was slowly increased, and to everyone's amazement, it reached its design capacity, for the first time in its four year life.

They waited for an hour while the furnace continued to produce steadily, at its design rate.

"Bloody hell Peter! This looks good, but now you are going to find worse problems," said van Breda.

"I know there's a lot more to do."

"It's the mine I'm really worried about."

"You can't produce this tonnage?"

"Not for long."

Peter stayed in the control room, checking and cross checking pressures and flows of gasses and of the ore. There were fluctuations which were expected because of ore variations, but the losses of combustion that had previously accompanied these events were now much more manageable because the patched control system was more capable of handling them.

One of Nelson's men was standing at the controller in the cubicle for the crane that handled molten matte from the furnace.

These huge cranes travelled on rails, high above the furnace floor and were critical to the operation; their failure for more than a few minutes would mean the smelter would have to be taken off line.

Excited at the prospect of action Nelson spoke into his cell phone. "Right Gerrit cut the controls."

Within a minute both cranes had stopped and sirens had begun wailing their protests.

Nelson watched Peter, through the dusty windows of the control room, like a predator, waiting for him to go to the crane control cubicle, he could see Peter looking at the furnace control panel.

An operator headed for the crane control cubicle, leaving Peter alone at the furnace controls.

At last, Peter moved away from the furnace control panel, but went toward the wrong door, heading for the feeder.

Nelson cursed.

Peter changed his mind at the last moment and walked briskly to the door that led to the crane control cubicle. He looked through the open grid covered walkway, at the ground, several stories below. It was bathed in the copper colour emitted by mercury vapour lights.

Nelson, covered in dust, wearing a hard hat and goggles, waited until Peter was out of the door and walking toward the cubicle, then followed.

The sirens were still blaring and there was a lot of smoke about.

Near where he had loosened a section of handrail, Nelson drew up behind Peter. He excused himself, as though he was trying to get past, then pushed Peter hard.

Peter fell through loosened handrail, managing to grab the kick plate with his hand, arm and his one foot. He hung painfully along the length of the kick plate.

Nelson holding onto the remaining solid piece of handrail lifted his foot, to kick Peter off the platform.

Peter managed to grab it as it flashed forward. Holding himself from toppling, he pulled Nelson by the ankle with all his strength.

Nelson, no longer in control, began to feel afraid as he was dragged toward the gap; strengthening his hold on the solid portion of handrail he jerked his foot free from Peter's grip.

Peter swung himself back onto the walkway, and Nelson turned and ran. The route he had chosen for his escape involved a short jump to another walkway. Unfortunately for him the man who was assigned to protect Peter met him there and hit Nelson as he leapt.

Nelson landed near where Peter should have been, never to move, of his own accord, again. At almost the same moment, the operator found the fault in the crane cubicle and the ladle cranes came back to life and the sirens stopped their high-pitched wailing.

A group formed around the limp form of Nelson, seemingly afraid to touch him.

Peter struggled back to the control room where the supervisor applied antiseptic to his grazed leg and hands. He accepted a cup of coffee gratefully and waited for the furnace to be put on line, trying to stop the shaking in his badly stressed muscles.

The control room supervisor filled the storage bin to half capacity and started the feeder.

They stood, quietly, watching the furnace normalise, mesmerised by the power of the conversion process.

The furnace was switched to automatic and the plant's production again steadied.

An ambulance was sent from the main security station by the duty sergeant, who was a direct employee of Andselc security and had known more about Nelson than his colleague in the smelter. He told the driver to take the body to the airport rather than the hospital and then phoned Willers.

Willers had no knowledge of Nelson or his mission, and this made his bad feelings about Ngami worse.

He thanked the security sergeant phoned van Zyl and told him what had happened.

Van Zyl offered no explanation, but gave Willers a terse set of instructions.

Willers went to the airport where he organised for Nelson's body to be loaded onto the twin engined corporate aircraft, as he had been told to do. He climbed into the cockpit and flew the corpse back to a remote base in South Africa, cold with fear. He could not get Anders' last comments out of his mind. Clearly the powerful executive was behind what had just happened and equally clearly Willers had not been informed about what was happening.

The fear increased as each moment passed. If Nelson had been in the plant without his knowledge, there would be others and if he no longer knew what was happening in his area of responsibility, then he had been moved from under the security umbrella.

He called his wife, who had made the trip the previous week with their valuables and had been staying with her parents as John's fears at his exposure had begun to increase, and asked her to meet him at a remote airfield

He then landed at an airport owned by GVN and waited there for the remains of Nelson to be taken from the aircraft by two agents.

He then flew to an airfield where he had arranged to meet his wife. Landed and turned the aircraft to face down the runway. He cut the engines and lights, climbed out and made his way to the office and asked for the tanks to be filled.

They climbed into the aircraft with the luggage she had brought with her and their two children and a friend from his air force days.

John took off, with his friend flying as co-pilot, and flew, not to Ngami, but to Northern Namibia where he had obtained another position. They landed early and John's friend then flew the aircraft back to the quiet South African field and left it there, before anyone at Ngami had noticed the absence of the security superintendent.

The furnace's successful run continued through the night and into the following day.

Peter went back to the hotel at about four in the morning, showered, and fell into a deep and dreamless sleep, only waking at nine. He got out of bed, showered and left for the site offices.

Anders and Heldebron received an email confirming John Willers' resignation before midday. He asked if his outstanding leave could be accepted as a period of notice, explaining that family pressures had forced his sudden departure.

Anders received the news of the resignation of Willers with ambivalence. He had mentally scrapped the security head and was contented to let him run to wherever he had gone. Willers knew too much about their activities though, and his own method of getting rid of the security chief would have been more permanent.

36

The increase in plant production, to near full capacity put ever more pressure for more ore on the mine. This increased the probability of another disaster. One so serious that it dwarfed the rest of their problems. Ahead of a critically important high thermal capability part of the mine was an ancient lake that had lain untapped for thousands of years. A fissure from the lake led into the stope and was slowly emptying the lake into the mine. The volume of water in the lake was immense, enough to flood the whole mine many times over if the flow rate increased.

Jeffery Nyasa had started work at Ngami, as planned. To allow him time to familiarize himself with the operation without drawing attention to his role, Charles arranged for him to be put in charge of the underground water management systems. This involved controlling a number of pump stations, several dams, and a network of pipes and drains that spread throughout the workings, and it allowed him to see for himself all the facets of the operation.

Goodwill, an afternoon shift supervisor, failed to arrive for work. His role was to ensure that someone would be there to manually operate the pumps if anything went wrong with the automatic control systems, and to supervise the cleaning of dams and waterways.

Jeffrey had filled in for him and headed underground.

After the shift started Jeffery briefly inspected the main pump installation at the mineshaft, then he walked toward where an intermediate set of dams and pumps were located.

He checked the drains that delivered the water from the mine workings to the dams as he walked. Unexpectedly he found the one was overflowing.

He walked on to arrive at the intermediate pumps to find they were working hard.

Two dams were full, with one of the three pumps running continuously, and a second intermittently.

The design of the pump system was such that a single pump running intermittently should keep the dam levels constant. This design meant that there was sufficient pumping capacity in reserve to cater for a pump failure and still be capable of handling an emergency of up to twice the design inflow.

Two pumps running at full capacity indicated that there was twice the design capacity of water flowing through the system.

He walked back to the source of the water along the drive, remembering, as he went, the underground workings of the mining estate where he had worked as an air-leg miner, as a part of his training.

Once in the stope with the extra water flow Jeffery stopped and watched the men working. Thinking how hard the life of a hard rock miner was, and had been for centuries.

The wet rock walls of the stope were shining in the light provided by the cap lamps, as, side-by-side, the drill operators drove holes into the rock-face, the deafening clatter of their drills rendered normal speech impossible.

At the start of twentieth century these people would have had a life span of thirty years, if they were lucky. They would then have died an agonizing death, smothered by layers of rock dust in their lungs. If they were unlucky they would die sooner, in a rock fall or burst.

The role was highly paid hard work and required both strength and considerable skill.

The holes they were drilling would be charged with explosives at the end of the shift and blasted from a remote station once the men had left the mine.

Heavy watering down of the drilling process now meant that the men he was watching would live longer, if the roof did not collapse or, they did not strike enough water.

A water ingress could come with a rock burst in which case they could be killed by the rock burst or the flood.

Jeffery noticed that the roof was heavily bolted, as though it was known to be more liable to failure than the rest of the mine. He looked again at the drain as he scrambled back to the main haulage-way. Several submersible pumps were sucking up the water and transferring it via flexible hoses to the strongly flowing drainage system in the haulage-way.

In a few hours the shift would end and explosives would blast the next batch of ore free from the rock face. Each blast at a point near the underground lake brought the mine closer to flooding.

The ventilation fans would clear the noxious air and the next shift would return to the stope, and the loading process would start again.

Over and over, in countless mining operations, throughout the centuries, the process of drilling, breaking and loading had been repeated; in a cycle that had brought immense wealth to some and death to many.

Jeffery walked back to the mineshaft, wondering if he should try to stop the next blast. He felt the danger as much as he worried about the water ingress. He checked the shaft bottom pump installation, more carefully this time. He found three of the four pumps were running continuously; then he looked at the pressure and flow gauges. These indicated that there was no problem with the condition of the pumps, which confirming that the inflow was twice as much as the maximum expected.

Jeffery phoned van Breda about the danger.

Van Breda was with Peter in the furnace control room. They had just witnessed a muffled explosion in the furnace, after which all indication showed that there had been at least a partial loss of combustion. The instability had forced the operators to take manual control of the furnace.

After the huge furnace had been stabilized, van Breda asked, "Was that the feeder?"

"I don't think so, they wouldn't have been able to get the furnace under control if it had been," Peter answered.

"Changes in ore characteristics then," said van Breda.

"Ore characteristics are certainly a problem if they can have such a big effect."

The call from Jeffery came as they spoke. When van Breda finished the conversation with Jeffery, he told Peter what Jeffery had found.

"So does that mean the water affected part of the operation will have to be closed?" Peter asked.

"It should at least be slowed and that will affect the furnace badly. Its ore has better smelting properties than that from the rest of the mine."

Peter contacted de Bruin to tell him about their discoveries of increasing seriousness of both the water and ore problems.

"That place is impossible. I just don't know what to do, I have to rely on Heldebron, and I'll talk to Ben when we're finished, but there's very little anyone can do from a distance. Please ask Jeffery to watch things as closely as he can. Obviously, aside of the danger to people, if the mine is flooded we are finished."

"Okay."

"How are the plant production improvements going?

"I've been making good progress but there is a lot to do. We need to arrange a complete shutdown for a week to get the most important work done."

The increasing danger presented by the water entering the mine provided Heldebron with an opportunity to redirect Peter's efforts.

Baker had told Heldebron that Peter had experience with a similar installation. He had been overheard by the consultant when discussing the water management system with Jeffery. Peter had been describing how he had designed and installed a similar facility.

Heldebron decided to ask Peter to help improve the safety of the people in the mine by looking at the design of the pumps and pipelines and asked him to come to his office.

Shortly after this, when Peter arrived to see the general manager, he was surprised by the enthusiasm with which he was greeted.

The welcome was followed by Heldebron saying, "Peter we need your help with the pumping installation. You have experience in pump design I believe?"

"I designed and operated several on one of the large mines near Rustenburg."

"We are facing great danger and we need your help."

Peter objected on the grounds of the urgency of the work program.

Heldebron insisted that the safety of the mineworkers was more important than the improvement program.

The truth of this was unarguable, so Peter agreed to look at the pump installation.

After a stomach-churning drop in a man cage into the mine, they walked to the shaft bottom pump station discussing the problems.

"The pumps to the surface are running at full load," Jeffery explained.

"Lets look at their design flow curves," said Peter.

Jeffery took him to the workshop that was attached to the pump station and found the information Peter was looking for.

"Another pipeline to the surface would help," Peter said after a few minutes.

"Yes, but how long would it take to install one."

"It could take a while. I'll work out if it can be done and if so, how. Do you know where the shaft drawings are?"

"There's a set in the drawing files somewhere," said Jeffery and looked through the drawing office files on the computer terminal in the workshop.

"Here it is," he said.

Peter checked the details of the shaft cross-section and found there was a provision for another line. Such an installation would still be time consuming. While it could possibly be done, an intense effort taking several days would be needed, the piping itself, and associated fittings and fixing components, would have to be ready before the work started.

He used the computer system to check the store inventory of such equipment and found there was nowhere near enough piping to complete the work. An investigation into the possibility of obtaining pipe from other operations and manufacturers was then set in motion through the supply department.

The work to prepare for the duplication of the pipeline was added to the list of work needed to address critical problems.

Peter's quick analysis of the water problems meant that there had been no delay in the improvement programs.

He went to see Heldebron and told him that they needed to shut the plant for a week to allow for the pipeline replacement.

"Shut the plant for a week. Sounds dramatic."

"There are a number of key activities that we can get out of the way in the processing plant at the same time as the pipeline is going in."

A telephone conference between Heldebron and Anders was held to discuss the potential of the shutdown.

After listening impatiently to the commentary Jack Anders asked, "So the shutdown increases the chance of improved production?"

"Almost certainly."

"But you said the water problems would interfere with his work to improve the place?"

"We thought that by using Connor to look at them we could derail the improvements," said Heldebron.

"The work hasn't been slowed?" asked Anders.

"No, he specified work to duplicate the pipeline during the shutdown. He's going to improve the security of the operation by doing so."

"I think we need him out of the way more than the woman."

"He's also got the furnace instability under temporary control."

"What's he done?"

"I'm not sure of the detail but he and Brett have discovered some way of steadying the furnace."

"Find out how permanent the fix is."

Heldebron then phoned Brett and asked how the furnace stability was being managed.

"We can hold on now but there is no way we can have men in and out making adjustments, like they are doing now for more than a few weeks," responded Brett. "We have to get something more permanent working during the shutdown."

"So it won't be enough without the more permanent work?"

"No."

And Connor is the key to success in the shutdown?'

"Yes."

Heldebron phoned Anders again and told him what Brett had said.

"Then there is nothing more to say, Connor has got to go," said Anders.

Heldebron did not answer.

"Well, think about it," Anders said, hesitated and then added, "I need to check on some other options."

Anders immediately contacted van Zyl and explained why Peter had to be got off of the Ngami site before the shutdown.

37

After her meeting with Chris Bain Rebecca phoned Ed Chalmers and told him that she needed his help in Africa.

"It's a long way away. Our company is talking about investing there though."

"I really need help,. I'm in bad corner."

"I've got some things to finish here, could you get to my office?"

She agreed as it was close to Binnetts.

When Rebecca got to Ed's office she found him tiding up after a busy day.

"So what help do you need?" he asked once she was seated.

"The project, I went to Africa for, has turned into a nightmare," she said.

"I thought it sounded odd when they asked you to go."

"Yes, you said so, and you were right," she said and went on to give him a brief outline of what had happened in Ngami.

"It sounds like you're in bit of a bad corner Rebecca," he answered, "Can we go back over what happened?"

"Of course."

"When you left here you said it was a basket case. If you proved it's worthless to the board, as you say you have, why didn't they just close the plant?"

"I recommended they close it, but the other shareholders had someone else carry out a technical review. He showed that there was a way to get it working, without as much effort as I said was needed. A major shareholder thought that what he was saying was worth trying and the bank extended the loan for a few months. Now between this engineer and myself, we've managed to improve production and the improvement is continuing."

"What's left to do then?"

"The whole exercise is very still shaky. Permanent improvements have to be made and will need to be supported by the people there, who are disillusioned and unhappy."

"What's that got to do with you?"

"The ball can still be dropped and members of the GVN contingent want that to happen. They don't want me encouraging anyone."

"So what happened to your effort that's upsetting GVN?"

"I helped get the whole unhappy lot working as a team and that infuriated the management of GVN. I was helping the people on site see that there was hope and the South African engineer was proving that the technical problems were manageable, so the site management made things difficult for me."

"It's hard to see what they did not like, and more importantly why are they working to shut the place?"

"I don't know and so I decided to come back here. The other partners, who will lose out badly if it's shut down, are now threatening to sue GVN for taking me off site."

"What on earth did you do to make things so much better?"

"It sounds odd, I know. I was looking into the failure of my grandfather's company because they were delaying the start of the work on site, and found there was some involvement of GVN in his failure. I was already annoyed by the attitude of the management of Ngami, in delaying my work."

"Sure sounds very odd."

"Thats putting it mildly, and then I was given a great deal of support and cooperation by Peter Connor, the engineer who's convinced he can get the place working."

"So?"

"At the kick off meeting the whole thing seemed to slip into a positive territory and Peter Connor and I were working togcther at the end of the meeting."

"You're normally the cool one."

"I don't know what to say, Connor is a very pleasant and cooperative person. He's not simply an engineer, his ability to direct effort where its most useful is very high. It's as though you thought of a step that you're taking and then realize he set it up."

"So he's some kind of very slick salesman?"

"Almost the opposite."

"Interesting."

"You could say that, but however you explain what's happened, I can't deal with the result."

"Why are they so eager to close the thing down?"

"Four years of hoping it will work and it just gets worse I suppose."

"But you say it's improving now? If it's something like your grandfather's loss do you think something dishonest is happening?"

"I can't say dishonest, just a bit hard for the partners who will lose out. Of course the similar failure of my grandfather's company worries me. It was shut down because of a failure to meet some contract."

"How do you want me to help?"

"After treating me like a wayward child, Wilson has changed his mind and wants me back there to avoid being put into court, but I don't want to go back."

"Can you explain why you need me though?" asked Ed.

"GVN are going to be sued and that will cause a key person there to lose face in a big way. So they have threatened to cancel all of Binnett's contracts if they don't get me back. That's more than half Binnett's business."

"That's a lot of reason to go back Rebecca."

"I really don't want to go."

"I can see why, but still sometimes you have to take difficult decisions, and this surely must be one of those."

"If you went instead we would fulfill our contractual obligations. You could spend two months in Botswana in my place. GVN are not happy with me, its just that they need my assignment to appear sound to stop the others suing them. You would look a good person for the specific exercise. I would pay you well and you could use the time to investigate opportunities for your company.'"

"What would be involved?"

"You would simply have to work on parts of the program of systems improvements. Peter Connor is very competent and there are good people on site who need good leadership."

Ed was silent for a few moments, thinking that he could afford to take a break and that certainly would allow him to investigate opportunities for his company, Genting. "There is one big worry for me though, I can't afford to have them harassing me about sabotaging the project," he said.

"I'll make sure they understand that, so you'll be there temporarily in my place, to help improve the image of management."

"It's a thought. The MD will need to approve," he answered.

"Could you speak to him?"

"I will."

"Thanks Ed, will you let me know what you want to do as soon as you can."

"I will, can we talk about it again tomorrow?"

"Okay, breakfast at Balmoral?"

"At the restaurant on the water where we went last month?"

"Okay, at eight thirty?"

"That would be great."

The next morning the weather was perfect, even by Sydney's high standards. The glossy leaves of Morton Bay figs that lined the Balmoral Beach promenade almost seemed to twinkle in the brilliant sunshine and to complete the idyllic picture, the creamy sand of the beach was lapped by smallish waves, that slipped in through the heads, from the Pacific.

Rebecca asked, "So what's it to be Ed?"

"I've spoken to the managing director and I've got his agreement that I can go. He decided that what I do in Africa can only benefit the company by improving their information on prospects there."

"Thats very good news, thank you Ed."

"I hope it works out."

"You will really be a help there."

38

Three days after the breakfast with Rebecca, Ed Chalmers was in Botswana.

Cecil Baker met him at the airport and took him to the main offices. He gave Ed a summary of the project and then introduced him to Heldebron and van Breda, the mine manager, who was with the general manager.

They spent some time discussing the project and by the time they were through, Ed thought that he was beginning to get a fair perspective of priorities and problems on the site.

They then went to the smelter where Cecil introduced Ed to Peter and Brett, who, after providing the Australian with their opinions, took him to the weekly smelter management meeting.

Cecil Baker gave the meeting a summary of Ed's impressive background, and explained that he would be filling in for Rebecca.

There was no questioning Ed's suitability from the account given by Baker.

The meeting went ahead as usual with key players reporting on the status of their areas of responsibility.

Whitehead, the maintenance superintendent, started off with his contribution by explaining the problems with one of the smelter's main transformers during the night. This had caused a large production loss. Brett asked him about the progress with a program to duplicate the transformer circuit that was being undertaken by a major Swiss contractor, finishing with a remark about the skill with which the specialist worked.

Peter had noticed the fair-haired Swiss technician himself. "You can understand how the Swiss are famous for their craftsmanship when you see him work can't you?" he said and then continued, "By the way, how are the failure statistics coming along?"

Whitehead, feigning confusion, looked toward the planning supervisor and said that the statistics had been recorded but not correlated.

The company had installed a comprehensive plant information system, on which better maintenance of production depended. This required a great deal of effort from a number of people.

Shawn explained the latest difficulties they were having with the accounting part of the package.

Peter was interested to hear Shawn's story, because of a scene he had witnessed the previous week: He had walked down to planning, to check an aspect of costing figures he had been sent. The planner had been communicating something wildly to his assistant, hands waving, face contorted, his few hairs standing on end and his glasses askew.

The plump attractive woman had been looking up at Shawn with large, very worried eyes, across a desk covered with untidy stacks of computer printouts.

"I really don't know Shawn," Peter had heard as he walked into the office.

They had both turned to face him, looking awkward.

"Sorry to interrupt," Peter had said at the time, deciding his question could wait. "I'll come back later."

Peter glanced at Ed as Shawn talked on about his difficulties.

Ed lifted his substantial eyebrows and rolled his eyes.

He glanced back at Shawn forcing himself not to smile

Shawn was looking more awkward than usual.

Peter liked and sympathized with the eccentric man, but could not afford to leave the issue, "So the problems are all under control and the new system is going in on schedule is it Shawn?" he asked.

Shawn was conscientious, in his late fifties, hated to admit weakness, and was genuinely overloaded.

"They'll be fully functional this month or we'll throw them out, Peter. You have my assurance on that." He said awkwardly.

Throwing them out was hardly an option, so Shawn's answer presented another problem. Peter was silent for a moment, as he thought about this. "I hope so, Shawn. You really looked a bit harassed the other day when I saw you. Perhaps we need someone to give you a hand with the data processing work, to free you up to carry out all these investigations?"

"That would be a help Peter," said Shawn looking relieved.

Peter made a note in his diary to see the information systems department about the progress being made with the package. Turning to Whitehead, he asked if they could ensure that the figures he needed would be completed before the next morning's meeting.

After some sideways glances and apparent confusion, this was agreed.

The meeting went on for another hour.

"That was a bit of a battle, Peter," Ed said as they left.

"If you think those lot were a bit slow, wait till you meet the people who do the work."

"It's hard to see how these people are the best that GVN can find."

"It's the culture more than their individual backgrounds. I believe that in a real world management achieve more by good example and supporting the real workers than is realized."

"I thought Rebecca was the expert at that?"

"She is and that's the way we've set it up, but I would not have done things the way she has. We are now dependent on her image."

"Is that a fact? I'm a bit curious to hear more about that."

"Let's just stick to the agenda now."

Peter had watched the thin self-contained man, clad in khaki longs and matching shirt, as the morning progressed. He thought that Ed would fit well in most field situations. He spoke clearly and more slowly than most Australians or South Africans and was quietly confident in his manner. He looked the part of a seasoned if not charismatic professional. He clearly belonged in a productive environment such as mining and construction and from the few moments Peter had been with him Ed had cut to the base of anything contentious. Peter felt intuitively that Ed would have the Australian ability to get things moving no matter what the odds. A leader from the front. He certainly seemed a good choice to replace Rebecca.

So that evening, when Peter phoned James de Bruin about the suitability of Rebecca's replacement, he said that Ed was providing a good image in Rebecca's place and that without actually having her back and working toward a positive conclusion this was probably the best way to keep the project on track. He described Ed's easy acceptance by the group and that he thought that he looked and acted as a thorough professional. He said the only thing missing that should be of any concern to them was that Ed did not have the same charisma as Rebecca. He was a leader from the front, or the boardroom, rather than a cheerleader.

Unfortunately for de Bruin, Ngami desperately needed cheering.

Heldebron had gained similar initial impressions of the Australian and had decided that Ed should not be approached about slowing the project. If Ed's contribution was to be minimized, and they were certain that it would need to be, then it would have to be done by providing something that would take Ed off site.

Peter went to talk to Ed later in the day and found him in the conference room, engrossed in the financial section of the local paper. Baker was out.

"How's it going Ed?" Peter asked warily when the Australian mining engineer looked up irritably.

"Bloody well pissed off," was Ed's abrupt reply. "I can't get anywhere near a decent response out of these people. It's like trying to force a herd of stupid sheep through a gate."

"No success with the team building?"

Ed rolled his eyes and sighed. "To tell the truth team building is not really my favorite activity, but you could say it was a bit slow."

They walked together to a planning meeting.

In that meeting, Peter could see the increasing pessimism that Ed had implied. He did his best to enliven the gathering.

"Wouldn't you agree that that was a bit slow?" remarked Ed, once they were on their own.

"At their level the loss of Rebecca is a disaster," said Baker.

Ed looked embarrassed. "I know she caught their imagination and like it or not that's what we have to deal with."

"I'm sorry Ed but I don't think you have her personality," said Baker.

"No. I know that."

"From my point of view we only have to do our professional best," Baker went on; rather pleased with the way he had put Ed in his place. "When companies like GVN want something they usually get it. I can't honestly see why they would have anyone at our level rewriting their agenda for them."

Peter, irritated by Cecil Baker' attitude toward Ed, had to bite back an expression of his anger. Baker was not his favorite person, but he wanted to maintain every bit of equanimity that he could.

"So what do you think about the project Ed?" Peter asked.

"Technically? You're the expert. Managerially? It's a basket case."

"I suppose as you say it depends on your point of view," replied Peter. "I've no doubt myself that this project is viable though, and you are providing a good image."

Baker shook his head slightly, and said he was not so sure, and then walked out of the conference room.

Peter went to an appointment he had with Brett, and when he returned he found Ed in an even worse mood, his face was flushed with repressed rage.

"What's the matter?" Peter asked.

"That bloody Baker, I've run operations bigger than this, I'm not his bloody servant."

"Come on, let's get over to the golf club and have lunch," Peter suggested, wondering what Baker had done while he was out, but did not ask, not wanting to further inflame whatever it was that was bothering Ed.

They drove the short distance to the golf club in silence, found a table and ordered lunch.

Peter thought as they sat down that Ed's black hair, thick black beard and handlebar mustache made his age difficult to guess. He looked, to Peter, like someone from a Russian folk tale. He was certainly a character.

Ed twirled the end of his mustache, like a slim, trim, representative from a past mining era as he decided what he wanted for lunch.

During the lunch Ed, in answer to Peter's question about what he did in Australia, explained the excitement of his recent successes, how he had over a period of several years improved mines' productivity, and obtained new leases expanding the company he worked for.

"Sounds impressive."

He went on to tell Peter that the company was now in a good position to take advantage of new opportunities.

"So why did you accept this role?" Peter asked.

"To help Rebecca in the first place, but also to look for opportunities in Africa."

"For your company?"

"Yes, and of course GVN is internationally accepted and as good a company, as any in Africa, to form an association with."

"You know the situation these people are in?" asked Peter.

"Yes, and I sympathize with the partners here. I also know that failures of companies are a part of business," Ed said awkwardly, wishing he had been less blunt the minute he'd expressed the thought.

"You feel failure is inevitable?"

"Not inevitable but they are in a bad position. The lack of combustible ore is a huge problem. The total failure that's been held in check by your work is not easy to understand. It seems ridiculous to me that a set of technical and management problems should have been allowed to hang about for years."

39

As Peter and Ed were talking over lunch, in the golf club, two Americans, clearly dressed for the bush, walked into the dining room and sat down near them.

The men were speaking quite loudly about new instructions and a different exploration pattern.

"That sounds a bit like they could be talking about an ore-body, I wonder if it's the one Ben found?" said Peter.

"Sounds as though they've been given a new lead."

"On the subject of exploration Ed, you said your company is looking for opportunities in Africa?"

"Yes, they are."

"The de Bruin's need help with geological work, would that interfere with your own agenda?"

"I suppose I could help interpret the geology but physically helping de Bruin find the deposit would probably be in contradiction with the agreements I've signed with GVN."

Peter contacted James de Bruin after they had parted and told him what they had overheard.

"I haven't heard from the laboratory about those samples yet. I'd better find out what's happened."

"I also asked Ed Chalmers if he would help with finding the ore body, and he says he can't because it would conflict with his company's agenda."

"And, his contribution to your work, are you still happy with what he's doing?"

"Until the shutdown he'll be fine, but during the shutdown and after it, he will battle. Ed's a mining engineer so the complexities of the metallurgical plant are too detailed for his training and experience. He is a reasonable sort of a bloke, positive in his approach, he wants to get things done, not worry about sensitivities. I just can't see that he will fully replace Rebecca's personality after the shutdown any more than I can. We will have to rely on the positive effect that steady production will have."

"We still need her then?"

"From GVN's perspective it's a question of the image they present to the World Bank, and it's not easy to fault the contribution that Ed would make on that front."

"So we have to accept him."

"For now, we are moving forward. The success of the shutdown will be an important factor and Ed will be a part of that, we'll work around his lack of mechanical and electrical skills. If it's a success he will be given a boost. The difficulty is that people who are able and willing to do routine maintenance are never easy to find. Here it's even more difficult. Rebecca's contribution would have added a spark we need to push the waverers to act like they would in a normal outfit."

"That still surprises me."

"She works with people. Her personality, her experience, or perhaps something about her, makes the average person believe in what they were doing."

"Oh well I suppose we will have to pray we don't need as much personality as that, and that what you create now will be enough," said de Bruin.

Ed made his way back to the office block, thinking about the potential of the missing ore body and sent a brief email to his managing director explaining this.

He received a reply within minutes. The managing director had welcomed Ed's suggestion. He was given the go ahead to look for the ore, but only on behalf of Genting Resources.

He decided to check the reserves of the project and drove to the geological offices.

He had met Ngami's chief geologist, Itzaak Bierman but had not spoken to him after that.

Bierman was not forthcoming when Ed asked about the company's plans.

Ed spent the rest of the day checking the department's records, explaining that he needed to know the potential for the report, which Binnett's were submitting. This was at least partially true. He could see that his efforts were annoying Bierman. Geology was not directly mentioned in his terms of reference. And, as he well understood, while such information certainly had connections to the improvement effort, the actual examination of geological records would have been unusual in an exercise such as theirs.

Bierman's manner did make him suspicious about wether there was something more than natural caution causing it.

His investigations of the records confirmed, to him, that there was a good possibility of finding more ore in the area not being explored by the Ngami geologists. He found that information and records indicating the possibility of additional ore to the Northeast seemed to have been put aside by the Ngami geologists, and that this probably added to the evidence of the fraud de Bruin suspected. He double-checked his studies. They firmly indicated the possibility of another ore body to the northeast of Ngami.

He left the geological section after thanking Bierman and went back to the conference room.

Baker was working on a set of statistics and greeted him absently, then went back to what he had been busy with before Ed had interrupted.

There was no sign of Peter.

Ed decided he needed more information on geology and that he would use the time available to check the files of the mines department in Gabarone. He left the office without saying where he was going and drove to Gabarone.

The department of mines was helpful when Ed explained that he was working for an Australian company.

His investigative work there confirmed what he had discovered in Ngami. He was not sure how to deal with the information but was certain that the de Bruin's exposure to a separate ore discovery was a problem for them.

He had lunch and then returned to the mines department to prepare a draft report for Genting Resources on what he had found in relation to their interests.

40

James de Bruin contacted the laboratory that he had commissioned to assay the samples, after Peter told him what the prospectors had said in the restaurant. The person who took the call told him that Jordaan, the managing director of the laboratory, who James knew personally, was out and would not be returning until the following week.

Not happy with the tone of the reply, he tried to work out what to do. He did not know the specific functions of the people in the laboratory, so he could not phone anyone else about the results. After putting the phone down, he closed the files on which he was working, trying to decide on a course of action. Eventually he concluded that there was one sure way to check the results from the samples and that was to go to Jordaan's laboratory himself.

He tidied his desk and walked into his personal assistant's office.

She looked up from the filing she was doing, and seeing his look of determination, felt a spark of hope, that he might have worked out how to solve the family company's problems. Not only because of her personal loyalty, but because much of her savings were invested in de Bruin Enterprises.

"Have you worked out what to do?" she asked hopefully.

"No, there's another thread come loose, but I'm going to get to the bottom of this one."

"How?"

"I haven't been given the Ngami sample results yet and his laboratory has told me that Jordaan was out and not expected back for a few days. That's what I'm going to find out about now."

She sighed, "How will you do that?"

"I'm going to see Jordaan's laboratory."

"Today?"

"Yes," he said.

He signed two letters for her, made his way to the car park, climbed into the beautifully maintained British Racing Green, 1964, Jaguar 3.8, and drove slowly to the city and the laboratory, thinking that of all the errors he had made, this was the least expected. He had not dreamed there would be any problem with Jordaan.

He was waved through the security gates at the laboratory by the guard who knew him, parked in a visitor's space, got out of the car, and climbed the entry stairs to the laboratory two at a time, then strode through reception without looking at anyone, and walked straight into Kim Jordaan's office.

Jordaan's personal assistant politely tried to stop him, but he was past her, and through the managing director's office door before she could complete her protestations.

Jordaan was there as James had sadly suspected his friend might be.

Jordaan looked up at his long time associate, in surprise.

The polished wooden floors of the office were partially carpeted with Persian rugs, making some steps sound sharp and deadening others. De Bruin reached the desk and leaned on it with both hands, bringing his face close to Jordaan's.

"I thought you were away for a week?" De Bruin asked.

"I've got some critical deadlines to complete, and asked them not to disturb me," answered Jordaan, a slim bespectacled man in his forties. He was sitting as far back in his chair as he could, trying, to get away from the angry face.

"What do you want James?"

"Kim." De Bruin replied without any preamble. "Why haven't I received the results of those samples from Francistown?"

"The head of your security company picked them up."

"My security company?"

"Andselc."

"Kim, I gave those samples to you personally. You know quite well that Andselc is not my security company."

"We do a huge amount of work for GVN James, I thought you were working with them. Security companies often pick up important results."

"I gave them to you personally and explained how important they were."

"Well, you are the same company as far as Ngami goes aren't you?"

De Bruin could barely control his feelings, "Kim, you and I go back a long way. You know I'm in a difficult position. How the hell could you give someone else those results?"

"I believed that they were intended for your joint venture. Weren't they?" Jordaan asked.

"I'll be damned. Could I have them myself do you suppose?" de Bruin asked abruptly.

"Of course James," Jordaan said as he double clicked with the mouse several times, then stood, and went to a printer that was located against the wall. He then handed the results to James mumbling something about how sorry he was

De Bruin took the pages Jordaan gave him, thanked him curtly, turned and walked out of the office.

He telephoned his personal assistant as he strode out toward the car park and asked her to book him a seat on the first available flight to Ngami, climbed into the car and looked at the results.

They looked good to him. The analysis showed that the samples contained high concentrations of platinum with nickel and copper together with what he thought were higher percentages of gold than in the existing deposit. He needed a more expert interpretation though. There seemed little doubt though, that if whoever it was that now knew this, and it seemed they must, had full knowledge of the value of Ben's discovery. He had no idea that Andselc could have had the influence to pressure Jordaan.

Rather than solve a problem he had found another unexplained situation. One that increased the need to find the ore before it was claimed by others.

He started the car and drove back out of the city feeling sure their life's work was slipping through their fingers. Whoever it was that was working against them seemed to be moving inexorably toward being able to claim the ore. After parking the car in front of the farmhouse he closed the door behind him and without looking left or right walked up the stairs, through the front door, down the passage and into the reception area.

His assistant asked what had happened.

He explained that Andselc Security had been given the sample results.

"How could they do that?"

"Apparently security firms often take information and valuables to and from the laboratory, for GVN and the joint venture.

"So where does that leave you?"

"No further ahead, I'll have to go up there and try to work through the mess with Peter Connor and Charles."

"How's your brother?"

"Making progress. They can't tell me when he's likely to recover his memory.

He turned to walk back into the living area of the house, where he collapsed into a chair in the lounge, feeling lost.

Michelle, his wife, found him hunched in his chair staring out the window.

She asked what was happening. She was getting progressively more frightened. She thought back to when she and James had met at an uncle's hotel in Paarl, the town closest to the de Bruin's farm. They had seldom been apart since their first meeting. He had sheltered her throughout their marriage and she had never questioned his strength or his ability to support them. Their youngest child was still in kindergarten, the oldest at university. Although she had a degree in psychology, she had never used it, having given her life to her family. She came from well-known stock herself, from people who had come to South Africa more recently, as refugees from a different purge. Her family were as committed to Ngami as were the de Bruins, their savings were also tied up in de Bruin Enterprises.

He told her that Peter had overheard prospectors talking about exploration near Ngami.

"GVN would have exploration teams all over the world, why would this one be so important?"

"Another ore body would simply represent an alternate ore supply, if Ngami has enough ore itself. If, on the other hand, the Ngami geologists cannot locate enough ore to supply the plant, then it's a different story."

"Surely that was serious enough to be worrying about in the first place?"

"There is no direct mention of inadequate ore reserves in the reports we have from GVN. Ben only became worried about the mine and the ore just before he was hurt. There have been no reports of problems from GVN."

"So where do we stand?"

"The samples show that there is a second source of ore. If we have to buy ore from outside, separately controlled, it would considerably reduce any possible profitability of Ngami."

"Can that be done?"

"I'm sure it can, by a completely different entity, and the way they've taken these results from under our noses indicates the worst."

"What do the samples show James?"

"I can't interpret them exactly," he said. "They definitely show that the ore Ben found is high quality."

He took the information he had obtained from Jordaan from his attaché case, read through the results more carefully, while she waited patiently, and then closed his eyes, and sighed. "Yes they're good," he said quietly. "There are high percentages of platinum, nickel, copper and gold but I'm not sure how big the deposit is. They also indicate the pyrogenous properties are good."

"Pyrogenous means ability to burn?"

"Yes."

"Sounds like it's a problem James?" she asked.

"Whoever gets control of this ore body will be very wealthy."

"What are you going to do?"

"I must go up there."

They spent the rest of the morning discussing the chances they had of disengaging parts of the company from the danger Ngami represented, but arrived at a series of dead ends and concluded that there were no alternatives, all their holdings would fail if Ngami were bankrupted.

41

Joseph, the herd boy, was woken one evening by a nightmare in his temporary home in the village. His dream had been terrible, death all around him. He was coldly afraid.

When he opened his eyes, Mma Kolwane, the mother of the family, was looking down at him.

His stay of several months with the family had mainly consisted of lonely periods looking after their cattle. The time in their home was pleasant, as the generous family had been most kind to him. At times he almost forgot his predicament.

"What is it Mma you look worried," he mumbled sleepily through the memories of the bad dream. He noticed that it was still dark outside.

"Joseph," she said, "they are looking for you. There is someone important coming here today. We are not sure, but think they are asking after you."

"I am afraid of this and I have been thinking that I must go away for a few days Mma. I am putting you at risk. I cannot avoid talking forever.

"This is an unexplained visit, we have never had anything like it."

"I will leave in the early light. So as not to be noticed."

She nodded and asked him, "Perhaps you should talk to Charles Obenta, he is a good man, is he not?"

"They are his cousins. Perhaps they don't work against him. Perhaps they work together and then where will I be?" Joseph replied. He and the people of the village knew about the interplay between powerful people that threatened their investment, but did not understand who was on their side.

The greed that had somehow grown strong in their community made Mma Kolwane sad. She sighed and nodded.

Joseph ate the hot meal she made for him, packed his few possessions and left.

He walked out westward toward a third well-sheltered cave on the side of a kopje, that he knew of. It was small, and enclosed enough to be safe from marauding animals and big enough to be easily checked for unwelcome guests such as snakes.

That evening he selected a comfortable raised place to sleep, made a small sheltered fire to keep unwelcome guests away, before he lay down, to fall into a restless sleep.

A visitor arrived at the Kolwane's at about the same time as Joseph was falling asleep.

Mma Kolwane showed him into the lounge area.

"Good evening Rra Obenta. This is a great surprise," her husband said.

"Good evening my good friend. I am sorry to bother you but I had heard that you had a boy staying with you?"

"We did indeed, he left today. Did you know him?"

"No, no I just like to keep myself in the picture about these things, you know."

Mma Kolwane thanked the great god of all and his son Jesus for the intuitive decision she and Joseph had made.

"Has the boy gone home?"

"We believe so," answered her husband.

"And where is that?"

"On a farm where my cousin once worked, I can't tell you exactly where, he came at the request of my cousin."

"Would I perhaps know this cousin?"

"I'm surprised at your questions," answered her husband. "Why this great interest in an orphan boy. Did he do something wrong?"

"No, no. Just curiosity, I'd been told you had a visitor who seldom speaks to anyone, and I was curious. I'm looking for a runaway boy from another village. I'll leave you in peace now my friend," he said and turned to leave.

He walked down the path deciding that the boy who had stayed with the Kolwanes was just another lost child of Africa, as they had said he was.

Joseph woke the next morning, and continued his march toward the desert, where he knew another tribe of Bushmen lived, having decided that a return to the tribe he was related to would put them at risk.

The journey into the Kalahari was slow. He walked steadily through the days, convincing himself as he trudged further into the dry country, that life on a remote farm would produce a potential to buy his own cattle. So that eventually, after the herd had expanded, one at a time, and with their offspring, his herd would provide him with his own wealth. He thought briefly of the money hidden in the cave. It would be a good start to his venture, but he felt firmly and sadly that it could never be his to use.

Even so he knew somehow he would be a farmer in his own right.

Each night along the way he fell asleep exhausted, after finding a sheltered spot, holding firm to his dream.

42

Stress, heat, the strong smell of Africa, and of aircraft fuel, were making James de Bruin feel dizzy as he disembarked at Ngami the next day.

He had visited the clinic where is brother was recuperating on the way to Ngami and had shown Ben the results he had collected from the laboratory.

It had seemed for a moment, during the visit, that Ben was on the verge of being able to remember what the results represented, but then he could not recall the vital information. He did however confirm that the reports from Jordaan showed the deposit was valuable, that the ore did contain bigger percentages of platinum and gold than the one the company was mining and it would be easier to smelt. Exciting news if only it could have been followed through to a claim. They discussed Ben's release from the clinic and decided he would be safer there while he underwent intensive physiotherapy sessions.

James carried his overnight bag through customs to the car hire desk. His personal assistant had arranged a four-wheel drive and he drove straight to the hotel, where he completed the arrival documentation and was given his room key.

His assistant had arranged a room next to Peter's.

He parked the hired vehicle as near to the room as he could, went inside, and unpacked. It was early in the afternoon and he decided to wait until Peter got back to the hotel to speak to him.

When he heard Peter's door open and close, James stepped quietly into the passage, went to Peter's room and knocked softly.

Peter opened the door.

James held his finger to his lips, feeling silly. Then led the puzzled consultant toward the Land Cruiser, telling him as they walked about the laboratory results.

"So Andselc, at least, know about the samples. The question is, I suppose, who else does?"

"If we could find the boy, and Ben's notes it would mean we could locate and claim the ore."

"Perhaps the security company is making sure you're not trying to do what you suspect someone else of doing? They are responsible for that sort of protection aren't they?"

"Afraid we would claim the other ore body on our own? Of course they would not take chances on that sort of thing. It's a possibility, but I don't think so."

"So the results are good?"

"They are. They mention platinum and gold in larger percentages than they are in the existing mine, which would mean the ore body is a lot more valuable than the one we are mining."

"If Andselc Security said that the samples belong to the joint venture, isn't that enough to allow you to claim the ore for Ngami?"

"I think we can be sure at this stage, that someone involved with Andselc, is planning to use the information to claim the ore in some way outside of the partnership."

"It surely isn't looking too good."

"No, I'm afraid not. How are the production improvements going?"

Peter gave him a summary of where they had managed to get with the preparation work for the shutdown.

"That sounds okay Peter."

The next morning Peter was given an urgent message to contact Heldebron's personal assistant.

He drove straight to the general manager's office.

Marie, the unhappy assistant to the general manager, met Peter in the passage way as he walked toward the general manager's office looking worried.

"What is it?" Peter asked.

"Apparently one of your children has been hurt in an accident."

Peter called Christine in Australia from Marie's phone.

She answered that their youngest child was in hospital in a serious but stable condition.

"What happened?" he asked.

She explained that, on their way to the supermarket, a car had hit the boy as he crossed the road. "It was in the car park. Someone accelerated as we were walking away from where we had left the car. They didn't stop. I think it was deliberate Peter."

"Did you get the license plate of the car that did it?"

"I hardly thought about the car, I was so worried about Nicholas."

Peter said he would get there as soon as he could.

Marie booked flights to Sydney and Peter phoned de Bruin, Baker and Ed on the way to the airport and explained what had happened.

James de Bruin could not believe the finality of the news, first Rebecca now Peter. He just could not deal with the forces at work in Ngami. He went to see Charles Obenta, simply to have someone to talk to, about what amounted to the failure of the project.

After a brief discussion about their options they called Ed.

He met them at the hotel.

"So what can we do Ed?" James de Bruin asked.

Ed said that he could not think of any way to replace Peter. "Perhaps Stone could be made more effective as engineering manager.

"Isn't Stone too marginalized?" asked Charles.

"Peter seems to have been working with him," said Ed.

"In my estimation, based on the opinions of the many people I talk to, Peter is irreplaceable," answered Charles.

43

James left Charles at the hotel and went for a drive to the river. He parked between the trees, on the firm part of the bank, and stayed in the vehicle, not feeling like going back to Ngami.

Looking almost unseeingly out of the vehicle's window he noticed that the repeated storms had provided enough water to create a flow in the normally dry channel. Watching the power of swirling brown stream, he took control of his desperation turning it to determination, to get through the seemingly impossible situation he now faced. There was one huge positive, the plant's production was holding at near design capacity, even if only by a thread; it proved that the target capability could be reached.

After his conversation with James and Charles, Ed had walked away from the two men, feeling most uncomfortable in himself. He could not see how they would survive.

Thinking about Peter, he decided to talk to his sister in Australia about the Connor family's plight, from the public phone in the hotel lobby. He told her that they were staying in a furnished apartment in the beachside suburb near where she lived and asked her if she could manage to go and see the family.

In reply to her questions, he said that he did not know what Peter was planning, but that he might not want to leave his family in Sydney on their own, so would probably not be too keen to return to Ngami.

"How do you want me to help them?" she asked.

"It might be easier for them if they knew someone there."

He then explained how Peter was not likely to return to Ngami if he thought his family was in danger.

"Would they be able to manage without him?"

"No, his failure to return would be the end of any chance they have of saving the project."

"I suppose some projects fail, don't they? You knew that all along Ed. That's why you went wasn't it? What's changed?"

"This is too bloody unjust. I find it hard to put into words, Rita. I like and admire both de Bruins, Obenta, and the Tswana who will lose out. I feel almost conscience bound to help them."

"I'll do what I can here, but be careful you don't get hurt in the process of trying to help them. You're normally so pragmatic. Lost causes have a way of drawing people down with them."

"I'll be careful."

Charles Obenta and James de Bruin met again at the hotel that evening. They realized that they would have to wait until they could talk to Peter about what he intended doing.

"We must do something about this ore body now though" said James.

"Yes, but what?"

"What about Marnie Stone, the geologist you said I should meet?" asked de Bruin. "Can we try talking to her? It might give us a better idea of what's going on."

They decided go to the Stone's house, and walked there along a common park and footpath. When they got there, Charles left James looking at an attractive part of the public gardens, went on his own to the Stone's and rang their doorbell.

Marnie Stone opened the door.

He asked her, quietly, if she could spare a few minutes to talk to them, away from the house.

Marnie looked at him oddly and walked into the garden with him.

He explained that his calls were being monitored. "I don't think they'll have any listening devices in your home but I think its safer to assume that there are."

Marnie would have believed anything about what she was convinced was a crooked set up, so she accepted his concerns without comment. Considering her state of mind, his arrival was almost as an answer to a prayer.

Marnie Stone was a very good geologist, with several international successes to her credit. Like many other experts recruited by Ngami, she had been treated like some form of intellectual fodder and had then been given a bureaucratic time filling role.

She knew her skills could have been used to improve the geological prospects for the company but, as far as she knew, she had not been able to get any part of them noticed by anyone who could or would do anything positive.

Her frustration had, coincidentally, been tested to its limit that afternoon.

She had tried, yet again, to get her thoughts about the ore reserves accepted by Bierman the chief geologist.

He had told her to get on with the database updating that she was supposed to be doing and leave the interpretation of the data to the man whose job it was to look at it.

"He could not interpret that data in a life time," she had replied.

"Look love, if it's woman's lib you want, this isn't the place. Please do what you're asked to do or you won't even see the end of your contract."

She got out of the suffocating man's office and sat down in her cubicle and sat for at least fifteen minutes, with her eyes closed, to hold back her tears.

Marnie had grown up in Zimbabwe but her family was from England. Her first degree came from the University of the Witwatersrand and she also held a Doctorate in Philosophy from Cambridge. Her field experience was extensive and she had undertaken exploration work in many parts of the world.

Marnie's position at Ngami, in geology, involved work on logging the Ngami drilling programs and, although repetitive and boring, it gave her a clear picture of the area's geology and capabilities. Ngami's exploration program was concentrated to the southwest of the existing mine, but her experience had shown the same as Ed's investigation, that the northeast offered a much better potential.

Charles asked her if she could meet him and de Bruin outside the recreation club to talk to them about the geological program. She said she would be there in a few minutes.

Craig asked who had been at the door and Marnie, now worried about the possibility of being listened to, mumbled an answer. She then went into the kitchen, put some cups out for tea before walking back into the lounge and saying. "Craig I feel like a walk, will you come with me?"

"Ah, I'm tired. I don't feel like it," he answered.

"Don't be like that, come on, let's walk," she said pulling him out of his chair.

She remembered, as she did so, how she and Craig had met in Zambia, on the copper belt, which lies in a beautiful part of the Central African highlands.

Marnie had been, and still was, a keen golfer. She had been more reserved than most women of her age and perhaps a little old fashioned.

Their first meeting had been dreamlike. One Sunday morning Marnie had fallen and hurt her leg in front of Craig's room. She had been walking to the golf course, on a path through the staff quarters. Beautifully landscaped gardens, natural rock outcrops, man made hills and carefully mowed lawns had made these into something more like a resort than a company village.

Craig had almost tripped over her as he walked toward the canteen, not looking where he was going. He had been watching a tiny antelope, a duiker, daintily nibbling at something in the garden, as he walked.

The morning air was warm and sultry with a heady perfume from the many frangipanis's in the garden.

She had been crying and dabbing the wound with a bloody handkerchief.

Craig, a tall athletic man, helped Marnie into his room, where he washed the graze and bandaged it.

He, like Marnie, had been brought up in lonely spots and had lived a sheltered life.

Bandaging her leg made him feel terribly awkward and he fumbled.

Feeling his tension, Marnie laughed, through her tears, at his clumsiness and touched his shoulder gently as he knelt in front of her.

He looked into her tear filled eyes and the touch had grown more firm.

One thing had led to another, and they had spent that day and the rest of their lives together.

Marnie now feared that Ngami would turn even their once fairy tale relationship to dust. She spent a large amount of her time trying to help him. However bad her job was, his position as engineering manager was a nightmare.

The people working for Stone paid lip service to him and ran a variety of private schemes for self-enrichment in the background.

Craig had been virtually a broken man having given up hope of influencing or controlling anything. His days were spent in his office shut off from reality until the arrival of Peter Connor, whose use of Craig's considerable skills to help prepare for the shutdown had been an unbelievable relief to him. To him Peter's departure represented a return to black despair.

She eventually coaxed him out of his chair.

The Stones walked along the path past the tennis courts toward Charles Obenta and James de Bruin who were sitting at a picnic table.

The two men stood to greet them, trying to act as though the meeting was completely casual.

"Can we walk toward your house while we talk?" asked de Bruin.

They walked slowly as Charles asked Marnie if she could explain to de Bruin what she had told him about the exploration program.

Marnie told them about her attempts to persuade the chief geologist to change the exploration pattern, and that he had said she did not know what she was talking about. She also said that Willers had spent more time in the geological office than any of the field geologists; and that he regularly took data from the office, in his portable computer, in files, and as complete drawings.

"So you are seriously concerned about their objectives?"

"Definitely. Work in the area we are exploring at the moment is showing reserves at a greater depth than the current operations. Exploiting them will take time, a large amount of capital, and a considerable development effort."

"We overheard two Americans talking about prospecting, sounded like they were onto something in the northeast."

"Nothing they're doing is being recorded in our logs."

"That confirms the problem we face. What to do about it is another question," de Bruin said. "Having to purchase ore from someone else will mean that there is no hope of recovering the situation here, even if we manage to get the plant going. We have to locate the ore ourselves and I'd like you to help."

"I would very much like to, just let me know what you want."

"Thanks Marnie."

"Is the plant still going well?"

"For now it is but Peter has just left for Australia, because his child has been in an accident, so the shutdown is looking to be more uncertain."

"I can assure you that you won't keep the plant's production up without him. Each link in that shutdown plan has been developed by him, he must check the work before we start, or we might not even start up again, never mind reach full production," Craig Stone commented.

"But, we're managing now?"

"Production at the moment is being held by a series of temporary patches. They must be made more permanent, or we'll be off line again, with every chance of the failure being more serious than any we've had so far."

"I didn't know you had been involved Craig," said Charles.

"Oh yes it's the best period I've had since I started here, Peter has included me completely."

"Can you take over from him?"

"Only to an extent. He's very familiar with the plant and the people, my involvement only started once he was fully in control, in the last few weeks."

"Will he be back?" asked Marnie.

"We don't know."

"If he doesn't get back the shutdown and the recovery effort will fail," Craig answered."

"We need to try to secure the ore supply," said de Bruin.

"Just let me know what you want me to do to help you."

He thanked her and asked if she knew what procedure was used in claiming ore deposits.

She said that she was not certain but would check.

Craig Stone said he would send Peter a list of items he could not deal with on his own.

They parted near the Stone's house.

Back at the hotel Charles asked de Bruin what he was planning.

"I can't think of anything else to do. If Peter has gone, and with Rebecca out of the picture, I didn't know Stone had been included to such a big an extent, that's good news at least. How much help will Ed be?"

"Not much technically but he's a huge help with management. He doesn't know enough about the plant."

"Perhaps I should call a meeting and try to involve Michael Anders?"

"I don't know what you would say, and there's still the loss of management and technical skill that needs to be filled."

At the same time as the meeting between the partners and the Stones, Heldebron was receiving instructions to contact Ed to tell him that GVN would like to offer his company an interest in a venture in neighboring Zimbabwe but that they needed him there to finalize the deal.

Heldebron spoke to Ed the next morning and told him about the prospective joint venture.

Ed knew that this was exactly the sort of endeavor Genting Resources wanted him to negotiate, and he also realized that it would completely neutralize his interest in helping de Bruin and Obenta. At very least he would have no option about disclosing any information about the missing ore body if the suggested arrangement were to be accepted by his company.

Since there was an eight-hour difference between the time in Sydney and that in Botswana, he could not advise Genting of the offer until later. So he phoned Rita, his sister, a few hours after lunch, from the pay phone in the hotel's lobby. He explained that he wanted her to tell the managing director of Genting about his difficulties. They both knew him personally. "They need to be very careful about a joint venture with GVN or I'm afraid they might end up in the same awkward situation as de Bruin and the other people in a few years time. But, having said that, what GVN is offering is exactly what Genting is looking for. I must phone head office and tell them about the offer. All I can do is talk about the offer itself, because the phone lines here are insecure, but the worries I have in relation to the dishonesty of GVN need to be understood by Genting."

"I think I understand, I'll talk to him. So what are you doing now?"

"This is the call box in the hotel lobby, they don't monitor call boxes, but not talking to them about the Genting offer on the office telephone system will look too unusual."

"I'll call him but it sounds a bit crazy."

"I know but I have to tell them what's happening here."

Rita agreed.

Rita's call to Genting's managing director, who she knew socially, was not particularly helpful.

The information about the problems de Bruin, the Tswana and other shareholders were having with GVN, in Ngami, was enough to convince him that the company needed to know more about the proposed partnership, but not enough to put him off the idea.

He remained keen on an association with GVN.

Rita wondered if the fact that Ed's company was going to ally themselves with GVN meant that she should not be helping the family herself.

44

Joseph's second flight from Ngami had taken place at about the same time as Peter's departure, to try to help his family in Sydney.

As the small boy wandered, on the following days, he began to realize that he was lost. He could not find any sign of the other tribe of Bushmen.

He was dead tired, too tired to stop, too tired to carry on, and very frightened.

Fully aware of the dangers a small boy could run into on his own, he forced himself through his doubts trudging warily along yet another track.

Almost delirious, incapable of protecting himself, staggering along the road, he noticed lights of a vehicle coming from behind, lighting the sandy, unmaintained road. He didn't even try to hide, as he had been doing since leaving the village.

The vehicle slowed and stopped. A man leaned out of the window.

"Where are you headed young man?"

He wasn't quite sure himself anymore, but said firmly he was going to a farm on the edge of the Kalahari.

The man turned to the driver and said something then called to Joseph to climb on the back of what he could now see was a pickup truck.

"We'll take you to the cross roads ahead. It will shorten your journey," the man said.

Joseph, too tired to think, thanked him and climbed through the opening at the rear onto the tray; which was enclosed in mesh, as some pickups are, when they are used for transporting articles that might fly away or escape. He barely noticed that the door to the back was tied open as he climbed in.

He found some sacks, near the cab end, and sat on them with his back against the cab.

The truck pulled away, and Joseph, relieved to be off his feet, hardly bothered about the discomfort of the ride on the rough road. He started to doze within minutes.

He woke to find the truck stopped, and then he heard the sound of a lock closing.

He scrambled to the enclosing cage's door and found it closed and locked.

He called out and was ignored, realizing that he was a prisoner, he panicked and shook, and shook the door, his mind filled with the stories he had heard about children being captured and meeting terrible fates; such as being sold to witch doctors for cutting up; to be used as 'muti', to provide magical protections.

No one seemed to care about the noise he made, so he stopped trying to attract attention.

The truck moved off.

He tried to calm down and think his way through his kidnapping. Although he had always been aware that witchcraft was practised, even in his home village in modern Botswana, this was his first direct experience of the danger it represented.

It was still dark, but the dawn's light was appearing in the East and he realized that the vehicle was now pointed back toward where he'd come from.

Joseph shivered in the morning cold.

He went back to his place on the sacks, sank into a fetal position and cried until his face was wet with tears. Eventually he fell asleep again.

An hour or so later, the sun was nearly up and the truck began slowing.

Joseph looked around to see where he was, and recognized the place. They were entering Ngami through the worst part of town. His heart froze. His fears grew stronger as he remembered that this was where several witch doctors practised.

The road was particularly bumpy and Joseph tumbled around in the back of the truck. At times he had to hang onto the tray and screen to keep his balance. He rearranged the bed of sacks into the corner so that he could hold onto the screen and his hand touched something hard. He caught his breath and pulled a small trenching tool from between the sacks and imagined with horror what it could have been used for, but it provided him with a spark of hope. He concealed the tool under his loose clothing and thought he could probably keep it out of the sight of his captors if he hunched forward.

The truck stopped a few minutes later and the men came to the back door to collect Joseph. The driver unlocked the door and said. "Get out, you," as though talking to a dog.

Joseph closed his eyes and lay still, feigning unconsciousness.

"The idiot's knocked out," said the driver and clambered into the tray to drag Joseph out.

The small boy pretended to be groggy and started to scramble forward awkwardly as though he was regaining consciousness, away from the driver and out of the storage compartment.

The driver, behind him, pushed him and the other man reached up to pull him down, holding his tattered coat firmly to stop him running.

As the man turned and lowered the boy onto the road, Joseph managed to find a foothold, and swing the trenching tool. He hit the man's shin with its edge, hard.

The man screamed and his grip faltered.

Joseph pulled free and ran down an alleyway toward the bush dividing the old and new villages.

The driver jumped down awkwardly from the confined space, and followed him.

The other man was in terrible pain and could barely walk.

The driver closed the gap between him and Joseph and reached out to grip Joseph's coat.

Joseph sidestepped and swung the tool again, upward like a cricket bat with both hands and hit the man's jaw.

The driver cried out and fell, his face bleeding.

Joseph ran on until he was in the part of the village where the senior company officials lived. He found a hiding place in the foliage of a thick hedge surrounding one of these.

He hoped, as he squirreled out of sight, he would not disturb the house's occupants, if there were any. The company houses for senior employees were sometimes left empty for weeks at a time. He eventually drifted into a restless sleep.

Joseph woke, with filtered rays of the morning sun warming him, to look around the biggish garden.

Seeing no one, he was about to slip away, to take cover in the cave when he was stopped by a question from a woman who seemed to appear form nowhere.

"Are you looking for something?" she asked, sounding a bit frightened but quite friendly.

His first instinct was to run, but the tone of her voice was so gentle that he turned to face her instead.

He saw a lady with a small child and thought quickly. He could not afford to have her call the police so he had to say something.

"Me want job," he said awkwardly.

"Who are you?" the lady asked.

"Me Joseph, work hard."

"Okay Joseph, I'll think about it, but as you can see my garden is just fine. I've already got two people working here."

Seeing his disappointed look she added, "Can you come back tomorrow morning and I'm sure we can find something for you to do?"

Claire Halliday thought the boy looked more ragged than most urchins in the village and thought she might be able to at least help him, perhaps with old clothes and some food, but wanted to ask Brett if it would be okay to do so.

Joseph walked firmly away and back to Mma Kolwane's house.

She was shocked by the state of the boy. "Joseph, what's happened?"

He explained, trying not to cry.

She told him about the visit they had had from the powerful cousin of Charles Obenta.

"I just don't know what to do." Joseph said still trying to hold back his tears.

"Perhaps you should see Charles Obenta himself."

"Will he believe me?"

"I don't know Joseph. Go and have a bath now and I will wash your clothes for you," she said kindly.

Her husband, who had heard her talking to the boy, asked what she was going to do.

"The poor boy, we can't send him away."

"They will finish us and him if he stays," he answered sadly. "We should really report his presence to that criminal who is Charles' cousin."

"Perhaps talk to Charles?"

"He won't be able to help us, they are too clever for him."

Joseph left at dusk to spend the night in the cave where the knife, diary and money were hidden. He wrestled with the idea of trying for the job with the woman he had met. He eventually decided that he would be too exposed if he returned and she checked on his background. He had no idea what to do and fell asleep praying, to the God of all, to allow him to find some peace.

He managed his forced return to Ngami by calling on Mma Kolwane every second day or so, after dark.

She allowed him to bathe at their house and gave him food items he could not find in the bush.

45

At Kingsford Smith Airport, Sydney, Australia, after a seemingly endless wait, Christine Connor awkwardly greeted Peter.

He looked as pleased to see her as she felt herself.

Their time apart faded and they slipped into each other's arms as they had done when they first kissed in the warmth of the sun and dry veldt. It was as though there had been no time in between.

"Is Daddy coming home forever?" asked Laura from the sideline.

Christine looked at her, and said, "We hope so love."

The delight of the children was best expressed by Desmond's leap into his father's arms.

Christine told him about the accident and about a second incident, when the children were out of hearing. She explained that Laura's teacher had called and asked her to collect the little girl because she had become hysterical in the playground, something about a man pointing at her through the fence.

"That's terrible, and you came here to avoid violence."

She started to cry, great wrenching sobs.

Peter felt crushed, he didn't know how to deal with this pain and the fact that the partners were relying so heavily on him.

After leaving the airport they went to see Nicholas in hospital. He had been badly bruised and had several unpleasant grazes, but luckily no bones had been broken.

His delight at seeing his father was limited by his injuries, but he expressed it as clearly as had the other children.

The doctor said that he was satisfied that Nicholas' injuries were largely superficial and healing well. He agreed that the boy could be discharged from the hospital.

They packed his books, and gifts they had brought him, left the hospital, and returned to the apartment Christine had rented.

The apartment was old and bordering on shabby, but had a restricted view of the Manly Ferry wharf and of the headlands that protect the harbor from the open sea.

When they had unpacked Peter walked through the apartment, out onto the veranda. "Nice view," he said as Christine joined him.

"Yes, fantastic, that's the ferry wharf for the Manly to Circular Quay service."

As they watched, a ferry started its journey back to the city, its powerful twin diesels churning up the sea in the cove. They heard the huge catamaran's engine crackle as it accelerated away from the pier, leaving a wide foaming wake.

"This is a good spot isn't it?"

"It sure is, nothing like anywhere I've ever been. Why don't we go for a walk and have lunch at the beach? Is there somewhere that we can eat?"

"Yes, there are quite a few places where you can buy takeaways and some good restaurants at the ferry wharf."

As they walked, their conversation came around to the most important issue facing them, their future.

"I don't know what to do," said Peter in answer to Christine's hesitant enquiry into what he was planning.

At the same time, instructions were being given to McTuffin, the driver of the car that had injured Nicholas, about the next course of action he should take, to make sure Peter was kept away from Ngami. The person at the other end of the line addressed him with a strong South African accent saying, "Forget the family for now, we need to stop Peter Connor getting back here and stopping him must be an accident. We can't have any speculation in the newspapers."

McTuffin replied that he would be careful to deal with Peter in a way that would clearly be seen as an accident.

"If he's going to head back to Ngami it will be soon, so you don't have much time."

Peter explained the desperate situation in Ngami to Christine; about the involvement of GVN, and the difficulties de Bruin and Obenta faced, adding, "Whatever, or whoever it is that they're dealing with is almost certainly linked to Nicholas' injury, and the incident with Laura. Yet if I don't go back the failure will bankrupt the partners, other than GVN of course."

"A big company like GVN wouldn't be involved with threatening children, surely? It might just have been some lunatic."

"I wish that were true but I've had three attempts on my life, a man is dead and one of the partners just barely survived. I think this must be treated as a deliberate effort to get me off the site."

Her face went white. "Three attempts to kill you? What are the police doing?"

"One was sort of a car jacking, once I was shot at and very slightly wounded, we didn't think the police would help and then someone tried to push me off a platform. The police would have had to shut the plant, potentially destroying the project, so we didn't report any one of the incidents."

"Peter what on earth are you involved in?"

"More money is involved than you would believe."

"Surely it's not being done by GVN itself?" she had worked part time for GVN when she was studying for her degree, in the company's head office, and had been very happy there.

"No, it seems impossible. I don't know who's behind what's going on. It is deadly serious though, and must involve an organization of some sort."

"It's like a bad movie or dream, but if so much depends on your contribution, it would be quite wrong for you to leave them now."

"I've been trying to work out what we could do and I think the only way that I could go back would be if you and the kids would come with me."

"Well, if you're the only hope they've got, that's what we'll do. Where would we stay? And it's going to cost a lot."

"The company has houses in Ngami but I don't know if we could just turn up there."

"Perhaps I could stay with the Lavers in Hout Bay, they've offered to have us there often enough?"

"I don't know. All your dreams would be shattered and what will we do after the work in Ngami. No. I think we need to be a bit careful. This country is very impressive. If I just tell them I'm not able to go back they will have to accept that."

"We must decide soon."

They walked in silence for a while, along the beach, and the years of stress began to slip away. They felt closer and happier than either of them had for years.

By the time they returned to the apartment they were all tired.

Peter sighed and collapsed on the couch.

Christine sat next to him leaning her head on his shoulder.

"I'll make tea mom," said Laura.

"Thanks my big girl."

Peter opened his laptop and checked his email to find a message from Craig Stone giving him the engineering manager's perspective of the hopelessness of the Ngami situation.

He showed it to Christine.

"They really seem to need your help," she said after reading it.

46

Rita, Ed Chalmers' sister, phoned the Connors as Ed had asked her to do and invited them to dinner, "I'll fetch you," she finished.

"Thanks," Peter replied, "but we can drive."

"You'll have trouble with parking, I'll collect you."

She asked about the attack on the child after she arrived.

When Christine finished her story, Rita said, "Good grief! I've never met an adult who was being threatened like this before, never mind a child. It's like some horrible newspaper story."

"So you can see I just can't go back to Southern Africa and leave them here," Peter said.

"Of course not, even if it's just a deranged person," Rita answered, thinking that this course of action would be very much in the interest of someone who was deliberately and dishonestly trying to close the Ngami project.

As they left, Laura started screaming and pointed to a grey Ford on the other side of the road, "That's him mommy, that's the man from the school."

Peter ran toward the car.

It shot forward, straight at Peter, who just managed to jump clear.

They put the children into Rita's car and closed the doors.

Rita telephoned the police and gave them the Ford's number plate.

After a few moments delay, the police officer told her that the number she had given them belonged to a car that had been scrapped.

Since both she and Christine had noted the number she checked that the number she had given to the officer was correct and it was.

"This obviously isn't someone with problems, Peter. The latest model Ford with false number plates means there is at least some organization involved," Rita said after she finished the call to the police.

Peter was silent as they drove to Rita's apartment.

Rita said, "Ed says that the plant won't work if you don't go back. I can't see how you can sit here frightened like this either, though, no matter what the source of the fear is."

"If I make it clear that I'm not going back I won't be any threat."

"I suppose that's true, but you don't know that, and more seriously neither do they."

Peter used his laptop to check the flight availability to Johannesburg and found the earliest they could go would be Tuesday evening.

Rita got them drinks and offered them the food she had prepared. Her phone rang as they sat enjoying her culinary skills.

It was Ed.

She walked into her bedroom as she spoke. "Ed, this looks very bad, almost like an organized terror campaign against these people."

"What makes you say that?" Ed asked.

She explained what had happened to the children and about the car with false number plates.

"What did the MD say?"

"He listened to what I had to say and decided to send a request for more information about the difficulties de Bruin is having. I tried to explain what you were worried about, but I don't think he really understood."

"If that's the case I have to do whatever they want me to do. Can I speak to Peter?"

Ed told Peter that GVN had asked Genting if they were interested in a joint exploration venture.

"In Botswana?"

"No, its for work they anticipate doing in Zimbabwe."

"So they want you to leave Ngami?"

"Not permanently, just do some geological investigations, but it will clearly exclude me from having anything more to do with de Bruin's geological problems. And it certainly looks as though what's happened to your kids might be a way of keeping you there."

"I think that's the reason for the attacks."

"What are you going to do?"

"If I stay here the de Bruins and Obenta are finished. I just don't know. I've checked the airlines, we can get on a plane on Tuesday evening."

"You're going to have to be very careful in the mean time. Anyhow I'd better be going, I'll phone you again," he said, and after a moment's hesitation continued,

"You know Peter there's a conference in Melbourne on Monday that I've been booked to attend for months now, perhaps you could go in my place, take a trip down there with your family. If you're going to be heading back you'll have to assume they're going to try to stop you. Going to Melbourne will make it more difficult for them to surprise you and it will keep you off the streets in Sydney."

"That's not a bad idea, will I be able to just turn up?"

"I'll phone them early on Monday and tell them you're taking my place."

"That's great thanks."

"Moving targets are still targets Peter. If they think there's a chance of your going back you will surely be in danger."

"I know, we'll be careful."

Peter told Christine and Rita about the conference, holding Christine's gaze, questioningly. She nodded her head firmly, "I think we should go," she said.

"Good."

They drank their coffees and spoke about what they could do while they were in Melbourne.

Peter emailed de Bruin and explained his situation.

De Bruin replied that he could arrange a company house in the Ngami village and that Peter would be authorized to charge the travel expenses to Ngami. He told Peter to book flights to Ngami, so as not to lose the time slot and then make up his mind what he wanted to do.

Peter sent another email suggesting that whatever he did it would be a good idea to delay the start of the shut down.

De Bruin agreed. His email concluded with a strong suggestion that Peter should consider his family before the problems of Ngami. He suggested that Peter's safest path would be to publicly declare that he would not be returning to Ngami.

Peter went to the kitchen where Rita and Christine were talking and showed them the email.

"So he's saying he cares more about us than his family's fortune?"

"Bit hard to believe but he is definitely a good bloke.'

Rita suggested that they should spend the night.

They left from her secure underground car park, for Melbourne, as the sun was coming up, driving a powerful V8 that Rita had arranged.

Their journey took them over the Spit Bridge; past the many yachts and cruisers that line the shores of the bay, past exciting looking restaurants, yachts, motor cruisers and brokerages.

47

Christine and the children parted from Peter outside the Melbourne conference center, which was located a short distance from their hotel. She walked to the tram stop to take the red tram to the Queen Victoria market, for a morning's shopping, and then attend a concert at the South Bank entertainment center.

Peter got to the conference as close to the official starting time as he could.

The venue was well attended so he felt reasonably secure.

Shortly after he registered, McTuffin was given his location and flew to Melbourne, planning possible 'accidents'.

He found the conference, run by the Productivity Commission, to be well worth his time. The economic model under discussion had been developed by one of Melbourne's prestigious universities to evaluate economic aspects of the industry concerned. It considered the relative efficiencies of the industry's efforts using reports from local and international consultants.

Several people contributed a freshness to the discussion that was as surprising to Peter as was the contention.

Productivity of people in the industry was compared to productivity in the United States and Peter noticed some surprising contradictions. The contrasts led him to wonder about this aspect of Australia's apparent brilliant future. It seemed at times to skirt the obvious, and the extreme antagonism displayed by some of the participants toward 'the workers' was hard to understand. It far exceeded anything he had ever seen in Africa. He would have liked to question some conclusions, but decided that an issue, as important as this seemed, did not warrant casual observations.

Ed had asked him if he would summarize the proceedings, and Peter made notes throughout the discussions, covering the facts as he found them. Conclusions would be a separate exercise.

That afternoon, after leaving the venue, he met Christine in a coffee shop located in the huge enclosed plaza of their hotel. They had two very good cups of coffee each and the children enjoyed their milkshakes.

Christine remarked on the impressive development; its scale, quality and appearance.

Peter agreed and asked how her day had been.

She described the markets in glowing detail saying that they were attractive, interesting and provided some very good value; then went on to explain how she and the children had spent time at a concert.

"It sure is a country with more aspects than I expected," said Peter.

They then retrieved their baggage and booked out of the hotel.

McTuffin had acquired a high performance, heavy vehicle during the day.

He and an associate were watching the Connor's every move.

When he reported to Andselc in South Africa as the Connors sat in the piazza, he was told, again, to make sure that he stopped Peter, but that it must be seen as an accident.

As he finished the call, the Connors walked out from the hotel, closely followed by McTuffin's associate, to retrieve their car from a valet.

The man moved quickly to the side of the vehicle and placed a homing device under the fender.

The two men then followed the Connors on their way out of the city.

Traffic was heavy and McTuffin lost sight of the family on a one-way street. A large truck had dragged a smaller one from an intersection, and across the one-way road into several cars, effectively blocking the road.

They had no choice but to wait for the road to be cleared and sat helplessly until the problem was resolved. The incident delayed them for more than twenty minutes.

Three and a half hours after leaving the center of Melbourne the Connors arrived in Albury.

McTuffin had closed the gap and was not far behind. He had picked up the signal from the homing device shortly before the Connors reached Albury-Wodonga .

It still being light, the family decided to explore a park they found on the way into Albury, next to the Murray River.

They found a small sandy road leading to the river's edge, followed it and pulled to a stop in a quiet spot near the northern bank of the river.

The sun was setting and Christine remarked, as they were getting out of the car, that the tranquil scene would have made a good painting.

The river current was clearly strong, despite the dry conditions.

McTuffin was approaching Wangaratta, the town before Albury Wodonga.

Christine suggested that it was being fed at a constant rate. "Lake Hume is shown on the map as upstream here, and it's quite famous for its irrigation capacity, perhaps water is taken off for irrigation downstream somewhere?"

He nodded and they walked along the course, with the children, who were throwing sticks into the dark, deep stream and followed them as they floated away.

Although their stick throwing game seemed fun, Peter decided to warn them back from the bank's edge, formed out of dark black clayey earth. The current seemed easily strong enough to sweep a child away. He asked them to move up toward the park.

The children listened cheerfully and went to the park's swings.

Peter and Christine spoke quietly about the trip ahead and the possibility of returning to the hope that Australia represented as the children played happily.

After a few moments of silence, Christine said. "We should get to the hotel."

"Yes, I'd just like to wander on a bit further down the river if you don't mind watching the kids?" he said.

"Always got to go a step further?"

He smiled, shrugged and walked a few hundred meters downstream after she had turned back toward their vehicle.

The pathway continued, closer to the river, with its steep bank overhanging the dark threatening current. Eventually Peter could go no further, finding that willows, growing up to the water's edge prevented further progress. The place looked like it was used as a fishing spot.

The sun slipped slowly behind the hills as Peter stood and dreamed. It reddened the bank where he stood.

The Victorian side of the river faded into darkness, as the sun's last rays sparkled through the sweeping willow branches.

High above, the clouds looked like candy floss, waves of pink, red and mauve.

He turned and strolled back, as the sun set.

He arrived back where he'd left Christine in the dusk.

She and the children were nowhere to be seen.

He quickened his pace and walked upstream toward a sporting complex, but could not find them, thinking, panic stricken, that they could not possibly have been swept away, he would have heard something.

He called Christine.

Nothing.

A cold fear gripped him. He ran up the river to where the road crossed the Murray. There was no sign of them.

Walking downstream again, terrified, he noticed there were children in a bigger playground further back from the river. He hopefully went toward the entrance, and with immense relief saw Christine and the children coming out of the main gate.

The children ran to him with Nicholas calling, "Daddy, Daddy where have you been we were getting worried?"

He surprised them with the warmth of his welcome, hugging each in turn, biting back the angry, irrational criticism he felt like leveling at Christine for walking away from where he'd left them.

They made their way back to the station wagon and drove to the same hotel they had stayed at on the way to Melbourne.

McTuffin and his associate arrived as they pulled out onto the road. He followed them and stopped outside the hotel parking ground while they went into the hotel, and waited there to make sure they stayed, and then called in to report that he would finish the family off the next day.

Early the next morning he followed the Connors out of Albury.

An hour after they set out, the weather changed. A storm broke, with a downpour that seemed to be enough to flood the relatively flat countryside. The bank of storm clouds spread out at the same speed as the car, in the direction they were traveling, looking like a nuclear bomb blast.

At a point he had decided on, based on his knowledge of the area, McTuffin brought his heavy four-wheel drive parallel to the Connor's vehicle and began forcing it left toward a gorge, that he knew was ahead.

Peter saw the vehicle coming at them out of the corner of his eye and reacted instinctively to the danger.

He became a part of the powerful vehicle, realizing that if he braked, or swerved left, he would go into the gorge. The heavy four-wheel drive was pulling in front of the station wagon to prevent him from going right or straight ahead.

He tried braking, briefly, sharply, but McTuffin stayed with him, driving them toward disaster.

Peter changed gear to get the engine at its maximum torque point and then accelerated, applying the vehicle's full power while swerving sharply left.

They shot forward to the left and then Peter pulled sharply right.

The V8 roared and they cleared the front of the heavier vehicle.

McTuffin could not ram the side of the station wagon because the four-wheel drive was not fast enough. He lost control and slammed into the concrete drain. Unhurt, he tried to pull away, but the vehicle was caught on something. He cursed and they got out to find that it had come to a rest on its differential and the fuel tank.

Peter, looking back through the wing mirror, saw McTuffin come to a stop through a break in the rain.

He breathed deeply, and drove on toward Sydney at speeds far greater than the limit.

"Wow Dad, where did you learn to drive like that," asked Desmond.

Christine told him to be quiet.

Peter phoned the police and explained that someone had tried to force them off the road and had ended up on the embankment.

They asked if anyone was hurt.

"I don't think so. They were trying to force me off the road, I was afraid to stop."

The police, after taking his number and license details thanked him for reporting the incident.

"Well, we have to decide whether to go to Botswana," Peter said.

"I think we should go," Christine replied, "These people should not be allowed to threaten anyone like they are doing. And anyhow what guarantee will there be that nothing else will happen."

"So we'll go?"

"Yes."

The Ngami shutdown had been delayed to the following week, as Peter had suggested, and James de Bruin was ready for Peter's return.

Once he was sure of the organizational efforts on site James returned to Johannesburg and went to talk to his brother.

Ben's memory was still a problem.

They discussed the progress that Peter's return promised.

"Thank goodness he's agreed to come back. It puts a hell of a responsibility on us to look after him though," said Ben, "How is the morale with the replacement for he woman from Binnett?"

"Ed Chalmers is managing but there's still the cynicism."

"It's a pity we lost her."

"It is, but we can only take things in stages, if the shutdown is handled as it now seems it certainly will be, we'll get both the furnace and water under better control," said James.

"The ore reserves are a desperate worry. I must get back there. If only my bloody head would work properly."

The Connors were booked on an evening flight and decided to spend the time that they had available within the security of the airport. They dropped their vehicle at the agency and did not feel safe until they had passed through customs.

48

Peter, Christine and the three children arrived at Ngami airport, as Joseph was standing in the bush nearest the near the arrivals area of the Ngami airport, dreaming of flying away to his pretend world. He had heard that Peter was coming back.

He was wondering if he should talk to Peter Connor who he knew was working with Ben de Bruin. He had heard Mr Kolwane talk of this the previous evening.

Whittling a stick into a walking cane, sadly thinking of the impossibility of his existence, "How long can this go on for?" Joseph wondered. He couldn't hide forever, having to keep out of the way of the people of the village was becoming a nightmare. He would have to get right away again, unless perhaps if he could perhaps return the diary, to the right person, his life might become more normal. Although he knew that Peter had been working with Ben de Bruin and Charles Obenta, for the improvement of the smelter, he did not understand the relationships between them. He just could not decide if it would be safe to approach anyone. He wished he had someone to advise him, he felt so lost and lonely. He sighed and irritably kicked a stone aside.

That evening, when Joseph went to the Kolwane's, he heard that the Connors had been given one of the senior official's houses.

Normally the quietest person there, he hesitantly interrupted, to ask where their house would be.

Mr. Kolwane's work related to housing so he knew where that house was, he told Joseph and asked, "Why do you want to know Joseph?"

Joseph said he had just wondered out of curiosity.

Mr Kolwane nodded and went on to talk about the reviving hopes for the project.

Joseph returned that evening to his sheltered spot, lit a small fire and lay down in his dusty blankets but could not sleep. What point was there to his life? Nothing was going to improve with this hiding, but, how to get above it? He grew ever more restless. He did not want a life as a hermit. It was so cold at night, he longed for a place of his own. If only he got a small job, with people who knew nothing of those who might still want to hurt him, he would perhaps be safe.

The next morning he went to look at the house the Connors had been given. Staying out of sight he saw that the garden was a mess. He wondered if he could get a job to clean it, and hoped, a hope that was more of a prayer, that the Connors would not have had time to worry about their garden. He watched, under the shade of a tree in the garden, out of sight of the road, until he saw Christine come out of the house to go to the shops.

He stepped out hesitantly and said, "Mma, me want job."

"Who are you?" Christine asked nervously.

"Me Joseph, I work very hard. Very busy, no time."

There was something appealing about the boy's proud stance and obvious awkwardness. "How much pay do you expect," she asked.

Joseph had no idea. "Don't know, you say," he replied.

She smiled. "Okay Joseph, let's give it a try. I'll find out from Charles Obenta what you should earn. Is that okay?"

"No asking please Mma," Joseph beamed, "Thank you Mma. I work hard."

Christine was slightly overwhelmed by the look of relief on the small boy's face, "I really should ask," she said.

"No please Mma."

"Why Joseph?"

He showed her the healed scar on his head.

"Charles did that?"

He shook his head and said, "Not know for surely, Mma."

Christine thought about the idea and decided to give the boy a chance. She had found a rake and a broom, left there by the previous occupants of the house, in the tool shed at the back of the house, and took Joseph to show him the tools.

Joseph thought for a moment and asked, "Where?" he said, indicating he needed a digging tool by miming a digging motion.

"I haven't got one," she said. "We'll buy one and you tidy the garden while we're gone." She said and made a sweeping motion.

Joseph nodded solemnly, took the broom awkwardly, not wanting to admit he had not used one before.

The guard who had been allocated the task of looking after Christine and the children had decided he should double check what was happening, and came across to them at that moment.

Joseph nearly ran but managed, with great effort to stay calm.

The guard asked if she needed help and Christine told him she was fine, that Joseph was going to do some gardening for them.

This was a common practice, and was accepted without comment, the man smiled and wandered back to the shady spot at the side of the house where he had been sitting.

An hour or so later Christine went to town accompanied by her children and the guard.

When she returned every loose leaf and stick had been removed and the entire garden seemed to have been swept or raked or both.

She showed Joseph the fork and spade she had bought.

He asked where she wanted him to dig.

She showed him the derelict vegetable garden.

That afternoon as she prepared the evening meal, Christine watched as he worked away at he barren patch, having some advice given to him, on digging, by the guard.

The vegetable garden was looking like a working operation by five, and she went out to tell Joseph that he could pack up and go home.

Joseph, by then, was feeling exhausted but managed a polite thank you.

She asked him to come again, at eight in the morning, and paid him what she had been told by someone in the shops would be a normal day's pay.

"Thank you Mma. I see you in morning," he said and walked off, trying not to seem too tired and sore.

Peter got home to find a strikingly more tidy garden and asked Christine how she had managed to clean it up so quickly.

"I've had the strangest day. A boy appeared from nowhere and asked if he could work in the garden. You can see the result. There's one thing though, he was desperate that we not tell Charles he was here when I explained that I was going to check."

"Perhaps he has a bad name?"

"I said we wouldn't talk to anyone."

"If he's got something to hide it's not going to be a good idea."

"He showed me a newish scar on his head, as though someone had beaten him."

"If you're happy, I suppose we can keep a close eye on him."

The next day Joseph asked if he might stay in the back room.

Christine, said she would think about the idea.

He tried to conceal his happiness by being very formal.

Christine knew the difficulties faced by African children, and resolved to find out about his schooling.

He was getting through the gardening at such a rate that it would hardly be enough work for a full day.

Perhaps, she thought, he could go to school with their children and asked him if he had ever been to school.

When she asked him, he pretended not to understand in case it was a reason not to keep him.

Joseph made friends with the children and, together, they started a project on the back veranda with Desmond's construction sets, and they managed to build a very reasonable set of structures in no time at all.

Christine noticed Joseph did much of the work, and wondered if it was a reflection of his intelligence.

49

On Monday, eight weeks after the World Bank meeting, the Ngami plant was shut down for a week of repairs.

Peter, with increasing help from Craig Stone, double-checked key aspects; Brett Halliday, Ed, and van Breda, each managed predefined aspects of the work.

On Tuesday, Ed found an email advising him that Wilson intended visiting the site to talk to him about the work GVN wanted to do with his company.

Anders had told the head of Binnett South Africa to get Ed to Zimbabwe to carry out the investigations they had discussed.

Binnett's South African principal arrived on Wednesday evening to discuss this with Ed.

Ed refused to go.

Wilson, unable to force the issue, said he would discuss the matter with the Binnett partners.

"Please yourself mate I don't work for them," said Ed.

Wilson, having no other business on site, left on the next flight and returned to Johannesburg, where he had a meeting with Jack Anders.

Anders contacted the managing director of the Ed's company about Ed's refusal to do the work in Zimbabwe.

Ed's managing director listened with some curiosity. A very accomplished operator himself, who could hold his own at any level, found the complaint odd to say the least. He said he would talk to Ed and, remembering Rita's warning, about GVN, decided to leave the issue to cool.

On Friday evening Whitehead, the smelter maintenance superintendent, phoned Brett to say that they had reached a breaking point in the critical drier area.

Brett arranged for Peter and Craig Stone to meet Whitehead.

They met him in a grassed area, at a table shaded by some of the only trees in the enclosure.

Peter asked what was wrong.

"I can't get them to do a lengthy exercise that will correct the drier head problem and they won't talk to me."

"What's the reason they gave you?" asked Craig Stone.

"I've tried to find out, and nothing I say seems to get through. They are on the edge of giving up. I don't think they're going to be any more keen on your involvement Craig, they see you as some kind of ivory tower puppet. Part of what is seen as the useless management."

"We still need to talk to them."

"I'm not going back there."

"Okay, perhaps that's better in the circumstances, thanks for letting us know. I'll go," said Craig.

"I'll go back to the control room," replied Whitehead.

As they got near the drier, there was a flare up between two of the men, one grabbing the arm of the other.

Peter stepped quickly forward to avoid an actual physical fight.

The men seemed partially relieved at the interruption and explained what was bothering them.

It turned out that the dispute was an ongoing one, related to family jealousies, apparently involving one of their supervisors. They said they would not talk to Whitehead because he was friendly with the supervisor concerned.

Craig Stone realized he could do something about the difficulty. He told them he would deal with the supervisor and let them know the result within the shift.

The problem was solved by transferring the problematic supervisor.

Craig got back to the group, in the large communal meal hall, during a break and told them what he had arranged.

The positive effect of his actions was immediate and work on the drier recommenced with increased commitment.

Stone commented to Riley about his lucky effort.

"Some luck and some skill Craig, much of the actual unhappiness in other areas came from similar problems and your effort has sent a strong signal that this aspect of the Ngami environment isn't acceptable to you."

On Sunday the full production capacity of the smelter was achieved, providing a further boost to morale.

The anticipated ore problems were then encountered, in the following days, the high production put an increasing load on the mining operation.

Heldebron was given instructions by Anders to meet the need for more ore by increasing production from the water-endangered stope.

"The pilot hole we've drilled shows there's a lot more water ahead of the mining operation. I've a legal responsibility here, deliberately endangering lives is insane," Heldebron answered, "More output from that stope will break through to the water. If anything we should be skirting the known danger in the stope, not mining there at twice the rate."

"You're doing it to improve production to help get the project's production up to specification. No one can complain about that."

"Well, I don't agree."

"Just get the bloody thing working at the highest possible production rate. You've been paid a great deal and will get the bonus you were promised when the project closes."

50

Peter met Van Breda, the mine manager, in the car park outside the Ngami plant a week after the Ngami plant's successful shutdown and asked him how the mine was faring.

Van Breda was clearly on edge and as they walked together toward the smelter control room, said, "They're steadily increasing the tonnage, I'm afraid to go down there myself. It's so dangerous."

"Are the pumps holding up?"

"Much better with the new shaft pipeline, and the motor upgrades will be ready soon."

"Is there nothing you can do to avoid the water problem?"

"As you know, the stope provides ore with better combustion properties," said van Breda. The instructions from Heldebron to double production of ore from the problematic stope was an area where legal responsibilities, meant that he, like Heldebron, had no way of escaping his responsibilities other than to resign his position, and he could not afford to do that.

"So we're going to lose the mine if we keep the smelter running?"

"There is no question about it Peter, if the rate of extraction from that stope is not dropped substantially it will break through to the water. Mining there should be cut right back and the defensive measures like cementation and rock bolding should be increased."

"Why is that not happening?

Van Breda shook his head and said, "Peter its out of my hands, all I can do is resign and I can't afford to."

Jeffery Nyasa noticed the increase in ore extraction from the stope with the excessive water ingress and drove to Peter's house that evening, calling Charles Obenta on the way to ask him to meet him there.

They discussed their options and emailed James de Bruin.

They also sent an email to Marnie Stone's personal address asking her to run a check on the assay data for the whole operation.

James read and reread their message, spoke to Ben in the clinic and notified Michael Anders.

Jack showed no emotion at all when Michael asked him about the danger. He explained almost without thinking that the water problem in the mine was part of the reason he wanted the project out of the way. "The dangerous stope is all that's keeping the project in production, I've asked Heldebron to develop a defensive program to allow the work to continue with less danger."

Michael thanked him, and added, "Please Jack, I've asked you several times to make sure Ngami does not blow up in our faces, it would help me if I did not get anymore messages from James de Bruin."

371

He then sent an email to James de Bruin explaining that his cousin had the water and mining problems under control.

Jack was feeling euphoric as Michael left his office. The failure of Ngami was guaranteed. He was on track to taking personal control of its wealth, and developing the additional ore deposit.

He phoned Heldebron and told him to create a defensive methodology and further increase mining in the endangered area.

"Defensive methodology? That's not practical the way we're going."

"I said plan it. Use your imagination."

Heldebron did not bother protesting. He knew he had to get away.

Jack was delighted for another reason, he had also been told that morning that the American prospectors he was employing had located the ore they were looking for, and would only require a few more days before it could be claimed.

He arranged to spend a few days in Francistown; to make preparations for his claim and to discuss the future with his associate, van Zyl.

51

Knowing that the operation was finished, Heldebron made one final move to increase his wealth.

He went to see the owner of Taylor Engineering, one of the factories in the village that served Ngami. He pulled his muddy Range Rover into the sealed visitor's car park, climbed out and strode across the crunchy, clean, crushed rock, that covered much of the yard, to the office door; wondering as he did so, at the contrast between its orderly status and the mess around the Ngami workshops.

Taylor Engineering was a good example of the many highly successful companies that grow with projects in remote sites that are difficult to service from larger centers. Taylor's neat and new looking building occupied pride of place in a Spartan looking yard. A spotless office block stood at the front of the workshops. Quantities of construction steel were stored in permanent looking racks behind the building. Heavy machines, in various states of disrepair, were neatly lined up next to the steel racks.

As he walked toward the building, Heldebron thought about his odd life. He had grown up in Indonesia where his father had held a position as a clerk. The pressures of growing up in a difficult yet wealthy ex-colony had been some part of the force that sometimes meant that he at times almost achieved miracles, and at others caused destruction.

In Ngami, he had recruited at least thirty specialists, chemists, metallurgists and engineers, during the years he had been there. He had used them, cast them aside, and destroyed careers, claiming credit for each castoff's least effort. It was not something he was proud of, but it was the path he felt he needed to follow to achieve his objectives.

Heldebron's time in Ngami had been forced on him.

Before joining GVN to run Ngami, he had worked in South Africa.

What he considered normal ambition, had led him to conduct a permanent campaign to move onward and upward at the expense of others. This ruthlessness, he had told himself, was not of his making, but a result of a system that encouraged the worst aspects of human behavior. He neither condoned it, nor criticized it. He had simply set out to work within it.

His move to Ngami had taken place after he had set out to discredit someone's capability once too often.

The 'someone' chosen had had enough of a support system to survive Heldebron's attack, which had then been turned back on him, and, as a result, Heldebron's position had become untenable.

The offer of the position of general manager of the Ngami project had been timely, just preceding his probable demise.

He put these thoughts behind him as he strode into the Taylor offices contemplating his profitable personal project.

Shortly after Heldebron's arrival in Ngami, Don Taylor had approached him about the scheme to milk millions from rock bolts, one of the main consumables used in the mine. At that time, Taylor had arranged to meet Heldebron for golf.

On the second tee Taylor had said, "Gerry I have a proposition that you might be interested in."

"Oh?"

"I've been offered an opportunity, to buy a consignment of rock bolts at a very good price. We would supply them to a shelf company owned by you at a greatly reduced price and your company could sell them to Ngami at less than they normally pay for rock bolts."

They both knew that the function of these bolts was critical to the mining operation, used, as they were, to control the pressure and stress in the rock that remained after the ore was removed. Poor quality material used in rock bolt manufacture would be dangerous.

In the case of the hanging wall or roof, large quantities of the bolts supported sections by being grouted into drilled holes then tensioned, The bolts tensioned to predetermined torques hold the rock back and transform the roof into an arch like structure.

A failure of a set of these would have the same effect as the failure of a part of an arch and huge quantities of rock would come crashing down. Not only endangering those in the spot below the failed bolts, but everyone in the area, and possibly everyone in the workings.

"How much would I make, if I agreed to the arrangement?" Heldebron had asked.

"Millions."

"Really?"

"You know the volumes just work out the cost figures."

Heldebron barely hesitated. "So what do I have to do?"

"All that's needed is an order to your shelf company for the rock bolts at a slightly lower price than the company normally pays."

"Where are you getting the bolts Don?"

Taylor had explained that the rock bolts had been purchased in Eastern Europe, for a mine in Central Asia, then been resold to somewhere in Africa and were now not needed there, due to that mine's closure.

"The quality of steel in rock bolts is critical. I wouldn't want any to fail and I wouldn't think of using them without proper testing."

"Of course not. The bolts have been certified in the country from which they originate. Somewhere in the old Soviet block, I believe. And of course we will arrange to have them tested here."

The bolts had been tested. Their strength had been satisfactory.

The decision to increase the ore extraction rate from the stope where water was a problem meant an increased need for rock bolts. This increased the return to Heldebron. The stope was using many more rock bolts per unit of roof area than the average, for a roof in the mine, because of poor conditions.

When he entered Taylor's neat office, Heldebron asked the entrepreneur if he would mind walking with him to where his vehicle was parked, to get Taylor out of the office. He then explained, as they walked, that he wanted to purchase a bulk quantity of the bolts, explaining that the critical nature of the application of the rock bolts in the dangerous stope was increasing their usage. This justified a bulk purchase to ensure that there were no support delays.

Taylor asked him for an estimate of what he wanted.

Heldebron gave him a summary of the approximate quantities that would be involved.

Taylor said they would have to involve the supply manager, Bert Thorn, to place such a large bulk order.

52

The exemplary run of the Ngami plant was brought to a stop by a disastrous electrical failure in the secondary crusher area.

This production calamity had a fortunate side effect, it allowed an extra day in the quest to control the mining of the endangered stope.

The secondary crushers were cone crushers. In these, pre-crushed ore is fed through the top of the cone crusher to flow over the mantle. The vertical cone crusher drive shaft rotates the mantle eccentrically, below the concave, or bowl liner, squeezing the product and crushing it between the mantle and concave. An electric motor drives the crusher through a set of V-belts. Two of these crushers would have handled the Ngami design production.

The investigation into the failure was brought to a standstill by the remark of one of the long serving workers in maintenance saying, "Most failures happen because of metal jamming the crushers. All your workings out don't seem to look at that?"

"What?" asked Peter at the unexpected comment.

He tried to continue, but was interrupted with, "Waste of time if they keep putting dozens of roof bolts through the system."

Peter caught his breath. "That is important, can you guys work on finding a solution? We can meet again in the morning to discuss it."

The electrical work was completed and the plant restarted, only to have a similar occurrence during the night.

Brett and Peter could not believe the difference in atmosphere and attitude at the next day's discussion. The core group had arrived early and had worked out what to do about the rock bolts that were getting past the magnets and jamming the crushers. Additional magnets were to be installed to remove them and a tighter cleaning schedule introduced to remove the offending rock bolts that became trapped on the magnets.

And most fortunately for everyone, the group insisted on an investigation into why so many rock bolts were arriving with the ore.

This forced a partial closure of the dangerous section of the mine.

53

Heldebron arranged a meeting between himself and the supply manager Bert Thorn, at a suitably remote, yet accessible spot, to arrange the purchase order for the extra bolts after leaving the supplier.

Jeffrey Nyasa, had gone for a walk, to stop at the same quiet spot and as he sat thinking about ways to mine the dangerous stope more effectively, some way up a kopje, watching the sun set over the bushveld, two off road vehicles pulled up below where he sat.

Bert Thorn and Gerry Heldebron got out of the vehicles.

Wondering why they were meeting in such a remote spot, Jeffrey supposed they might be going climbing or walking together, but it was late and the bush could be dangerous at night. He could hear every word they said, and was not sure what to do. He would have felt silly jumping out to say hello, so he waited.

Heldebron said, "Let's take a walk Bert."

"What's this about?" Bert asked.

"Its about the bank overdraft you're so worried about. I may be able to help. Let's head up the kopje a bit, as though we're going climbing."

They turned and walked slowly upward, past Jeffrey, toward the crown of the kopje and were within a few meters of him for several minutes.

Heldebron was explaining that he, like Bert, was in a corner and that there was an opportunity to make several million and told him about additional rock-bolts he wanted to purchase.

"We're getting some from that source already Gerry. Why the need to buy so many now?"

"Never mind the detail, take the chance while you can, it's not even as though we're paying as much as we would normally."

"Several million is hardly a small deal, I'm in this remote spot looking after purchasing because I've never done a dishonest thing in my life." Bert answered. "I need that record for the future I'm still only in my fifties."

"You were telling me you needed money because your manager has ruined your pub?"

"I'll borrow the money somehow."

"You said you had problems with your credit rating?"

"That's why I asked if the company could pay me part of my contract, in advance, as a loan."

"As I've explained Bert, they would never dream of it."

Jeffrey wished he had shown himself when they had first arrived. He simply did not need another problem to think about.

"Let's treat the rock bolts as an opportunity for both of us and, the company, who'll save money as a result of your buying them," said Heldebron.

Bert stopped walking and turned, looking unseeingly toward where Jeffery was sitting. Making Jeffery want to pull further out of sight but he managed to stay frozen.

Bert had always believed that integrity was one of the most important parts of character. He also believed that bent purchasing officers were of no value, to good companies, or bad, but, he was desperate. Bert turned back toward Gerry. "I suppose I don't really have a choice, I'm in such an impossible position," he said quietly. "How do we go about organising the deal?"

"I'll talk to Taylor. Don't worry about it, Bert, you'll be safe for the first time in years," Jeffrey heard Heldebron say, before they parted and left.

Jeffrey waited awkwardly for a few more minutes, then climbed down from his ledge and moved quietly through the bush, to make his way back toward the village. As he walked, he heard baboons barking raucously above the spot where he had been sitting, such a row could mean leopards. Baboons being a food source for the beautiful spotted cats.

They were a special fear of his. Near his home in Malawi they hid in the tall cedars, waiting in ambush for their meals. He remembered how, when he first climbed M'lanje as a teenager, he had heard the cough of a leopard in the trees above the path they were following. He could clearly remember the fear that the sound had brought with it. He had never seen a leopard in the Ngami area but had heard there were fairly large numbers of the beautiful cats in the hills.

Bert Thorne met Taylor the next day to finalise the order.

"What about the underground people, they might notice the difference?" asked Thorne.

"They won't know a thing about it. The name on all the invoicing and packaging is well known," Taylor replied, "And they use them already."

"How are you getting such a good price?" asked Thorne.

"They're coming from a mine in Central Africa that has closed and we repackage them before they get here." Taylor replied. "Just get me the order and you'll have the bank off your back and your family business will be safe."

"Hell," said Thorne "a lifetime of working and only one partially odd deal. I suppose it's quite safe if Gerry's happy. He is, after all, responsible for the technical aspects and if it were not for my pub manager's failure I wouldn't even consider your offer."

"Of course not Bert," Taylor replied, "and as you well know its just one more deal in this place."

Bert knew Taylor was right but had never had any wish to be involved in anything not completely above board. "OK, Don," he replied, "I'll arrange the order today and you'll have the bolts within the week. When can I have the money?"

"You'll have it the day after I get the order. It will be paid directly into a Channel Islands account that you will have to organise. Don't worry about it, write to your bank now and tell them they'll have their money by next week," Taylor said and turned to walk to his Land Cruiser.

Bert watched as Taylor drove away feeling as though he had lost something, but he also knew, as well as Taylor did, that, who owns what can become confusing in a project like Ngami. Having made his one dishonest move, he never intended repeating the exercise and as the minutes passed his worries about the deal changed to elation at having found a way to survive a nightmare. He walked slowly back to his office, thinking of ways to explain the sudden windfall.

54

The shadows of the oncoming dusk were almost complete as Jeffery got back to the village. The smell of wood fires and cooking drifted out to greet him. He went to Peter's house and told him what had happened.

"It means they're thinking of increasing the extraction rate in the area that's likely to cause a flood, doesn't it?"

"Definitely."

"Let's see what de Bruin says."

They composed an email to James de Bruin, explaining about Heldebron's deal for rock bolts from a non standard source and the apparent intention to increase the rock bolt use.

When James de Bruin's heard about the bulk purchase of rock-bolts, so soon after being told by Michael that Jack had the Ngami mining situation under control, it baffled him. He sent a message to Michael expressing his surprise at the planned purchase of extra rock bolts, seemingly to be used in the area they'd agreed to pull back in.

The de Bruins decided Ben was needed on site to sort out the odd situation. They called Ben's specialist and the subsequent discussions ended with the medical professional agreeing to Ben's going to Ngami.

The specialist warned Ben to be careful and not involve himself in anything that would be too physically demanding and he provided him with a set of exercises that he wanted him to do in the Ngami gymnasium.

Ben's relief at getting out of the clinic helped lighten the load on James. The younger de Bruin's infectious enthusiasm had always been a big part of their ventures.

James called Peter after he and his brother arrived at the hotel in Ngami.

They arranged to meet for dinner, together with Charles, at Peter's house.

Joseph was in the garden when the brothers got to the Connor's house, at about five in the evening, and heard their car pull up. He put his head around the corner, to see who was there, saw Ben de Bruin and recognized him. He rushed into the house, found Christine and asked her, "Excuse me Mma. Is Ben in the car?"

"Yes he is," she answered warily.

Joseph was silent as he thought for a moment about what he should do, and decided he was going to give Ben his notes, money and knife. He asked awkwardly if he might leave the work he was doing to get Ben's possessions. Christine could not understand much of what he was saying but agreed.

Joseph shot out of the house to return to his cave and collect the items he had been looking after.

After James, Ben and Charles were warmly welcomed by Christine, she mentioned that Joseph seemed very pleased to see Ben, but had run off to get something.

Peter asked them what they wanted to drink.

After they were settled, they talked about their options, until Christine called them for dinner.

Their meal was interrupted by the return of Joseph. He popped into the room with a plastic bag containing Ben's diary, some notes, the money and the pocketknife. He apologized in broken English for interrupting and handed them to Ben, deferentially, as is the custom of his people, saying, "Good evening Mr. Ben, I've saved your valuables," then he sadly told them that the samples had been taken by someone.

Ben looked at the items in the plastic, and they triggered a memory, he recognized his diary and realized that this was a much less dusty Joseph, the missing herd boy. He could barely believe the luck. He laughed happily, and, remembering Joseph's original introduction, of himself, after the crash, said. "Thanks Joseph how's the herding going."

"Unfortunately not at all Mr. Ben I'm a fugitive now. A gardener fugitive," he said looking awkwardly at Christine.

There was a surprised silence, as Charles and the rest of the company realized that the Connor's gardener was the missing boy.

Charles asked Joseph, in Setswana, how he had obtained the diary and money.

Joseph explained and told Charles about his fear of the people from his village and of Charles' cousin.

Charles thanked him and explained what had been said to rest of the group.

After hearing what Joseph had told Charles, Ben looked through the notes trying to remember what they were about. They'd been made for his own use and were not easy to follow with a poor memory.

James looked on anxiously.

Ben looked blank.

"Can you follow them Ben?"

"I can't work out where they are referenced from. I just can't remember."

Charles asked Peter if he had a survey map of the area.

Peter said he did and went to get it.

Joseph stayed in the background, excited and pleased, about his dutiful action, and how it had gained the attention of the group.

When it became clear that Ben could not interpret the notes they decided to look through the data with Marnie Stone the next morning. They thanked Christine for the dinner and left as a group.

Ben took the diary to bed with him and tried again to work out what he'd done, but could not find the basis to which the notes referred. By ten he was exhausted, showered, climbed into bed and fell into a restless sleep.

In the moments before Joseph fell asleep he realized, from the events of the night, and the parts of the conversation that he had understood that he might be able to help his Ben find more rocks like those he was so interested in.

The next morning Christine phoned Peter at work to ask him to come home urgently, with Charles and Ben, to talk to Joseph.

"All of us?"

"He wants Ben and Charles, he's excited about the rocks. I can't understand everything he's saying but he's insistent about talking to Ben."

When they got to the house Joseph told Charles he knew where to find rocks exactly like Ben's.

Charles translated this for them.

"Surely not?" was all James, who had driven Ben from the hotel, could say.

"Come on let's go," said Ben. "We should be able to work things out between us. We'll collect any equipment we need in Francistown."

James asked Peter what he intended to do about the work on site.

"It should be okay. Van Breda will manage with Jeffery and Craig Stone."

"You can talk to Marnie Stone if you need information from the geology department."

"What's happening about the water problem?" Peter asked.

"A section of the roof collapsed this morning," James answered.

"Was anyone hurt?"

"Luckily not, but that stope, and because of it, the entire mine, is a very dangerous place. The rock bolts are not being installed properly and that increases their usage rate, that's why the crushers keep jamming."

Peter decided to stay with James, and Ben left for Francistown with Charles and Joseph.

Charles drove.

Peter phoned Jeffrey as the group left, "Jeffery with all the interest in the ore I haven't had a chance to talk to you about the mine."

Jeffery told him that the roof collapse seemed to have been caused by corrosion of the rock bolts as much as poor installation. This meant that others, in the same condition, under less stress, still performed their function but were also likely to fail.

"What's van Breda doing?"

"Nothing, I don't know what's got into him."

"Shite Jeffery we must stop them somehow."

"I have been working on it but although they are being slowed by the falls and the crusher investigations we're not getting anywhere fast enough the engineering of the mine at that point must be rethought if it's not going to fail catastrophically."

Jeffery asked Peter where he was and Peter said he would see him in a few minutes.

"I hope Joseph will be able to find the way from where we're going and quickly," said Ben as they drove.

"I find," said Joseph.

Charles parked next to the Jamieson's office in Francistown and they went into the building. Aware that there was a possibility that the building was bugged they were careful what they said.

Their arrival was noted by van Zyl and he phoned Jack Anders.

The receptionist in Jamieson's office greeted the group from Ngami and said that the technician, Rob's assistant, who had been running the agency since the agent's death, was not there yet. She offered to help them find whatever they needed.

They worked with her to stock up on the geological equipment that they needed.

Van Zyl was able to hear everything that was said.

They then went to the nearby general store and bought the food, drinks and camping supplies that Jamieson's did not have.

On their way back to the Jamieson office they met the technician in the street and told him about their expedition.

"Where are you going?" he asked.

"We need to claim the ore I found, to meet the increased smelter throughput."

"It's that urgent?"

"There's another group looking for it. We must make sure that the new ore is not claimed by someone for themselves or Ngami and our company will lose out badly, without the smelter problems entering into the equation."

"So how are you going to find any ore, if you can't remember the trip?"

"Joseph believes he knows the area where they come from."

"How would he know something like that?"

"He's a herd boy and takes his family's cattle over large distances to find food and luckily for us he collects rocks. He's certain he knows where he can find what we're looking for."

"Well, that'd be one for the record books," the technician replied doubtfully.

They arrived at the office as they were talking.

Van Zyl was sitting behind his desk in Francistown when he heard Jack Anders abruptly enter the facility.

Anders barged into his office and asked without preamble, "What are our prospectors doing?"

Van Zyl radioed the Americans, who assured him that they were nearly finished.

By then, the two men and the boy had loaded their vehicle and, in a very short time, were where Joseph thought they had to go.

Ben used what he could remember of the district, and the information Marnie Stone had provided him, to decide their route and Charles translated this for Joseph.

Joseph helped by telling them by pointing out paths through particular kopjes. His directions became steadily more confident and they soon located the outcrop.

Ben's memory of what his notes meant had improved as they progressed.

He realised that he had already marked the claim and they found his markers.

So all they had to do was return directly to Francistown.

It was so early that they decided they might as well keep driving to Gabarone.

All this time, Jack Anders was speaking to van Zyl about what he was planning, waiting for the American prospectors make their next report.

Eventually the call came in, and it was not what Anders wanted to hear.

Questions had arisen, about the continuity of the orebody they had found.

"Oh shit!" said Anders and collapsed back into a chair.

Van Zyl phoned someone while Anders was hunched back into the chair, and told him to stop the de Bruin group of prospectors, but more than three hours had passed.

Joseph and his mentors were on their way to Gabarone before the man van Zyl had despatched left Francistown.

Ben booked the group into a good hotel in Gabarone.

Then made the official claim the next morning, using the de Bruin's lawyers and information emailed to them by Marnie Stone.

Ben phoned James and told him their claim had been made in the name of the Ngami clan and the de Bruins.

James emailed the information to Michael Anders, and, in the email, again asked him again to stop the mining in the dangerous stope.

Michael called him back after he had read the email. "Hello James, good news about the ore."

"Yes terrific, GVN are not mentioned in the claim, though, because we did not have the authority to include you and with the confusion we've been going through we did not want another, shall we say, mix up."

Michael was silent for a moment then said that Jack was about to claim an ore-body in the general area.

"I think it's probably a bit late."

"I see," He replied, "this mining problem sounds bad?"

"I've tried to tell you that several times now."

"I think it's time I came up there," answered Michael.

55

Michael arrived in Botswana in the evening of the day after his conversation with James.

The problematic stope had been restarted after the investigation forced by the crusher group and bolting failures had caused yet another major rock fall during the night.

Water started entering the mine at a higher rate.

When Michael got to Heldebron's office the general manager explained the failure.

Well-qualified to examine the site himself, Michael organized to inspect the underground site himself, with the general manager and van Breda.

The inspection party looked like something of a celebrity tour, with Heldebron and the senior mining personnel following Michael in a procession.

Within minutes of his arrival in the problematic area, Michael found some broken bolts and noted that they were thinner than they should be because of corrosion. He realized that the extent of their corrosion was certainly be related to the collapsed roof. He turned to van Breda and asked what he thought had caused the corrosion.

"Not the water?"

"Perhaps its because they come from an unusual source?" said van Breda.

"Unusual source?"

"You need to talk to purchasing, I only use the things."

After getting to the surface and changing into clean clothes, Michael went to the supply office, with van Breda and Heldebron, and checked the documentation for the bolts.

Bert Thorn showed him the recent bulk order, explained what had happened and apologized for his part in the purchase, including the reason for his desperation, "It's the only dishonest thing I've ever done Mr. Anders," he finished, looking as downcast as he felt.

Michael turned to van Breda and asked, "Did you know about this?"

"It's been a worry of mine, but I'm not in any position to confront management myself."

Michael looked hard at the straightforward manager then turned back to Thorn. "You could have asked for a loan from us, you've worked for GVN for more than twenty years."

"I did and it was refused, this purchase was suggested as an alternative."

Michael was silent, as he looked at the large amount of money involved. He noticed that there had been no competitive tender, as required by procedures when such a large sum was involved. The order had been signed by Heldebron, as general manager and had been approved by his cousin Jack Anders as managing director.

"Let's forget your involvement for now. I'd like copies of these please."

Michael left the purchasing office and flew back to Johannesburg with copies of the documentation.

He went straight to Jack's office.

The meeting was short and to the point, there was no questioning the documentation about the rock bolts and no need to discuss other issues.

Jack laid the blame squarely on the shoulders of Heldebron saying his counter signature was a mistake made because he was signing so many documents at the time.

Michael could not disprove this. The counter signature could have been a clerical error. He knew that his cousin was dangerous. A threat, at least to himself, if not to the corporation, but had no evidence.

"Jack, I'm taking control of Ngami, Botswana is too important for Ngami to be allowed to slip."

Jack was silent for a moment, then said, "It will make my work in Johannesburg more effective, Ngami is taking too much of my time."

"Will you speak to Heldebron?"

"Let's get him on the line now."

They contacted Heldebron using a conference telephoning facility. The Ngami general manager was given the option of accepting a cash pay out or facing prosecution for the bulk buying of the rock bolts. Since there was indisputable evidence of his failure to comply with company purchasing policy.

Realizing that he had no reason to expect Jack Anders to fall on his own sword, Heldebron accepted, knowing he would leave Ngami with the considerable fortune, made up of his pay out from GVN, and his profit from the rock bolts.

Michael told Heldebron to hand over the operation to Brett Halliday, who he had spoken to before seeing Jack. He told Heldebron that he wanted him off site immediately.

After Michael left, Jack phoned van Zyl, his associate in Andselc. "My cousin Michael has worked out what's happening and he's taking over the Ngami operation."

"And GVN?"

"No problem, I carry on here."

"Are you sure."

"Absolutely. As you know it's essential that nothing unexpected turns up," he said.

"Don't worry yourself."

"I can't afford, under any circumstance, to have any detail of our operations there brought into the open. We need to remain completely in the clear."

"Nothing will surface Jack."

"If that can be achieved our other ventures will hold up."

"Don't worry Jack, I've as much to lose as you, if not more."

Having decided to make sure that Ngami was run as an important part of the corporation's empire. Michael spent extra time there. This was at the expense of his attention to the overall company.

The disaffected and uncoordinated Ngami team felt the road ahead for themselves was becoming more secure.

Jack was left to look after more aspects of the GVN corporation than Michael had initially intended.

As the weeks progressed Michael appointed Brett Halliday as general manager of Ngami, and van Breda assistant general manager, with Jeffery taking over the management of the mine, each with considerable increases in pay. They were warned to report any odd instructions given by Jack Anders.

Together they contained the problems within the mine, reduced production from the endangered stope and carefully nursed the feed to the furnace.

Peter Connor was asked, by the de Bruins, to take responsibility for engineering of the new mine that had to be got off the ground, and be made operational in a very short time

The World Bank approve ongoing finance.

ABOUT THE AUTHOR

Thomas Bagot PhD, (MGSM), MEngSc (UNSW), BSc (UNISA), NDT (UNISA) is an expert in fine tuned engineering, risk, management, communication and control and has worked as a manager, an operator, an engineer and in management and engineering consulting, in Southern Africa, Canada and Australia; on large and small plants in mining, power generation, dam building, generation planning, engineering, engineering planning, commissioning and problem solving. He is married with five children and lives in Sydney, Australia. His interest in writing developed from a wish to show the immensity and the beauty of the efforts of people who contribute a great deal to the world and yet are hidden by the scale and complexity of their efforts.

TomBagot@bagotbacl.com